OPERATION
ALEPH BET

D.H. STONE

aethonbooks.com

OPERATION ALEPH BET
©2024 D.H. STONE

This book is protected under the copyright laws of the United States of America. No part of this publication may be reproduced, stored in a retrieval system, or transmitted, in any form or by any means, without the prior permission in writing of the publisher, nor be otherwise circulated in any form of binding or cover other than that in which it is published and without a similar condition including this condition being imposed on the subsequent purchaser. Any reproduction or unauthorized use of the material or artwork contained herein is prohibited without the express written permission of the authors.

Aethon Books supports the right to free expression and the value of copyright. The purpose of copyright is to encourage writers and artists to produce the creative works that enrich our culture.

The scanning, uploading, and distribution of this book without permission is a theft of the author's intellectual property. If you would like to use material from the book (other than for review purposes), please contact editor@aethonbooks.com. Thank you for your support of the author's rights.

Aethon Books
www.aethonbooks.com

Print and eBook formatting and design by Kevin G. Summers. Artwork provided by Steve Beaulieu.

Published by Aethon Books LLC.

Aethon Books is not responsible for websites (or their content) that are not owned by the publisher.

This book is a work of fiction. Names, characters, places, and incidents are the product of the author's imagination or are used fictitiously. Any resemblance to actual events, locales, or persons, living or dead is coincidental.

All rights reserved.

For Harry, Sofia, Leo, Clara, Diego, Amelie, Marla, Lavi and Ariyah

[1]

Clutching a mug of fresh mint tea as though her life depended on it, Sofia Lopez-Weiss gazed out of the French windows of her Hampstead flat at the lush arboretum framing her back garden. The fresh dew sparkled in the early morning sunshine and even the pulsating hum of nearby traffic failed to spoil the idyllic scene. It had started to drizzle but that didn't matter; the beauty of suburban nature seemed immune to the vagaries of the English weather. A couple of hyperactive magpies were skipping around the lawn, squawking and pecking in the direction of any of the smaller birds that threatened to invade their self-declared fiefdom. She smiled at this minidrama that she had witnessed many times before, taking comfort from its daily predictability.

Sofia needed comforting today more than ever. Being married to a Mossad agent wasn't in itself the problem. She had become accustomed to living with a man whom she loved with all her heart but whose covert professional activities she didn't fully understand and about which, if truth be told, she had always preferred to know as little as possible. Tamir's repeated short absences were just about tolerable. Over these past two years following their return to London from Australia, the intermittent 'time-outs' (as he called them) had become an unavoidable fact of their family life. But this latest disappearing trick had crossed a line.

He'd been gone for five weeks and she hadn't heard as much as a squeak from him. Their little daughter, Clara, was coping with her Israeli dad's sudden truancies as well as any six-year-old would—badly. Her sleeping pattern was erratic, her eating habits picky, and her social behaviour unpredictable; her friends' parents were expressing mounting concern at Clara's outbursts of unprovoked violence—mainly spitting or scratching—towards her classmates. Sofia didn't need to consult a child psychologist to understand the roots of this aggression. The child needed her father where he belonged—pottering around the home, eating at the kitchen table, and sleeping in her mother's bed. *Not good enough, Tamir, not by a long shot.* Something would have to change and fast. Tamir needed a sharp reality check and that was what Sofia had in store for him.

Acting out her newfound resolve, Sofia made a fist of her right hand and slammed it with a loud smack into her left palm. That seemed to jolt her into a decision. She found herself rehearsing the words. *You have to choose, Tamir. It's either your job or your family. You can't have both.* How would Tamir react to such an ultimatum? Wasn't she playing with fire? Was it worth placing all their futures at risk?

As the sun emerged from behind a large cloud, the fog in her mind lifted and the elusive answers to those questions became as clear to her as the sunbeams that danced that morning over the verdant expanse of Hampstead Heath.

For all its fearsome reputation at home and abroad, Israel's foreign intelligence agency, the Mossad, had suffered its share of failures since Israel's rebirth in 1948. More than a few of these glitches had fatal consequences for the hapless agents in the field. These anonymous heroes and heroines were, on too many occasions, left exposed and defenceless as a result of some blunder perpetrated either by an incompetent or sleepy desk-bound operative at the agency's Tel Aviv headquarters or, more often, by a negligent politician.

New recruits quickly appreciated the dangers of poor decisions by remote superiors and of the consequent need for everyone, whatever their rank, to remain in a state of perpetual hypervigilance. Instructors went to great lengths to inculcate in their trainees the habits of personal initiative and out-of-the box thinking. The result was that all agents venturing into hostile territory, whether for the first or hundredth time, were equipped with a default mindset that involved a readiness to take rapid evasive action, however unorthodox, in the face of an unanticipated hazard. That skill was indispensable for any Mossadnik hoping to enjoy anything like a normal life expectancy.

Since his earliest days in the agency, Tamir Weiss had developed, for reasons he had never quite understood, an uncanny knack of detecting imminent threats to his survival. *A charmed life* was the envy-laden epithet that his colleagues deployed whenever his name cropped up. Another was *Tomcat*, referring to his nine lives. Tamir knew well that luck was only one of several factors that had kept him alive. Three other essentials were his advanced training, his formidable physical strength, and an exquisite mental attunement to any incipient sources of serious danger. This last had become so refined that it amounted to a sixth sense; it was now his closest and most trustworthy companion.

Today, Tamir knew that trouble was approaching. Barely

halfway through this latest mission, his internal red lights were flashing. While this was far from a new sensation, on this occasion he diagnosed a qualitative difference from his previous escapades—he couldn't discern any possibility of escape. Throughout his years of service to the Mossad, he had never succumbed to negativity and he hated himself for contemplating the possibility. Yet here was failure staring him in the face; however hard he stared back at his most feared adversary, it refused to budge.

The mission itself wasn't the problem. After a sticky start, he'd made huge progress in the last month and was on the verge of achieving a breakthrough. Another couple of weeks and he'd have exciting news to report to his bosses. He couldn't turn back now. Yet continuing would throw up an imminent and painful dilemma.

The truth was that this latest project was taking a heavy toll on his personal life. Unable to contact Sofia, even for the briefest of phone calls, he could sense the earliest rumblings of a major marital crisis trundling down the tracks towards him. It was all but inevitable. While he was criss-crossing Europe in hot pursuit of his Jew-hating quarries, his wife and child were languishing in a North London suburb. On his most recent visit home more than a month earlier, Sofia had read him the riot act, making it clear that she wouldn't tolerate that degree of enforced separation for much longer. He didn't blame her in the slightest. She had displayed remarkable forbearance in the face of repeated provocation. His provocation. Not that he'd had any choice—an enforced silence was almost *de rigueur* in these sorts of operations as Sofia well understood. That was little comfort to either of them. Something in the complex but delicate fabric of their relationship would have to give, and he knew for certain that the stability of their marriage was the weakest link in the chain.

Tamir's gloomy reflections were interrupted by his phone's ringtone. He checked the screen. It was Sofia. He closed his eyes and inhaled deeply. *Here we go, the great reckoning has started.* For the first time in weeks, he answered her call.

[2]

IDIOTS, MUTTERED PROFESSOR PIERRE CAMBON, STRUGGLING TO constrain his anger below the threshold of audibility. *Don't these people understand what they're doing? They are leading us all to disaster.*

Almost more than anything else in life, Cambon treasured his mid-morning stroll along the boulevards and bridges of his beloved Paris. He always made a point of including a half-hour interlude to refuel with a couple of shots of espresso. His portly figure was well known in the *Quartier Latin* where he could be spotted wrestling with the unruly sheets of *Le Monde* across an outside table or two at any one of a dozen of his favoured cafés, peering hard through his rimless spectacles at the latest national and international news. What he read there was invariably depressing but many years earlier, in his early twenties, he had discovered a reliable antidote—caffeine. In normal circumstances, the merest whiff of the bittersweet elixir would be enough to lighten his spirits and re-energise his zest for life in this, his ninth decade. Today was different. The circumstances were far from normal and his mood was plummeting to the depths of his boots.

'*Un café pour Monsieur, comme d'habitude?*' a young

uniformed waiter inquired, placing the tiny cup and saucer, along with the customary glass of water, on his table. Cambon nodded, casting his crumpled newspaper aside to continue his internal musing as though the many troubling events unfolding in the external world amounted to a mere trifle, a distracting irrelevance.

Cambon was out of sorts that day. The project to which his name had somehow become attached was not just distasteful, it was absurd. No, worse, it harboured major potential dangers. That smug Austrian tinpot dictator, Christoph Berg, had barged and bullied his way to the top of a political movement that had once shown such promise. Cambon had long been a strong supporter of radical, anti-establishment causes but he now realised—too late—that this one wasn't just pointless, it was toxic; he shouldn't have touched it with a bargepole. The root of the problem was that Berg had surrounded himself with a bunch of sycophantic idiots who viewed him as the returning Messiah. Well, they'd all soon be in for the shock of their lives.

These blinkered people claimed—and maybe some of them even believed—that they were embarking on *un grand projet* to rid Europe of its troublesome elements—apologists for colonialism, governing elites, venture capitalists, media moguls and, above all, Zionists. This 'enemy' was a large and rather ill-defined group, but the common denominator was clear enough to all if only whispered in polite company: Jews. Cambon had, after initial hesitation, accepted the proposition that the world would be better off without them, but it had become obvious that the clear-out would be messy. It could even amount to a kind of Final Solution, twenty-first century style, undertaken in the full glare of public scrutiny—with all the unpleasant consequences that would entail for anyone stupid enough to be associated with it.

And now he, notwithstanding his giant intellect, epitomised that stupidity. How, he wondered, had this come about? The ageing professor, despite his innate conservative instincts, had always tried to align himself with the radical European left. He thought of himself as a liberal and lifelong opponent of all forms of bigotry, though he had never gone out of his way to prioritise the issue of racism. There were so many more important challenges—global capitalism, western imperialism and the looming destruction of the planet by rapacious commercial conglomerates and bankers. But he couldn't acquiesce without protest as he watched *Destiny*, the mass political movement over which he nominally presided, evolving into what amounted to a cryptofascist organisation. In any case, the whole concept was so deranged, so detached from reality, it wouldn't stand a snowball's chance in hell of being implemented. Yet he couldn't ignore it. Here he was sitting in the heart of Le Marais, a district still almost synonymous with the Jewish population of Paris, about to unveil a policy that contained an implicit plot—the details of which remained sketchy in the extreme—to launch a frontal attack on Europe's Jews. The irony of the setting wasn't lost on this crusty warrior of the left.

Everyone concerned, up to and including his de facto boss, the *patron*, aka Operations Director of *Destiny*, the despicable Christoph Berg, had assured Cambon more than once that his fears were groundless. Cambon could forgive the hangers-on, the groupies who had found an appealing, albeit illusory, channel through which to express their anti-establishment identity. Berg, on the other hand, was smart and knew precisely what he was doing. When the whole operation went belly-up, as it would as surely as night follows day, Berg was the one man who should be held responsible. Yet he was also the one man least likely to face the charge sheet.

A tabloid journalist, Berg had a way with words and explained to anyone who would listen that their target was Zionism, not Judaism, and that there was no question of Europe's Jews and their fellow travellers being subjected to any form of physical violence. Berg was adamant that the Third Reich's 'misguided' programme of mass murder was not about to be emulated (though he always stopped short of condemning the Holocaust outright). He had used soothing phrases like *adhering to humanitarian principles* and *offering fair and sympathetic treatment* without elaboration. Such pledges played well in the media but they didn't fool Cambon, nor were they likely to reassure Europe's Jews.

Cambon had challenged Berg on his facile *anti-Zionism is not antisemitism* claim. He reminded Berg of the inconvenient fact that upwards of 90 percent of Europe's Jews were ardent Zionists and that *Destiny*'s repudiation of antisemitism was a sham. The real sticking point for Cambon wasn't the targeting of Jews *per se*. He had always regarded them, when he thought about them at all, as an arrogant race who had never committed themselves to full assimilation into French secular culture in the spirit of *laïcité*. And their reactionary creed of Zionism, he believed, was the ultimate colonialist endeavour, an anti-progressive pollutant that had to be removed from the face of the earth. Cambon sympathised with that end; his doubts lay only with the means. But while Cambon attempted to draw a firm line between the old-style Jew-hatred promoted by the Nazis and his modern, progressive anti-Zionism, the Austrian had no time for such niceties. *Jews are Jews*, insisted Berg, *whatever you want to label them*. Worse, Berg couldn't or wouldn't spell out to Cambon how Europe's Jewish-Zionist problem would be solved without violence.

Cambon recalled Berg's facile response to that concern. *They will be offered a choice—and what could be fairer than that? They can either abandon their repulsive ideology or pack their bags and leave the continent of Europe for good. Problem solved. They will simply melt away.* Cambon's next question hit the nail on the head: *What will you do if they refuse?* That challenge was answered with a shrug. Berg couldn't—or wouldn't—elaborate. That could only mean one thing: he was lying just as his Nazi predecessors had lied decades earlier. Cambon recalled the chaos of the German occupation that he had experienced as a young child in Vichy France, but he could remember few of its darker details. His parents, however, had always instilled in him the precious national values of *liberté, egalité, fraternité*. All three were at now risk, and if they were trashed by Berg and his followers, he would be complicit.

No, he couldn't be a part of their disgraceful plan, but neither could he see any way of derailing it. He had been placed in an impossible position. None of this madness was of his making, but he had been cajoled into becoming a figurehead for a trans-European political movement that had started out with such idealism, only to descend into potentially murderous intolerance. From the outset, he had grasped the uncomfortable truth that they had appointed him president of *Destiny* purely for the purpose of public relations. He had lent his academic gravitas to Berg's crackpot ideas that had energised *Destiny*'s rag-tag army of bigots, misfits and criminals. Berg had, from the start, recognised the need to broaden the movement's base, and the mere mention of Cambon's name achieved that aim as it guaranteed the recruitment of large sections of the European Left to the cause. Cambon berated himself for having agreed to it. How had he allowed himself to get into this godawful mess?

That was a rhetorical question as he knew the shameful answer: vanity. He had fallen hook, line, and sinker for their flattery. What a fool he had been to take Berg at his word that *Destiny* was a force for good in a world that was collapsing under the weight of the globalised New World Order. It had taken him too long to discover that *Destiny* was the opposite of the embodiment of the progressive revolution they claimed. Berg and his cohorts were, in reality, quintessential reactionaries who threatened to tear down the very institutions they professed to cherish. And they had designated him, a high-profile but ageing intellectual, the celebrated anti-establishment *enfant terrible* of French academe, as their president. What could be more respectable than that? It was a brilliant ploy to disguise their true colours and it had worked. Until now.

Merde. Cambon cursed his own imprudence. If he, the respected Professor Cambon, doyen of the French intelligentsia and one of the sharpest minds of the modern era, could be duped so easily by their slogans and half-truths, what hope was there for the ordinary men and women, decent working-class foot soldiers of the socialist cause, on the streets of Paris or Berlin or London?

Destiny's elevator pitch had been impressive: *Where chaos rules, we will bring order; where corruption flourishes, we will enforce the law; where alienation is the norm, we will enfranchise the masses.* This was their manifesto for bringing about a new, prosperous and exciting Europe, one in which every citizen could participate and take genuine pride. The old tribal divisions between left and right, royalist and republican, secular and religious, they denounced as anachronisms, irrelevant vestiges of a fading reactionary era, and all such barriers would be dismantled. The *ancien regime* of self-destructive capitalism would be consigned to the footnotes of history and a new, progressive, anti-imperialist, anti-Zionist Europe would emerge—wide-eyed, ambitious and optimistic—into the sunlight of a glorious collective future.

What a message! The stuff that dreams are made of. Or nightmares? The scales soon fell from Cambon's eyes. The movement's leading activists were nothing more than immature, self-regarding fantasists, whether spouting Marxist or fascist utopian platitudes. The co-option of a bunch of radical Islamists—trumpeted as demonstrating *Destiny's* support for inclusiveness and tolerance—was a propaganda coup that had disarmed many of the party's liberal critics and had merely injected another strand of violent ruthlessness into their ideology. Cambon knew that these so-called Muslim 'idealists' were actually jihadist thugs who had made common cause with Berg because of the one thing that united them all—their virulent antisemitism. Much of the senior echelon within *Destiny* could detect this foul aroma but were prepared to hold their noses as long as their Islamist friends could muster substantial political and, above all, financial support from their unsavoury Middle Eastern backers.

Now that Cambon understood how he had been tricked, he felt wretched. He was trapped. If he tried to walk away, they would denounce him as a hypocrite and a traitor. They would threaten him and his family with dire consequences and might even kill him. If he stayed, he would compromise every moral principle that he had spent his life, personal and professional, promoting. As Professor of Moral Philosophy at the Paris-Sorbonne University, he had expounded his neo-Marxist, post-modernist hypotheses to successive generations of adoring students who had lapped up his imaginative scenarios in which all individuals were caught between two equally compelling but conflicting imperatives, the revolutionary overturning of the hegemony of the current oppressive elites and the seductive allure of pragmatic conformity to the well-oiled but flawed *status quo*.

The challenge he confronted now was no mere hypothesis and his dilemma was all too real. And if he, *le grand philosophe* of his age, couldn't find a solution, neither his reputation nor his integrity would emerge unscathed. His students would be fascinated by this cognitive conundrum; one or two of the brighter ones might even be capable of devising a workable exit strategy. He could do with their intellectual athleticism right now.

He drained the last of his coffee and looked around him. The Place des Vosges looked as elegant and tranquil as always. Its diverse population of Chinese, Africans, Indians, Latinos, Arabs, mixed-race and the ever-present Jews, all blending effortlessly with the native French, represented the best of twenty-first century Paris. The third-rate mob he was about to address represented the worst. Could he stop the putrefying rot from within *Destiny*? He would do all in his power to do just that as the alternative was to watch in despair as Europe became convulsed yet again in a psychotic fit of murderous racism. But what, in practice, could one man achieve in the face of mass hysteria? He needed a plan and time was against him. There was only one course of action that he could live with: he'd have to square up to Berg and demand clarity on the details of the fate that awaited Europe's Jews and the other minorities that were about to find themselves in the firing line.

Having made his decision, he felt better. But it was a brief respite. The cloud of anxiety that had clung to him for weeks refused to dissipate; he was far from convinced that his approaching showdown with Berg would end well. But it had to be done, and soon.

The professor sighed, shook his head, grabbed his walking stick and gestured to the waiter to bring his bill.

[3]

LATE NOVEMBER MORNINGS IN TEL AVIV CAN BE DAMP AND chilly even in bright sunshine. Senior commander Dr Keren Benayoun shivered on her uphill walk towards the lobby of the Institute for Intelligence and Special Operations (aka Mossad) but the goose bumps on her arm weren't caused by the weather. When she had requested an urgent meeting with the agency's avuncular director, Moshe Lunenfeld, to discuss a problematic agent, his response had been unsympathetic. Although she had been around the higher echelons of the agency for long enough to detect many of the nuances of the director's style, she had no idea what that coldness signified except that it wasn't a prelude to a convivial chat. She prepared herself for the looming confrontation with her boss in the only way she knew how: total defiance. As she entered the building, she held her head high and her back straight, a posture that sent an unmistakeable non-verbal message to all around her: *I'm here on serious business so you'd better get out of my way. Fast.*

Keren had enjoyed a good relationship with Lunenfeld from the start. She had earned his trust through years of effective teamwork and her fearlessness in challenging his opinion when the need arose. She knew that he admired her analytical mind and her intellectual honesty—he had revealed as much to her when he had plucked her out of relative obscurity to place her at the centre of Israel's most sensitive counterterrorism activities.

Giving up a successful medical practice in child psychiatry had been a wrench. A committed clinician, she had enjoyed participating in multidisciplinary research with psychologists, paediatricians, and neuroscientists. Her most recent publication on the unexpectedly high prevalence of severe post-traumatic stress disorder among young Israeli children living in proximity to the Gaza border had caused something of a stir both in Israel and around the world. The word on the academic street had been that she was on course for a professorship at Tel Aviv University's medical school.

When she decided, with almost no notice, to abandon that path to join the intelligence services, even her closest family members were amazed. Little did they realise that she had surprised herself. But the decision had been taken for her by a cruel twist of fate: her closest friend and partner for more than two decades had been reduced to a blood-drenched heap of mangled body parts by a terrorist bomb that had detonated in a bustling seaside café.

Shimon had been a fellow psychiatrist whom she'd met at a Jerusalem conference when they were both starting out on their specialist careers. They had hit it off instantly and shared a similar liberal world view. Along with a growing sector of the Israeli public, both believed with a fervour verging on the fanatical that the only road to peace in the Middle East was through the implementation of far-reaching Israeli concessions to a raft of Palestinian demands. When successive Israeli leaders agreed and negotiated with PLO chief Arafat to do just that, the response of Hamas and other rejectionists was unequivocal: They sent wave after wave of suicide bombers into Israel where they blew up restaurants, supermarkets, nightclubs, and buses. By the early 2000s, they had murdered more than a thousand Israeli civilians —including Keren's lover, partner, and best friend.

Shimon's death plunged Keren into a deep depression from which she would emerge weeks later a changed woman—heartbroken and hardened in equal measure. Gone were the dewy-eyed political ideals and the accompanying conviction that all human beings were in essence good. Her innate naivety had been blown to smithereens the instant Shimon had met his fate one sun-drenched afternoon in Netanya's Independence Square. That was the spot where a teenage *shahid*—groomed into launching his final journey to paradise to meet his maker flanked by seventy-two dark-eyed virgins—pressed the detonator on his rucksack tightly packed with a judicious mixture of explosives and ball bearings. As well as causing unfathomable carnage and grief to his dozen or so immediate victims, the misguided adolescent had also vaporised a potentially illustrious psychiatric future: Dr Benayoun's career path had been diverted in that ear-splitting moment away from tending to sick minds towards what seemed to her a more pressing priority—the defence of her country.

By the end of the *sheloshim*, the prescribed month of Jewish ritual mourning, she had made a few tentative enquiries. When Moshe Lunenfeld heard about the disillusioned young psychiatrist, he invited her for an interview that lasted exactly eight minutes, at the end of which he offered her a job with the Mossad. She accepted without a moment's hesitation.

Keren turned out to be a gifted spy—'a natural' was how Lunenfeld had summarised her talents following his appraisal of her progress towards the end of her six-month probationary period. Appointing her as field manager of *Operation Aleph Bet*

—or AB, standing for *Ain Brera*, Hebrew for *No Alternative*—had been his most recent vote of confidence in her talent. That decision had raised a few eyebrows within the agency's higher echelons, but the director had an unassailable reputation for reliable judgement.

In the world of espionage, there is a disclaimer that echoes the world of high finance: past performance is not indicative of future results. Today, Keren understood that her stellar record offered little protection from future adversity. She was about to take an enormous risk, one that guaranteed that her job was on the line. It wasn't too late to turn back, but that wasn't in her playbook. It had to be done.

After a smooth enough start, the European operation wasn't going according to plan. Her confidence in the abilities of her chosen field officer, Tamir Weiss, remained undiminished. He had been, beyond doubt, the right man for the job and she had amassed extensive data to prove it to Lunenfeld and any other sceptic who cared to look at the evidence. He had all the requisite skills to fulfil the aims of the mission and had appeared on course to deliver every one of them. Until now.

Operation Aleph Bet was entering its most critical, decisive stage. Weiss and his small hand-picked team of agents had already achieved two-thirds of their ambitious objectives. One final push over the coming weeks and they would be home and dry. The existential threat to the Jewish people and their state was on the verge of being crushed. Now was not the time to rock the boat. Yet that was what Tamir had done in his devastating message to Keren: *Sofia knows. I had to tell her to save my marriage. I know I'm breaking the rules. As we Israelis have a habit of saying, there was no alternative.*

If Tamir had intended to inject a touch of ironic humour into that last sentence, it was a bad mistake. Keren had reacted with undisguised fury. Her reply was curt: *You've blown it this time. Stand down and await further orders.* She had nursed her roiling indignation for the full twenty-four hours since Tamir had dropped his bombshell. One thought preoccupied her as she pushed open the door of the director's office: it was high time for Tamir Weiss to suffer some serious blowback.

'Doctor Benayoun, so good to see you again,' gushed the director with jarring faux-enthusiasm. 'Come in, come in, please take a seat. What's on your mind?'

Keren forced an unconvincing smile as she arranged her papers on the director's table. Dispensing with small talk, she pulled a file from the bundle and handed it to Lunenfeld. 'This is the background dossier on agent Tamir Weiss. I suggest it be amended.'

'Really?' Lunenfeld raised his eyebrows at his colleague. 'Explain, please.'

'Certainly, sir. You'll see that the first line of the summary stated that Mr Weiss has long been regarded as one of our most outstanding and reliable field agents. That description no longer applies, to my great regret.'

'Ah, so he has displeased you in some way?'

'That would be putting it mildly. He's violated a cardinal rule in the agency's workbook.' Keren bit her lower lip. 'He has broken cover.'

'That's a serious allegation. Please elaborate.'

She hesitated, then shook her head as if terminating an internal conversation. 'He's told his wife. You remember her? Sofia Lopez, the English journalist? It seems she now knows everything there is to know about *Aleph Bet*.'

What Lunenfeld said next took Keren by surprise.

'Oh, I doubt that very much, doctor.'

'Excuse me, sir? What do you mean?'

As Lunenfeld peered at her over the top of his rimless glasses, a mischievous smile played on his lips.

'Mrs Weiss knows exactly what Mr Weiss wants her to know. And that isn't the whole picture by any means. Agent Weiss broke no rules and was following orders. We've decided that the presence of a talented English journalist on the team would be most helpful to the ultimate success of the operation.'

Keren froze. *We've decided.* The words rattled around her brain like a swarm of locusts. *We've decided.* By which he meant that *he* had decided. And she had been kept in the dark. This was intolerable. Her pulse rate was increasing by the second.

'I see,' she whispered, struggling to control her seething emotions. 'Let me get this straight. If I have understood correctly, in making your decision you have bypassed me and undermined my authority.'

'Come now, doctor, don't be so melodramatic. No one is undermining your authority. Quite the opposite. We need you more than ever. Sometimes high-level decisions have to be made at speed before all the interested parties have been consulted.'

'Is that what I am, an interested party? I thought, as field manager of this project, I was rather more than that. And if you haven't undermined my authority, what do think you have done?'

'We have simply made a tactical change in the field plan. Come off your high horse, Keren. It doesn't suit you. You feel slighted but you'll get over it. It happens to all of us from time to time. Now if you'll excuse me...'

'Slighted?' Keren's expression was thunderous. 'You have embarrassed and humiliated me.' Unable to control her agitation, she collected her papers and stood up. 'You can't behave this way towards me, sir. It's unacceptable. I will have to consider my position.'

'Ah, that's such a pity,' Lunenfeld sighed. 'I'd hate to lose you, doctor. Look, if you're determined to resign your post, I can't stop you. But you'd be making a grave mistake. And as I'm sure you know, a Mossad commander of your elevated status can't simply walk away. You would be bound by Protocol 48.'

Protocol 48 was the legally sanctioned device the agency used as an absolute last resort to silence troublesome ex-employees. It had rarely been applied in the nearly eight decades of the history of the State of Israel. Although most Mossad employees were aware of its existence, few understood its practical implications. Keren didn't relish the prospect of finding out.

'Look me in the eye, Officer Benayoun, and tell me that you are about to turn your back on your country and your people.'

She declined to respond to either instruction. Lunenfeld spoke softly as he always did when he wanted to emphasise a point. 'Listen carefully to what I'm saying. I understand that you are upset. But there is no room for bruised egos in this organisation. You must trust me when I tell you that I had no alternative in taking this decision about Sofia Weiss. I am sorry you feel slighted, but I can't help that. Look, I don't want to lose you. You are one of my best commanders. And my respect for your abilities remains unbounded.'

Keren said nothing, her mask-like expression unyielding. Lunenfeld stood and checked his watch. 'This is a distressing situation for all of us. Permit me to make a suggestion, doctor. Take a fortnight's leave. Or a month's. Get away from this hothouse and reflect on your future. I'm confident that you'll come to the right conclusion. We need you. And your country needs you. Now, if you'll excuse me, I have a busy schedule today. The PM awaits.'

[4]

THE VENUE WAS VAST, MORE LIKE AN AIRCRAFT HANGAR THAN A conference hall. How, wondered Professor Pierre Cambon, the figurehead president of *Destiny*, had they found such an enormous space right in the centre of Paris? Who was paying for it? Cambon had demanded an answer from Berg, whose cryptic reply referred to *profiting from the prophet*—meaning, suspected Cambon, that the reactionary royals of Saudi Arabia or Qatar were bankrolling the event (and probably much more besides). He'd have to take this matter further with Berg but that would have to wait until he had delivered his speech. In the wings of the sprawling proscenium stage, Cambon leafed through his sheaf of notes and tried to concentrate on the key words, but he couldn't focus clearly on his text so distressed was he by his predicament. To make matters worse, the humming chatter of the enormous crowd of delegates distracted him—it was incessant, like a school assembly anticipating the arrival of a popular head teacher who was about to address his excitable pupils.

The lights in the auditorium dimmed and the throng fell silent. All eyes turned to the front of the hall. A side door at the opposite end of the stage to Cambon was flung open. A tall, partially bald,

23

goatee-bearded, black-clad man with a slight stoop strode onto the platform to the accompaniment of whoops and cheers. Christoph Berg, operations director of *Destiny* and the movement's undisputed leader, waved in acknowledgement of the ovation and joined the applause in the manner of a TV celebrity—which, indeed, he was rapidly becoming.

Cambon had to admit that Berg cut a striking yet somehow menacing figure, his steely blue glare transmitting a clear message to all who saw it—don't mess with me. Berg turned to Cambon and gestured to him to make his entrance. That was the moment when Cambon's mind flashed forward to contemplate an unsavoury scene in which Berg prepared to address a gigantic Nuremberg-style rally; this was, after all, a man who would not hesitate to model himself on his fellow-Austrian hero, *der Führer*. Cambon shuddered. Berg was in his element, wordlessly working the crowd into a frenzy of adulation, making ostentatious eye contact with several individual members of his reverential audience and offering them approving nods of encouragement. It was an undeniably impressive performance. Like the maestro of a symphony orchestra, he was patently in meticulous control over every detail even before the first note had been played. He turned and stared hard at Cambon, hissing *schnell, schnell*. The Frenchman was no lipreader but he understood Berg's hand gestures beckoning him to make his entrance. Cambon swallowed hard and limped, with the aid of a walking stick, onto the stage towards the star attraction, blinking under the uncomfortable glare of the spotlights.

Both men gazed out at the adoring multitude. Berg beamed a toothy smile, his gold fillings glinting, and stood to attention, his back ramrod straight as though he were guarding the crown jewels. By contrast, the corpulent old academic at his side looked nervous. On receiving the signal from Berg, Cambon approached the microphone. He coughed and tapped the microphone, which responded with a volley of minor explosions followed by a horrible high-pitched feedback whine. When that eventually settled, he pulled out his sheaf of notes and began to read from them.

'*Bonjour mesdames et messieurs. Bienvenue à Paris. Je vous remercie...*' That was as far as he got before he felt a hand grasping his elbow with far more force than necessary.

'Stop!' hissed Berg in his ear. 'Speak English. On second thought, don't bother. I'll take over. Move away.' The Austrian pulled the professor away from the microphone, raised both hands above his head and applauded with theatrical enthusiasm, a cue to which the expectant audience responded with whistling, shouting and stamping. Berg ushered his bemused elderly colleague from the platform as though he were guiding a demented old patient back to a closed psychiatric ward. When he resumed what everyone present knew was his rightful place centre-stage, Berg turned to face the crowd. He waited for his listeners to calm down before addressing them in a tone of amicable bonhomie laced with sarcasm.

'Thank you, Mr President, dear Professor Cambon—Our Esteemed Genius—for your inspiring opening remarks. We all appreciate your invaluable leadership of our wonderful organisation. Thank you, thank you, thank you!' He nodded vigorously and mimicked a clapping action that launched another round of staccato applause, this time rather more subdued than the first.

'Dear friends, we have arrived at a momentous phase in the history of *Destiny*. Until now, we have been patiently arguing our case with some success. Why? Because we have been fearless. We have been honest. We have been speaking truth to power. And our words are being heard and endorsed in the capitals across this great continent. That is because we, my friends, are unafraid to speak of things that have for too long been considered taboo. My friends, I have wonderful news. I can confirm to you all today that we have reached a tipping point in our quest for wider support.'

The crowd gasped in surprise and approval. A few whistled and roared, stamping their feet in delight.

'Yes, my fellow Europeans, I am serious. I have here in my pocket a document, a copy of which you will all receive shortly. This is our manifesto, *Our Glorious Birthright*, and in it you will read of our exciting plans for the future. Our policies will address the urgent economic and social issues that have been scandalously neglected across this continent for years, for decades. To give you just one example, we will ensure that every European family has a decent income, enough to feed and clothe their children, and to end the obscene inequalities that blight all our nations. But that is only the start of our ambitious programme.'

That announcement was met with muted applause, just as Berg had anticipated. He raised his arms, the palms of his hands towards his listeners as though wishing to snuff out any premature triumphalism. His oratory had been restrained, by his standards, up to that point, and he knew it. Now he turned up the emotional thermostat. At first, he spoke quietly so that the audience had to strain to hear him. 'My dear friends, let me remind you of our mission statement: *Destiny* will strive to serve the many, not the few. Let me repeat that.' Now he turned up the volume: *'Destiny will strive to serve the many, not the few!'* Those words will, I promise you, soon resonate around the capitals and parliaments of Europe.' Then the dramatic, climactic crescendo. 'If that prospect strikes fear into the capitalist fat cats and Rothschild bankers who have controlled our lives for years—no, centuries—we can live with that, can't we? Let them quake until their jewellery rattles!'

He had delivered that last line with such energy that it echoed around the enormous hall like a thunderclap. His listeners stood *en masse* and cheered. He nodded and raised both arms. The noise instantly abated.

'How will we achieve this radical transformation? First and foremost, we will address the serious matter that patriots across the world have been told for years is off limits for discussion. My friends, there are no such limits in this hall. We will not be intimidated. Not by anyone—nor by any vested interest. I speak, of course, of the powerful Jewish lobby, or more accurately, the Jewish-Zionist axis.' The audience fell silent as they absorbed this new revelation.

'Let me address the Jewish question head on. I must stress that we have no argument whatsoever with adherents of the Jewish faith or with individual Jews—indeed I am happy to report that some courageous young Jews have joined our movement and we welcome them with open arms and warm hearts. I know I speak for all of you when I proclaim that, contrary to the unfounded claims of our enemies, *Destiny* is not an antisemitic movement. Perish the thought! God forbid! Like everyone in this room, I do not have a single antisemitic bone in my body!' The audience responded with a burst of applause that lasted a few seconds and then petered out once more on Berg's command.

'Judaism was, after all, the forerunner of our beloved Christianity. It was, and remains, a flawed religion and cannot be compared in any sense to the far more civilised beliefs that our dear mother church has promoted for two thousand years. But Judaism, for all its many faults, is really not the problem. It has had its day and is bound to wither on the vine. And Jews as individuals are not the issue. As good Christians, we may disagree fundamentally over their rejection—and indeed calculated murder —of our Messiah, our Saviour, the Lord Jesus Christ, and we may find some of their bloody rituals, such as circumcision and animal slaughter, utterly barbaric. But these are relatively trivial matters for which I am confident we can find compromises. No, my friends, we are facing another threat, another level of danger entirely.

'We all know that we have to address the disproportionate individual and collective influence of the morally depraved Zionist politicians, of the manipulative global Zionist media, and of the despicable Zionist arms trade. All of this loathsome activity is backed to the hilt by the criminally aggressive, usurping, apartheid State of Israel. For us—the majority of Europeans, white, God-fearing Christian Europeans, along with our many Muslim friends—this state of affairs is unbearable. The Jewish-Zionist Axis must be stopped if our continent, indeed our world, is ever to return to its former glory. What is more, many other good people—Hindus, Buddhists, and people of no faith—find themselves agreeing with us. Most have been cowed into silence by—you-know-who.' Berg theatrically cupped his left ear as a ripple of applause coursed across the room accompanied by a staccato chanting of *Jews, Jews, Jews.*

'I know, I know, I'm not allowed to criticise any of those of the Jewish persuasion despite their plotting against us ordinary decent Europeans. At least that was true in the recent past. Happily, however, we have succeeded in smashing this politically correct censorship. So let me be frank with you.' Berg paused, drawing energy from the tense silence that had enveloped his audience. When he resumed, he spoke in a near-whisper. 'We will soon be in a position to deal with this poison at its source, once and for all. This will be done efficiently and decisively but also sensitively, humanely and legally. The precise methods have yet to be determined but, I promise you, we shall do it. How do I know?' He ratcheted up anticipation of the answer by pacing the stage for ten seconds. On returning to the microphone, he delivered the punch line with an unrestrained, booming fortissimo. 'Because, my friends, we have found a way! We have succeeded in mobilising strong and widespread support from ordinary men and women right across the continent of Europe for the immediate implementation of this radical and necessary policy!'

The audience rose to its feet as one and bellowed its endorsement. Berg gazed into the middle distance as if he had momentarily lost his bearings. As the ovation petered out, he recovered his poise and returned to his rousing theme. 'Comrades and friends, brothers and sisters, this brings me to the reason I have called this historic meeting. I have a tremendous achievement to report to you today. I am truly thrilled to announce that our manifesto has been signed by senior politicians and officials from at least twenty countries across our continent. More are sure to follow. While not all these brave individuals represent their governments, they carry sufficient weight for us to be able to declare to the world, *We are here, and we are significant, and we are winning.*' He inhaled deeply and thrust his chest outwards to deliver his next sentence. 'Yes, my friends, we are finally on the verge of grasping the levers of power.'

On hearing the magic word *power*, the crowd rose as one, with a handful of cheerleaders in the front row whistling, stamping and chanting. Berg raised his arms and the noise subsided. 'You see it turns out that we, *Destiny*, are indeed the authentic force of destiny. We are Europe's destiny, and soon everyone across the world will see how inevitable our revolution has become. It is, literally, as our manifesto proclaims, *Our Glorious Birthright*. And it's all thanks to you, the visionary, pioneering, loyal supporters of our great movement, for without you, we are nothing, we are insignificant. With you, everything, and I mean everything, is possible.'

By now, a Mexican wave of adulation had swept through the ranks of the faithful, extending from the seats nearest the stage to the very farthest corners of the auditorium. All were now on their feet, clapping, whistling, stamping, shouting and embracing, drunk on the news of their latest triumph. Someone in the middle of the room started chanting: '*Bravo Berg, bravo Berg,*' and soon all had joined the mass accolade, generating a deafening cacophony that caused the floor to vibrate and the lights to flicker.

Not everyone in the room had been roused to a state of frenzied enthusiasm. In the near darkness of the back row, two inconspicuous figures, a man and a woman, declined to join the party. Instead, they were listening intently to the speech, jotting down a few notes and snapping occasional photos with their phones.

Tamir Weiss and Keren Benayoun, both senior employees of Israel's intelligence agency, the Mossad, glanced at each other, rose from their seats and slipped unnoticed out of the auditorium.

[5]

'IN THAT CASE, WHY DON'T YOU JUST BRING CLARA WITH YOU?'

Sofia's jaw dropped at Tamir's question. 'Are you out of your mind? You know why—education, safety, continuity, consistency. Everything a six-year-old child needs. And that doesn't include a grand tour of Europe living out of suitcases and sleeping in a different bed every night. Why can't you get that, Tamir?'

'What's your solution if you won't ask your sister or mother for help?'

'It wouldn't be fair on them. Luisa has her own young family to bring up and my father's been ill, so my mum has her hands full. No, I won't do it.'

Ever since Tamir had returned to London three days earlier, they'd been engaged in the same circular, futile argument about their daughter's welfare.

'In that case, *ahuvati*, you'll have to stay at home with her. Whatever the consequences for...' His voice trailed off.

Sofia helped him out. 'For us, you mean, don't you? For our marriage. Why don't you just say it?'

Sofia closed her eyes, as though trying to conjure a solution out of the ether through sheer willpower. Having engineered this showdown with her husband, could she finally convince him to take her into his confidence? That, she realised, was the crunch question. She knew he wouldn't do it without further coaxing.

'Listen, Tamir, I'm not ruling out parking Clara with Luisa again. She's a resilient child and my sister is a gem. But how do you expect me to make such a big decision without knowing why? Just talk to me. I can't stand the secrecy anymore. Either we're real partners or this marriage is a sham. You disappear for days or sometimes weeks on end and I don't even get a phone call. You have to tell me what is going on.'

'You're right.' Tamir sighed in apparent capitulation. 'Come here, *ahuvati*, and I'll tell you as much as I can.'

Sofia hesitated, but only for a moment. She needed to try to dismantle the barrier between them. She snuggled close to him on the sofa and let him place his arm around her shoulder.

'But before I start, you must understand something. Just having this conversation could cost me my job. I'm doing it because I don't want to lose you—and Clara. You'll have to treat this information as the most confidential you've ever heard in your entire life. Got that?'

Sofia nodded. 'Yes, one hundred percent. Thank you, darling. Go on, I'm listening.' She shuffled further down into the depths of the large, upholstered sofa and adopted her favourite fetal position while enfolded in the protective embrace of her muscular husband. Tamir lightly caressed her shoulder as he began his story.

'When we returned from Australia, everything was up in the air. I didn't know what the future held—for us as a family, especially. And I can tell you now that I wasn't at all certain that I wanted to stay in the agency.'

'Until Keren convinced you otherwise, I suppose.' She hadn't meant to invoke the name of Tamir's Mossad handler, but it somehow spilled out.

'No, it wasn't just Keren. I know this is hard for you to understand, *ahuvati*, but we Israelis can't just walk away when our country calls on us for help.'

'And patriotism trumps family every time?'

'It's more than mere patriotism. You have to place today's events in the context of the past. The Jewish people waited two thousand years to get our homeland back and it's still not certain that we've pulled it off. There are a lot of bad guys out there who want us to fail. We won't let that happen for one reason. It's a matter of life and death. We tried trusting in the good will of others for centuries and it ended in catastrophe.'

'Please, Tamir, don't give me a history lesson. I'm not an idiot.' A note of exasperation had crept into her voice. 'You're committed to defending your country and I respect that. But you have a family now. Where do we fit in?'

Tamir responded in kind. 'I can't believe you can even ask me that question! You and Clara are the centre of my universe. I can't do anything without you. No, don't sneer—I mean it. And the last thing I want is for either of you to feel excluded. That's why I'm telling you this. I want you to join me. Both of you. Starting with...' He paused as though unsure whether to continue. 'Starting with citizenship.'

'Are you serious?' Sofia was studying her husband's face in detail. 'You are, aren't you? You mean you'd like us to become Israelis? Is that even allowed for non-Jews?'

'Sure, it's allowed. You'd have to go through a few bureaucratic hoops but the Law of Return can fast-track the whole thing as you are my family.'

'Hold on, you're going too fast,' said Sofia, her eyelids flickering. 'One step at a time, please. Before we start filling in the forms for Israeli citizenship, you'll have to tell me about this European project you're currently involved in.'

Tamir seemed to recoil, almost imperceptibly, at that question.

'OK, but it's complicated. I'm not sure it will make much sense to you.'

You're mansplaining again, she wanted to say, but instead said, 'Try me.'

'Let me get this straight,' Sofia said twenty minutes later. 'You're afraid that a new Hitler is about to take over Europe?'

'Not yet. Not imminently, at least. But he's making preparations. Or rather they are, the entire group. It's not just one man. And we're pretty sure we know who they are. The figurehead is a famous French academic called Pierre Cambon. But the real threat is his official deputy, an Austrian journalist. He is—how do you say it?—the power behind the throne. His name is Christoph Berg and he's one very nasty piece of work. Together, these two characters run an extremist organisation called *Destiny*, but it was Berg's brainchild and he is the real boss.'

'You mean they're neo-Nazis and it's your job to stop them? By fair means or foul?'

Tamir nodded. 'That just about sums it up. And I'm asking you to help me do it.'

'You want me to join the Mossad?'

'No, not exactly. At least not straight away. I don't have the authority to invite you to join us. And even if I did, you would have to start off as a kind of associate member. You wouldn't officially be on our books and you wouldn't get paid. But we'd protect you if we had to, and that's worth more than any salary, believe me.'

Sofia rose and circled the room, clasping and unclasping her hands several times as if attempting to capture an elusive thought between her palms. She walked behind Tamir, placed her hands on his shoulders and gently massaged his tense muscles.

'Mmm, that feels so good,' he said. 'Keep doing it.' He closed his eyes and smiled.

'Look, Tamir, when we married, you promised me you'd put all this derring-do behind you.'

'Derring what? Is that even English?'

Ignoring his question, she continued. 'I never signed up for this. And more to the point, neither did Clara. You have a family to think of now, not just you or your country. But it's your decision. You know that I'll still love you, whatever happens. Though you make it hard for me at times.'

She paused waiting for his reaction. When none came, she abandoned the massage and wandered back to the sofa. They sat in glum silence for half a minute.

Finally, Sofia said, 'What I'm trying to say is that I'm not prepared to keep farming Clara out to anyone, even to Luisa. Period. That's my position. And you'll do what you have to do. I know that. But I want to save this marriage too.'

'Thank you, *ahuvati*.' Tamir was visibly relieved. 'Looks like we're on the same page. Does that mean you'll join us?'

'Hold on. Let's assume, for the sake of argument that I agree to get involved in your operation—what do you call it?'

'*Aleph Bet*, the first two letters of the Hebrew alphabet. They stand for *Ain Brera*, meaning "no alternative." It's an apt phrase. We have to neutralise them, Sofia, or they will do untold damage, not just to Jews but to the whole of Europe and to the democratic world.'

'Yes, I see that. Listen, Tamir. I'm prepared to help you, if I can, on one condition. I want to be based here with Clara in London. Is that an option?'

Tamir scratched his head. 'I can't promise but it's possible, I suppose. Maybe you could do something useful for us here, using your journalistic skills or checking out how *Destiny* operates on the publicity side. I'd have to look into it and get the approval of my bosses and that may not be easy. They're not keen on involving outsiders. But they might accept some form of compromise. I'll raise it with them, but it will be risky. As I said, I could get fired just for discussing these ideas with you. It's strictly against protocol. But I think I can talk them round.'

'You mean talk Keren round.'

'Not just Keren but she'd have to give us the green light. Then she'll discuss it with the director. Give me a day or two, *ahuvati*, and I'll do my best to sort something out. Deal?'

'Deal.'

[6]

OUTSIDE OBSERVERS (WERE ANY PERMITTED) WOULD BE surprised to discover that Israel's security cabinet was an ad hoc body of only eight or nine people comprising (usually) the prime minister, the Israel Defense Forces' chief of staff, the ministers of defence, foreign affairs and the interior, and the heads of military intelligence, national security, and counterterrorism. Political, legal and security advisors were invited when their input was necessary. On this occasion, Moshe Lunenfeld, the head of Mossad, had been informed that his presence was required from the start of the meeting.

'Good morning, friends,' boomed the prime minister, Yoav Adar, his burly frame occupying much of the centre of the long rectangular table. 'Let's get started. There's only one item on today's agenda. *Destiny.* How appropriate that name is. Moshe, over to you.'

Lunenfeld nodded. With meticulous care, he pulled a few sheets of paper from an inside jacket pocket and placed them on the table in front of him. Peering, as was his custom, over the top of his rimless glasses at the assembled company, he cleared his throat. That had the effect of attracting eight pairs of eyes in his direction.

'Thank you, Prime Minister. My purpose today is to review for you the history and nature of a dangerous political entity called *Destiny* that has been gaining momentum in Europe in recent months. Though it's a relatively young movement, we can trace its ideological roots all the way back to the early twentieth century. I will explain why we in the agency believe it poses a serious and even an existential threat to the Jewish people and the State of Israel, as well as to several other minorities. This will take me a little time so please bear with me.'

Everyone around the table knew that this was code for *don't even think of interrupting*. Lunenfeld spoke slowly and with authority. He outlined the tumultuous effects of the financial crisis of 2008 across the world and the impact of subsequent upheavals in the Middle East and Africa that had driven millions of asylum seekers to pursue newer, safer lives in Europe. Other factors—especially climate change—had reinforced the phenomenon. Mass migration had, in turn, generated a deep-seated social malaise, a populist xenophobic backlash against the newcomers. The reactionary trend was magnified tenfold by the entry into Europe of thousands of radical Islamist ideologues, a minority of whom perpetrated periodic barbarous acts of terrorism. Just as national economies were recovering, a second shock occurred in 2020—the catastrophic Covid-19 coronavirus pandemic. This resulted in draconian lockdowns and the cessation of almost all economic activity across the world. That, too, heralded huge consequences—surging unemployment, poverty, chronic ill health and political instability. All of this was exacerbated by the expanded reach of social media that facilitated the spread of conspiracy theories, hate-filled discourse and political extremism...

Lunenfeld paused, ostensibly to sip some water. Glancing around the room, he observed a malady common to almost all political gatherings he had addressed over the years: a short attention span. Was he was losing them? Their glazed expressions told him all he needed to know. A collective torpor had descended on the group and anything he said now would dissolve, unnoticed and unmissed, into the ether. It was time to change gear. He laid his notes on the table and removed his spectacles.

'Gentlemen, you have just heard the essence of my message. I could elaborate but I prefer a more interactive approach. I am sure you have many burning questions. Please feel free to ask me anything you wish. Over to you.'

His listeners blinked with surprise at being handed the baton with no notice. But politicians are a competitive breed and they soon overcame their diffidence in order to avoid appearing wrong-footed. The foreign minister weighed in first.

'Thank you for that summary, Moshe. One thing puzzles me. The entire world has been affected by these various crises you have so clearly outlined to us. Why has Europe, of all places, spawned this poisonous phenomenon that calls itself *Destiny*?'

'An excellent question, minister, to which the answer must, of necessity, be unsatisfactory. Let me start at the end, as it were, with the impact of the pandemic.

'The global public health emergency affected all continents, but Europe was traumatised by the event to a greater extent than elsewhere. Many people died, as we know, and the survivors had to cope with the pandemic's disastrous socioeconomic and political consequences. The virus itself was believed to have originated in China. That country's lack of transparency and its resentful response to the international finger of blame that was pointed at its authoritarian leaders—along with the other factors to which I referred—generated suspicion, anger and racism across the European continent. The public reaction was fierce and vengeful. It found expression via social media that in turn helped propel a range of extremist parties to prominence. Some of these were far-right or far-left ideologues who fell out with each other with predictable frequency. But all shared the same ultimate objective —to create a revolutionary transformation of their societies. In this brave new world, the majority, or the so-called indigenous citizens, would—and here I must reference the Brexit Britain slogan—"take back control." That notion was always delusional but the sentiment appealed to millions of people, not just in the UK but across the continent.'

'Are you saying that Brexit was a racist ideology?' asked the interior minister.

Lunenfeld pursed his lips. 'Not necessarily. But it resonated with pre-existing racist attitudes. It also generated an atmosphere of xenophobia in its own right. We have to ask ourselves what that mantra 'take back control' implied for the future of minorities, including the recent wave of Middle Eastern and Central Asian immigrants. At best, they would play a marginal role in the planned utopia; at worst, they would all be sent packing. These views were promoted by a few political disruptors who enjoyed transient success but failed to gain sustained traction for one reason—globalisation, both economic and political. The world was just too interconnected for any old demagogue to achieve a decisive seizure of the reins of power.'

The head of military intelligence jumped into the conversation. 'The EU never stops lecturing us about how civilised they are compared to us. Is that hypocritical of them?'

'Until recently, I would say no. The supranational European Union was itself a manifestation of liberal globalisation, and a highly effective one at that. From its inception, the EU fulfilled its mission well. Let us recall the vision of its founders. It had been formed after the Second World War as a monolithic bureaucracy to forge tight and unbreakable bonds of governance across the continent as a means of preserving peace and ensuring that a new Adolf Hitler or Joseph Stalin could never sweep away democratic institutions. Working with the giant global financial institutions—the World Bank, the International Monetary Fund and the Organization for Economic Co-operation and Development—the EU succeeded for many decades in preventing the lunatics from taking over the asylum and destroying European institutions. From time to time, radical elements emerged but EU institutions stepped in and stopped them in their tracks.'

'What changed?' asked the foreign minister.

"The radicals didn't disappear,' continued Lunenfeld. 'Instead, they regrouped, redrew their plans, and waited. When the multiple crises I described struck, these extremists re-emerged from the chaotic melee that had threatened to submerge them. This time, they were more determined than ever to establish their vision of a New World Order. How did they intend to achieve this? By learning from history. They adopted a commonplace yet powerful strategy—cooperation. The far right and far left were, after all, used to getting into bed together; Hitler and Stalin had paved the way for that tactic around a century earlier. It had long seemed a far-fetched idea that such an alliance would ever be repeated. But something had changed. There was a new kid on the block, as our American friends might say. The purveyors of a fundamentalist, radical and violent version of Islam wanted in on the action and offered manpower, intelligence, arms and, above all, cash. Let's all work with each other, they argued, and we will prove irresistible. Separately, we're doomed, but together, by forming a three-way red-green-blue alliance, we'll succeed beyond our wildest dreams.'

'That sounds to me like a sure recipe for disaster,' said the defence minister.

'On the contrary, Minister, it worked like a dream. That

message of subsuming differences for the sake of a common goal hit its target and the Islamists were drawn, in tight secrecy at first, right into the heart of this wall-to-wall populist collaboration. The immediate need was threefold: a well-organised, well-financed mass movement; a charismatic leader who would channel this international resentment; and an obvious target. The first two could be achieved quickly. Identifying the target—enemy number one—was the top priority.'

'I think we all know where you're going with this, Moshe,' said the prime minister, studying the ceiling.

Lunenfeld ignored the comment. 'What could it, or they, be, this enemy of the people? European history again provided the answer—the Jews, as always, the eternal scapegoats, the perennial outsiders. The Nazi Final Solution had not resolved the Jewish question but had merely displaced it temporarily. The time has come, screamed these old-new ideologues of the twenty-first century, to deal a final, mortal blow to the exploitative bankers, the greedy speculators, the bullying employers, the rapacious multinationals, the trouble-making writers, the lying journalists. These are all synonyms for the conspiratorial Jews—correction, 'Zionists'—who were accused of ruining lives, disrupting the environment and threatening all our futures. The world's oldest hatred was on the march once more.'

'You're saying that antisemitism is the *raison d'etre* of this new organisation, *Destiny*?' asked the counterterrorism head.

'Indeed, it is. Out of this febrile, deranged vision of a single, overarching enemy, the first rumblings of another dangerous political earthquake in Europe could be felt. The red-green-blue alliance emerged from the far edges of politics and merged into *Destiny*, a superficially respectable political alignment that is, in effect, nothing more than a great lumpen battering-ram aimed at crushing the Jewish people once and for all. We know that the leadership of *Destiny* draws its energy from that reliable old standby, antisemitism.'

Lunenfeld opened his briefcase and pulled out a sheaf of papers that he placed in the middle of the table. 'In this report, which I urge you all to read at your leisure, I have summarised for you the results of an as yet unpublished Europe-wide survey that confirms, in stark statistical terms, the reality of this trend. You will see that the rates of antisemitism and a willingness to vote for extremist politicians are, in both cases, over 50 percent of the adult population, especially in younger age groups. A similar pattern is observable in all the surveyed countries. In other words, European anti-Jewish sentiment, combined with a willingness to elect antisemites to high office, is higher now than at any time since the 1940s. These results are based on sound scientific methods and point to one inescapable conclusion. *Destiny* has strong winds behind it and nothing will stop its ship from sailing —apart from the State of Israel.'

Prime Minister Adar stood and the not-so-subtle cues from his body language signalled to the Mossad director that it would soon be time to wrap up this part of his presentation. Lunenfeld refused to be rushed. He had more to say.

'Gentlemen, my analysis, albeit a provisional one, is profoundly gloomy. Hatred of our people is a permanent reality that tends to infect those on the fringes of society. We don't like it, but we have learned to live with it over the centuries. Most of the time, it is confined to the fringes of society and is manageable. But we have also learned a hard lesson—that when it enters the mainstream via the media and broader civil society, we need to sit up and take notice. And when it becomes harnessed to real political power, as it is on course to do today, it becomes a threat to both the Jewish people and to the established democratic order that we have come to take for granted in Europe since 1945.'

The prime minister folded his arms, as was his custom in preparing to make what he regarded as a profound statement. 'Moshe, I must insist on greater clarity. Please be more specific. Are we, the Jewish people and Israel, facing a potential or an actual threat?'

Lunenfeld poured himself a glass of water and took a couple of leisurely sips before answering. 'My friends, I regret to inform you that political power is now within reach of those who again wish to promote hatred towards us. We already have populist politicians of both the far left and far right in influential positions across Europe. Some have even been elected to the highest offices of government. If they manage to join forces with the Islamists and their wealthy supporters from our part of the world, their collective impact will be far greater and more dangerous than the sum of their individual parts. They understand this reality and are working day and night to achieve that end.

'The three necessary preconditions for reaching their goal have been met: They have an organisation, *Destiny*; they have money from many individual and institutional backers; and they have a scapegoat—us. By which I mean the Jewish people, not least our last line of defence, the State of Israel. A new front is opening in our endless war of survival. This one is not sitting directly on our borders for a change. But it is as dangerous as any threat that we have faced in the past. We must challenge it and draw its fangs—or it will rise up and seek to marginalise and even destroy millions of our people. Again.'

Lunenfeld scrutinised his audience. Not for the first time in his career, he found himself in a roomful of Israelis whom he had stunned into total silence.

The PM spoke first. There was a marked tremor in his voice. 'I don't think anyone in this room would disagree with your diagnosis, Moshe. But what's the most effective treatment? What must we do to cure the disease?'

'Indeed, Prime Minister, that is the critical question. And, as you know, we are already seeking ways to answer it. We have developed a detailed plan to counter this menace. It is, I assure you all, appropriate to the scale of the challenge we face. We have called it *Operation Aleph Bet* or *Ain Brera*. We have no alternative.'

[7]

CHRISTOPH BERG, OPERATIONS DIRECTOR OF *DESTINY*, ADMIRED Hungary—a country that had, after all, once been ruled from his native Vienna—but he detested Lake Balaton in midsummer. Once an elegant watering hole for Hungary's affluent middle classes, it was now an escape for the great unwashed of Budapest's slums who headed in droves to its shores for cheapskate holidays. Like so much of Europe, the lake and its environs had seen far better days. How sad it was, thought Berg, to observe the fate of great swathes of territory that had once comprised a great empire; so much of the landscape had sunk into a state of tragic decline and squalor due, he was convinced, to the noxious influence of immigrants who dragged their alien cultures into the once-pristine towns, cities and villages of what was once the world's most civilised continent. That process of relentless degradation would have to be stopped and he, Berg, knew in his gut that he was the man to stop it.

He fixed his gaze on the glassy surface of the water, trying to ignore a bunch of noisy teenagers who were knocking back iced vodka shots at the other end of the terrace of his hotel. Without such riffraff, this little place, Keszthely, could be a half-decent resort, he reflected ruefully as he lit his third cigarette of the morning.

When Cambon demanded an urgent face-to-face discussion with Berg, the Austrian had insisted, for reasons of security, on meeting at this specific spot, though it was inconvenient for both of them. 'Now that our manifesto has been published, we can't be too careful, Professor,' he had stressed to the elderly Frenchman. 'The forces of darkness have eyes and ears everywhere. We have to keep them guessing day-in, day-out.'

Berg stared at the small paddle steamer wending its way slowly across the lake, producing a rippling wake on which several white birds were bobbing in playful unison. The deck was packed with enthusiastic and exuberant trippers. Who were these young holidaymakers, he wondered, pointing and taking 'selfies' and shouting at nothing in particular, and why did they come here, of all places?

Suddenly, it hit him. Were those the ugly, guttural sounds of Hebrew he could hear wafting across the water? He might have guessed it. Those damned Jews again! Israelis to be precise— same thing. He would have to be careful. While this lot didn't much look like the Zionist interlopers he knew them to be, they were adept at deception, passing themselves off as ordinary low-class tourists that this part of the world attracted over the holiday period. He clenched his jaw in resentment at their sheer *chutzpah*. Let them enjoy themselves while they could. They and their ilk were soon in for a surprise. It would be the biggest shock of their pointless lives.

'Solving the world's problems again, are we, Herr Berg?'

A rotund, silvery-haired man was standing at his table. He was wearing an onion-seller's beret and clutching a gnarled wooden walking stick. It was the movement's eminent president, *Our Esteemed Genius,* as Berg had himself christened him in a spirit of *schmaltz* dripping with irony.

'I really wish you wouldn't creep up on me like that, Pierre!' snapped Berg.

'Nice to see you too, *patron*,' replied Cambon. Been here long?'

'I got here forty minutes ago, at the time we agreed to meet. Don't you remember? Or have you turned even more senile in your old age since we last met?'

Cambon declined to rise to the bait. 'We are in a good mood, aren't we? What's bothering you today, apart from your big head being stuck up your own arse?'

Berg ignored the insult, lit another cigarette and inhaled from it deeply. Cambon searched out a metal chair, scraped it along the wooden deck, placed it next to the Austrian and awkwardly manoeuvred himself into it. Both men were now facing the lake. They sat in silence for a full minute. Finally, Berg said, 'Explain yourself, please. Why are we here, Pierre?'

'You mean apart from the sheer unalloyed pleasure we take in each other's company?' Cambon sniggered at his own comment. 'We are such a strange pair, you and I, aren't we?'

'Whatever you say. Come on, what's this all about, old man, I haven't got all day,' muttered Berg, glancing at his watch.

The 'old man' leaned forward, placing his elbows on the table. 'I'm here to tell you some home truths you may not want to hear, *patron*.'

'Is that so? Let me tell you something you may not want to hear either. I don't have to sit here and listen to you pontificate.'

'On the contrary, that's just what you have to do. So at least have the courtesy to hear what I have to say. First, this whole madcap scheme of yours will fail. Your dream child, *Destiny*, is going nowhere. Targeting Jews, blacks, Roma, gays and anyone else you dislike isn't just immoral, it's impractical. These ideas are contrary to the *zeitgeist*. They won't gain traction nowadays. You'll never get any serious politician, whatever their party allegiance, to accept it. We both know that all your boasts of twenty countries signing up to our manifesto is pure bluster, a tabloid journalist's fantasy. Let's be honest for a change, eh, Berg?'

'Oh, you're the great expert on strategy, are you? We'll see. I'll prove you wrong. Just leave the politics to me. What else? Or is that the sum total of today's great thought?'

'There's more, Berg. I've helped you as much as I can. Above and beyond. I've gone the extra mile for you. But it's getting too dangerous. Even this country, Hungary, the most xenophobic in Europe, is turning against us. The writing is on the wall and I've had enough. From now on, you can count me out.'

Berg stared out at the lake and bared his teeth in angry frustration. 'What did you just say? Count you out? That's funny, hysterical actually. No deal, old man. I'm sorry to disappoint you, but you don't get to decide. You're in this up to your stinking French armpits and that's exactly where you'll stay until I tell you otherwise. Got that?'

'I see. In that case, Berg, I'll just walk away right now. I don't need to sit here and listen to your codswallop. Who do you think I am? Your cut-price whore?' Cambon's face was scarlet as he struggled to his feet.

Berg muttered something under his breath and rose to address Cambon face-to-face. Though only a couple of inches taller than the Frenchman, Berg's powerful build was an intimidating presence. When he spoke, he almost spat out the words. 'Stop this nonsense right now! You will do exactly as I say, old man. You know the score. You may be president of *Destiny* but I am the one who put you there with strict conditions attached. Or perhaps you've forgotten? Allow me to refresh your memory. You can enjoy being in the limelight as much as you like, but I call the shots in this movement. All of them. If you try to defy me, sir, you'll soon discover that you've made a very serious mistake. Understood? Good. Now, shut the fuck up and sit down.'

Cambon stood stock still, defiantly trying to outstare Berg, who had turned the colour of boiled beetroot. '*Scheisse!*' spat Berg. 'What the hell are you playing at, Pierre? How dare you dispute my authority. You know the penalty. Believe me, I won't hesitate to enforce it.'

Cambon glanced around the terrace. It was empty. There was no possibility of escape, at least not for the moment. With a deep sigh, he slowly resumed his seat, as did Berg.

'That's more like it, Professor. As you see, I'm a reasonable man. I'll put that little tantrum down to your age, though it's more than you deserve. But I won't be so tolerant next time, I assure you. Now listen carefully, I have some good news to cheer us both up.'

[8]

TAMIR KNEW THAT KEREN BENAYOUN, LIKE MANY ISRAELIS, WAS not one to mince her words. It was a quality that he admired even if it was hardly her most endearing one. Nevertheless, Tamir was taken aback by the acidity in her voice.

'I nearly got fired because of you, Agent Weiss.'

They were seated near the window of a large bustling café located just north of London's Oxford Street next to Selfridges department store. In keeping with Mossad good practice guidelines, they had selected a crowded space to maximise their privacy. They spoke mostly in English, reserving Hebrew for their more heated exchanges.

'Hey, that's not fair, Keren. I think you're bending the truth a little. Weren't you sent off on a month's leave to cool down?'

'Excuse me, what exactly did you hear, and who told you?'

'Let's just say a reliable source gave me the impression that you threatened to resign. Happily for all of us—including me—you changed your mind.'

'What source? Lunenfeld? Surely not?' Keren's eyes widened.

Tamir remained silent but couldn't help smirking as he studied the depths of his coffee cup.

'Bastard!' hissed Keren after a brief pause.
'Who—me or him?' asked Tamir, smiling.
'Both of you. You can both go to hell.'
'If there is a hell, we probably will both be going there. And so will you.'

Throwing her head back, she laughed mirthlessly, her eyes smouldering with rage. Tamir had always enjoyed that gesture of hers. He found something alluring about a beautiful woman who was uninhibited about displaying anger while keeping her cool. He had an inkling of the source of that appeal—somewhere in the depths of his memory, he could almost recall his mother expressing a similar combination of emotions. Keren caught sight of his admiring glance and wordlessly communicated her approval. He coloured slightly as he made a conscious effort to block his hormone-fired imagination from wandering down a forbidden path. He needed no reminding that Keren, beyond doubt one of the most attractive women he had ever met, was almost twice his age.

'Fine, mister wiseguy, we're both upset by recent events, but let's not play the blame game. What's done is done, so let's move on. We have much work to do.'

Tamir was puzzled. 'Wait a second. We just established that you're on holiday.'

'This is my holiday. Who said I couldn't spend it in London? I love it here. I have a ticket for the theatre this evening. A musical. Anyway, enough of this chit-chat. Has there been anything new since the Paris event?'

'Yes, as it happens there has.' He pulled out his phone and clicked. 'Take a look at this video. Freshly delivered this morning. You see the guy with the beard seated at the table? You'll recognise him.'

'That's Christoph Berg, isn't it? Where was this taken?'

'It's Berg all right. He's in Hungary, enjoying the view of

Lake Balaton from his hotel. A pretty scene, isn't it? That must be why he chose to go there.'

'I hope he chokes on his goulash. Why are you showing me this?'

'Keep looking. Someone is about to join him at the table.'

The clip ran on. A few seconds later, a stouter figure sat down next to Berg. 'And here he is, just as you predicted,' said Keren. 'Is that Pierre Cambon?'

'Good to know that your eyesight is still in working order, doctor. Those two are our targets. Especially Berg. He's the big chief. Cambon is probably just a figurehead.'

The video ended after around fifteen seconds. Keren asked, 'Is that it?'

'That's the only visual we have. Our asset was a waitress. She couldn't risk being spotted so she couldn't run the video for long. But she managed to place a bug near enough to pick up an audio signal.'

'I assume she recorded something worthwhile?'

With a flourish, Tamir clicked the phone a couple of times and placed it on the table. He attached an earpiece and handed it to Keren who placed it in her right ear. 'It's a bit fuzzy but it's good enough. Luckily, it's all in English.'

'I can hardly hear anything. It might be the noise in here. Can you amplify it?'

'Never mind. Here's the transcript.' He pulled a sheet from his pocket and offered it to his superior. It was densely typed. She shook her head irritably, removing the earpiece.

'Give me the gist, please. Bullet points only.'

'OK. There are three. One, they had a big row. Berg threatened Cambon with some sort of punishment for dissent. He didn't spell it out. He didn't need to.'

'That confirms that Berg is the real boss of *Destiny*. Go on.'

'Two, some serious money is coming their way from the

Middle East. Some wealthy sheikh, a strong supporter of the movement, has dug deep into his pockets. We're talking big money, several million dollars. It's a huge breakthrough for them.'

'Wow, it sure is. Do we have the donor's name? Or the country?'

'Tamir shook his head. 'Berg didn't mention either and Cambon didn't ask.'

'A pity. But this is gold dust. we'll get our techies back home on the case. They might be able to extract more information from the recording. Anything else?'

'Not much. Just one last little detail. A rather significant one.'

'Really? Go on, spill it. The tension is killing me.'

'An unfortunate choice of words, Keren. That's exactly what they'd love to do to you. And to me too.'

She frowned. 'What's that supposed to mean?'

'Brace yourself. They know about us. And they've discovered that we're on their tail. I don't know how it happened, but it has. Our phones may be compromised so we'll have to replace them. Anyway, we have to deal with an uncomfortable new reality. *Destiny* know about *Operation Aleph Bet*. And they're coming after us.'

[9]

'I SUGGEST WE TAKE A BREAK. FIFTEEN MINUTES, FRIENDS. Moshe, a word in your ear.'

The prime minister of Israel rose from his place at the cabinet table and placed his hand on Lunenfeld's back, a patronising touch, thought the Mossad director. Lunenfeld was uneasy. He didn't appreciate being interrupted in mid-presentation. The PM must have had good cause for calling this unexpected intermission.

The two men rose and headed for the coffee urn at the far end of the room.

'I must compliment you on your presentation, Moshe. As we have come to expect, it was a model of insight and intelligence.'

'Thank you, Prime Minister.' Lunenfeld's antennae were twitching. Lavish praise was not something he expected to hear from this source. There had to be an ulterior motive.

'If I may, I'd like to clarify a couple of points before we embark on the next part of the meeting. The purpose of *Operation Aleph Bet* is to decapitate this *Destiny* monster, rendering it impotent, correct?'

'Correct, Prime Minister. As I explained, history suggests that totalitarian movements depend on a small number of fanatical leaders. *Destiny* is no exception. They have just such a leader and he is our prime target.'

'You mean this man, what's his name, Berg? An Austrian?'

'Yes, that's him. He's the so-called operations director and nominally subordinate to their president, Professor Pierre Cambon.'

'And Berg, you believe, has the necessary charisma and hence the real power in the organisation?'

'Correct again. Cambon is merely a figurehead. He's a famous philosopher in France and, from what we hear, is completely out of his depth. In reality, Berg is his boss.'

Adar looked pensive, almost crestfallen. 'Hmm. That's a pity.'

'Is there a problem, Prime Minister?'

'Indeed, there is. It's to do with Berg's nationality. Let me be frank with you, Moshe, this puts us in an awkward position. After a difficult start in the late '40s—for obvious reasons—we've developed good relations with Austria in recent years. They've been most helpful to us in various ways in the UN, trade, security and other matters. I'd hate to jeopardise all that. If we are seen to be involved in a targeted assassination of one of their most prominent citizens, it won't exactly help our case with that country.'

'I see that, Prime Minister. But don't you think that neutralising a major threat to the Jewish people and the State of Israel is far more pressing than the risk of a temporary diplomatic rift with Austria, of all countries?' There was genuine alarm in Lunenfeld's voice. 'I hope you're not seriously suggesting that we abort the operation?'

'No, not at all. Calm yourself, man. And keep your voice down, please. I want this conversation to remain strictly between ourselves. I just need you to be extra careful, that's all. We can't risk a smoking gun that leads back to us. If this man is killed, there will be a massive police investigation. Is there really no alternative? Can't we have him arrested for inciting hatred and violence?'

Lunenfeld fought to conceal his impatience with the turn the conversation had taken. 'As you know, Prime Minister, we've explored that route in great detail. Berg is a clever character. He has a knack of making his intentions crystal clear to his supporters without actually breaking the laws of any country. He knows how to stay on the right side of the red line. And he has nurtured close connections in high places right across Europe, not just in his own media profession but also in politics and the judiciary. That's what makes him so dangerous. You are right that an assassination is risky and best avoided, if possible. But how? We've explored all the alternative options. We can't discredit him in the eyes of the public because he thrives on all forms of publicity, good and bad. We can't persuade any police force in Europe to charge him because he hasn't broken any laws or they've had instructions from their governments not to touch him. I know it sounds ridiculous, especially in the light of European history, but nobody will lift a finger to stop him unless we do. This man is forging ahead with his murderous plans and will stop at nothing until they are implemented. By that point, it will be too late. I fear that we will reach that point very soon, perhaps within months or even weeks.'

The prime minister absorbed Lunenfeld's dire prediction before responding.

'Very well. I'm still unhappy about all this though I trust your impeccable judgement. Assuming we get the green light from our colleagues today, and that remains to be seen, you will have official authority to go ahead. But under no circumstances must any of our people be implicated in the public arena. Can you guarantee that, Moshe? It's extremely important.'

'In my line of business, Prime Minister, there are never any absolute guarantees about anything. But I get the message.'

'Good. Let's rejoin the others. I may have more to say on this subject. As for my cabinet colleagues, they'll be keen to hear what more you have to say. And so am I. Choose your words with care.'

Lunenfeld smiled weakly and tilted his head in acknowledgement of the instruction. 'I always do, Prime Minister. That's in my job description, is it not? It's what you pay me for.'

As they returned to the cabinet table, Lunenfeld prepared himself to grapple with one of the most hazardous moments in his long career.

[10]

VIENNA IN THE 1960S, WHEN BERG WAS ENTERING HIS FORMATIVE adolescence, was a strange and dysfunctional place. Rooted in a distant past, and embarrassed by the post-*Anschluss* collaboration with Hitler, the citizens of Vienna tried to live a normal life. But somehow their sordid love affair with the Third Reich kept returning to haunt them. While their German neighbours won plaudits from the international community for their collective *mea culpa*, the Austrians' strident insistence that they had been unwilling victims of National Socialism was greeted in most quarters—including most Jewish survivors of the Nazi nightmare—with scepticism verging on disdain. Helmut Berg, Christoph's ill-tempered father, had no doubt who was to blame for this exasperating state of affairs. And he was pleased to share his theory to all who would listen.

Berg Senior was a rather typical 'old school' Austrian. He was a small-scale businessman, a shopkeeper who struggled to keep his head above the water financially. Despite his best efforts, the appeal of his wares—which he advertised as 'fancy goods'—waned over time. Never averse to a *schnapps* or three before lunch, Herr Berg took solace in gambling and womanising whenever he had accumulated enough money in the till. The result was that he and his hapless family sank ever deeper into debt, poverty and despair.

Helmut was man of strong opinions and was fond of expounding them at length to anyone who would listen. The young Christoph heard his father voice the same complaint at the family dinner table every single day of his life. 'We're not allowed to say it, but I will not be silenced. Every decent Austrian knows the truth. These people still have a stranglehold on us, always wagging their sanctimonious fingers, always whining about their so-called victimhood and demanding what they call justice. "An eye for an eye" is their primitive creed, though—mark my words—they can be bought off easily enough with a nice fat cheque paid for by us, the ordinary, upstanding, hardworking taxpayers of Austria. These leeches will never let go until they've squeezed the lifeblood out of this country.' Helmut's listeners knew exactly who *these people* were without anyone having to spell it out.

Frau Berg knew better than to contradict her husband, so she held her tongue. Young Christoph had always interpreted her silence as approval. In later years, he began to wonder whether the opposite might be the case. After all, her best friend was an elderly Jewish lady, a retired nurse who had survived the concentration camps that had destroyed her entire family. Christoph couldn't begin to fathom why his mother defended this pathetic old crone in the face of Helmut's disgust at her defiant association with the woman. The resulting domestic rows were troubling to the boy, yet he never hesitated to side with his father for upholding traditional Austrian moral principles. His stupid and weak mother was reduced to tears whenever she found herself on the receiving end of his father's justified wrath. Perhaps the old man did resort a little too readily to the odd slap across his wife's face. As for Helmut's occasional deployment of a heavy leather belt across her plump backside, what did she expect? The stubborn cow deserved every blow. And more. How could she have been so unpatriotic as to stand up for a snivelling, half-dead Jew?

After leaving home and following a disastrous first term at a third-tier university that resulted in his unseemly expulsion from his accountancy course, the angry young man became reconciled to the reality that he would always be a loner. No one would lift so much as their little finger to help him. So be it, he decided. He had no choice but to forge his own path. His first stop was the Austrian army, or rather what remained of it—the military had been so emasculated after the war that it had barely survived. His fellow soldiers turned out to be such a feeble bunch of lily-livered pussies that young Berg resigned, disillusioned, after only three weeks.

Next, he travelled to Paris and applied to join the French Foreign Legion. Except that the effete fools wouldn't admit him due, they claimed, to unspecified personality issues. Somehow, he found his way to Belgium where a kindly recruiting officer of the Belgian Security Service spotted a vestige of potential in the opinionated Austrian and whisked him off to a part-time undercover unit of the intelligence corps. Berg never progressed beyond the rank of sergeant but he loved the cloak-and-dagger exercises that gave him the opportunity to make useful friends and acquire skills that would stand him good stead for the rest of his life.

By this time, Berg was earning a decent living as a freelance journalist. Right-leaning tabloid editors approved of his dogmatic habit of dividing the world into two competing blocks—white and black, saints and sinners, decent conservatives and wicked socialists—locked in a permanent battle for supremacy. Readers' reactions were mixed but the circulation figures didn't lie. Soon every

European politician, whether conservative or liberal, wanted Berg onside.

But Berg's growing success in the popular media failed to satisfy him. He remained restless and unfulfilled. Words were, after all, just words, and were worthless unless accompanied by deeds. Following the passing of both parents within six months of each other, Christoph became imbued with a sense of mission. He knew that his father's dearest wish would have been for his son to play a central role in the harsh struggle against the expanding miasma of evil that was closing in around them. The ever-cunning Hebrews were, as everyone knew, ruthlessly single-minded in their quest for gold, power and revenge. He was determined to find a way to defeat them. But how?

One glorious autumn afternoon, he found the answer. He picked up a book that his father had bequeathed to him and started casually flicking through its pages. It was a dusty old hardback, a biography of one of Vienna's most famous sons, Karl Lueger, who had ruled the city as mayor in the early years of the twentieth century. *Der schöne Karl* ignited young Christoph's imagination. He concurred with Lueger's brilliant analysis of the toxic nexus of power between Jewish socialists and bankers who, between them, bled the ordinary working folk dry. Every word of the writer's plain yet vivid language—that even Christoph's uneducated father would have understood—rang so unarguably true. And Lueger's message went further than mere truth-telling: firm intervention was essential. His oratorial skills were a means to an end—the acquisition of power. He was a man who craved action rather than philosophising, yet was smart enough to recognise the potency of a rousing speech. Berg didn't just admire this gifted politician who had risen through the ranks of Viennese officialdom to become one of the most powerful figures in the Austro-Hungarian empire, he wanted to emulate him.

How had Lueger achieved high office? Berg found the answer in the book's account of the great man's early career: by bringing together like-minded political factions, none of which could have achieved victory alone but whose combined impact proved decisive. Only his premature death from diabetes prevented him from implementing his programme to rid his city and nation of the oppressive burden of Jewry. That task had to be handed on to a younger man, a fellow citizen of Vienna called Adolf Hitler.

Tragically, in Christoph Berg's eyes, through a mixture of incompetence and bad luck, the Nazi programme that became known as the Final Solution had not been fully completed. There were still far too many Jews left in the world and, to make matters worse, they now had their own state that the UN had been duped into recognising. The loathsome entity they called 'Israel' was still a tiny, insignificant apology for a country, but it was growing fast; Berg had no doubt that it was bent on regional hegemony as a prelude to world domination. For what other purpose had it established one of the fiercest fighting machines in history, the so-called Israel Defence Forces? With every passing year, the challenge posed by this new breed of Jew-conspirators was becoming that much tougher, but someone would have to muster a counter-balancing force to overcome it. The alternative was, he had no doubt, the end of humanity.

Berg felt the hand of destiny—yes, *Destiny*—on his shoulder. His great new trans-European political movement had virtually named itself. One day the world would acknowledge that he, Berg, had more than lived up to that title. He always knew he had been born to fulfil a sacred task. Only the means of fulfilling it had eluded him. Until now. Historians of the future would credit one man with the accolade of having realised the magnificent, sacred vision that he had inherited from his ideological soulmates, Karl and Adolf. The reputation of those two great figures had been cruelly besmirched by the Jewish cabal that controlled the media and academia. Fortunately for civilisation, their legacy would be preserved by a third great statesman whose name would resonate down the generations, evoking awe and fear in equal measure.

That man, the hero for the ages, would be Christoph Berg.

[11]

FOR AS LONG AS SHE COULD REMEMBER, SOFIA HAD WANTED TO be a journalist. A Cambridge University graduate, she felt destined to achieve greatness. She had known she could write readable prose from an early age and that skill, combined with a flamboyant personality, gave her the perfect foundation for a career as a professional communicator. In adolescence, she found two inspiring journalistic role models—the BBC's intrepid Kate Adie and *The Sunday Times'* courageous Marie Colvin. Both had been elite war correspondents in their day, the latter having lost her life in the Syrian civil war.

Sofia's fascination with the power of the written word was matched by another driving obsession—to explore as much of planet Earth as she could manage in whatever lifespan was allotted to her. Her mixed Anglo-Spanish heritage may have been the driving force behind her wanderlust and her fascination with travel to far-flung and exotic locations. Or perhaps that was attributable to an overactive imagination, combined with a penetrating intelligence, that refused to be confined within the straitjacket of a conventional suburban English lifestyle. Whatever the explanation, Sofia yearned to see as much of the world as she could within the shortest possible time. In the process, she would wield her metaphorical pen to describe what she observed to countless readers who would hang on her very word. In short, she was determined to create a splash, to be noticed.

Her Spanish father was the wisest man she had ever known. On their drive to her university lodgings, he had been in a philosophical mood. 'You'll discover that the world is a larger and more complicated place than you thought. You could easily get lost in it and no one would even notice.' Then came this gem. 'If I have one piece of advice for you, it's this: make an impression, wherever you are, whatever you do. Don't be a shy English wallflower. Remember that sentence and you will achieve great things in your life. The sky is the limit, *mi amor*. Don't be daunted by it. Aim for the stars.'

She had taken her adored father's words to heart. She hadn't doubted for a second that she would make an impression, and that it would be a big one. After the graduation celebrations had died down, she had written in her journal, *What is to stop me from becoming the most fearless and famous foreign correspondent the world has ever seen?* She'd have to work hard, and there would be setbacks. But she was in her optimistic early twenties, brimming with energy and self-confidence, and more than up for the fight. That was her unshakeable mindset as she headed for the metropolis to embark on her great adventure.

Several years on from that adolescent journal entry, Sofia's aspirations were evolving fast. As a self-styled cub reporter, she had offered her irresistible talents to the global media. To date, the global media had resisted. Her ambition remained as lofty as ever, but had become somewhat blunted by contact with reality. She recognised that the early years of her career had been undistinguished aside from a few well-crafted articles in the posher Sunday supplements. These had been well enough received but were, in her view, trivial achievements and insufficient to catapult her to stardom. She knew she would have to raise her game.

From the outset, Sofia had viewed herself as an investigative reporter on a global stage, but finding exciting subjects to investigate proved a more elusive task than she had expected. With increasing desperation, she had searched far and wide for that one juicy exposé that would launch her career. When she had stumbled across a secret British government memo about covert Israeli-Saudi military cooperation, she had recognised her discovery for what it was—a journalistic gem—and Sofia hadn't been in any mood to let that opportunity pass her by. This was, she had sensed in her bones, the breakthrough moment she had been awaiting.

She had been about to go public with the story when half a dozen foreign intelligence agencies somehow got wind of her intentions and crashed down on the young journalist like a torrent of ice water. One of these shadowy organisations was Israel's Mossad. A crack unit of that legendary outfit had scooped her off the streets of London and whisked her away to a safe house in Scotland. That had been the unlikely setting for her first encounter with her future husband, Tamir Weiss. The handsome young Israeli secret agent had been her principal kidnapper.

Stockholm Syndrome—that's how a psychologist might have described her infatuation with her captor. Tamir was tall, slim and charming, the kind of action-man hero who was just too good to be true. And so it turned out. Sofia discovered that his first priority was—and always would be—to serve his country rather than his partner. She was forced to confront a challenge. She had fallen in love with a man whose job had been to incarcerate her— or worse. The adventures that followed could have filled the pages of a hundred tabloid newspapers. She couldn't publish a single word.

Why did she stick with him? Two reasons: first, she was still besotted with her Israeli superhero; second, the tantalising promise of a normal future beckoned. Quite unexpectedly, the perpetual storm that swirled around the couple had abated for a couple of years. That had lulled both of them into a false sense of security. Marriage and childbirth followed quickly and the Weiss family seemed destined to a life of contented middle-class respectability in Sydney, Australia. Until Tamir received a call from his masters and the idyll ended. *Once a Mossad agent, always a Mossad agent*, Tamir tried to explain to his uncomprehending wife. Nevertheless, Sofia was a fighter and she was determined to win this battle. The marriage survived that test. Just.

Following their return to London, Sofia had felt a sense of *deja vue*. She was back to square one. Except that she now had a demanding six-year-old to look after as well as an ever more challenging marital relationship to fret over. Not that she had regretted motherhood for a moment. Clara had been a source of unremitting delight for the whole family. (Tamir's relatives, all of whom were in Israel, complained endlessly, according to Tamir, that they never got to see his baby girl.)

Today had been another turning point in their relationship, a make-or-break moment. The *status quo* had been untenable and had run its course. She had issued her ultimatum to Tamir in the full expectation that her marriage was about to end. His initial hesitancy had done little to placate her, but his eventual decision to call her bluff and bring her into his confidence had been a surprise. It seemed he wanted to hold his family together and she had to credit him with that at least. He deserved one more chance. She would reluctantly stop the clock and see where events would lead them, for better or worse. She knew it was pointless to speculate, but she couldn't help pondering the question that kept demanding an answer she couldn't provide. *What does the future hold for us?*

She didn't have to wait long to find out.

[12]

'TO SUM UP,' LUNENFELD ANNOUNCED TO THE CABINET WITH AN air of finality, '*Operation Aleph Bet* has reached a decisive moment. We can't proceed further without government approval. The ball is now in your court.' Lunenfeld removed his spectacles and moved closer to the ministers to scrutinise each of them in turn as though they were unfamiliar museum specimens. A few reciprocated in kind. Most ignored him, more intrigued by their phone screens than anything happening in the room around them.

'Thank you, Moshe,' said the prime minister. 'That was most illuminating. And worrying. Now, if I may, I'd like to make a few points of my own.' The prime minister stood up and began pacing back and forth behind his chair. 'As you have heard, we—by which I mean the Jewish people and the State of Israel—face an imminent and serious, perhaps even existential, threat from this neo-Nazi movement, this quasi-political organisation that calls itself *Destiny*. I am confident that we will all agree with director Lunenfeld that they have to be stopped in their tracks or we risk facing a disaster on a scale that we have not experienced for many decades. However, I have to tell you that, in my opinion, the plan as it stands is highly problematic. Certain adjustments to it are needed...'

'Prime Minister, I must protest!' exclaimed Lunenfeld rising to his feet.

'No, Moshe, please wait. I haven't finished.' The prime minister glared at Lunenfeld and gestured to him to resume his seat. In an instant, the atmosphere had changed; all ministers were now focused on this unprecedented stand-off. The two men eyeballed each other until Lunenfeld complied and sat down with undisguised reluctance.

'Thank you. I'd like to express my appreciation of the director for the important work he and his colleagues do day in, day out. He keeps us all safe. Without the Mossad, there would be no Israel. Period. We are all grateful to you and your fellow defenders of the state.' He paused as if expecting a burst of applause. None came.

'Let me make something clear. There is no question that the plan Moshe has outlined to you is needed and has been successful up till now. We have identified the true and dangerous nature of this organisation, its *modus operandi* and its key leaders. We have infiltrated their meetings and have discovered their ability to operate under the radar of both the media and the law in a way that poses a serious threat to all of us. A threat that cannot be ignored.' He paused to allow this dramatic assessment to sink in, then resumed his seat. But he had more to say.

'It seems, my friends, that these dangerous people are on the verge of seizing political power, through the forging of secret political alliances with so-called populist governments across Europe. As Moshe has explained, we have a window of opportunity to stop them, but I fear it won't stay open for ever. We must act with resolve now. The director has requested our authorisation to implement the final stage of *Operation Aleph Bet*. As you have just heard, that will involve neutralising their leadership using all available means.' The prime minister paused again and looked around the room. 'I am sure we all understand the implications of that statement. In case anyone is in doubt, let me call a spade a spade. We're talking targeted assassination.'

There was a low-pitched murmur in the room that could have indicated approval or disquiet. Or both. At least two members of the cabinet indicated their desire to speak. One of them, the powerful defence minister, General Arkady Volkov, tried to attract the attention of the PM who, to the astonishment of his colleagues, denied the minister that opportunity. To reinforce the point, Adar stood and turned his back on Volkov.

'My apologies, gentlemen, we will have no general discussion on this issue today. You will hear why in a moment. As your prime minister, I must take account of a range of factors that could influence our decision-making here in this room and in the government as a whole.' He was pacing back and forth again.

'Let me enumerate some of these for you. First, this man Berg is an Austrian citizen. We currently enjoy good relations with that country—in fact the best in our history. They are a small nation, like us, but they carry disproportionate weight in the international community. They argue our case at both the EU and the UN, places where our true friends are as rare as hen's teeth. And as my good friend, our esteemed defence minister, has pointed out, in just the last few weeks we have signed scientific, commercial and, above all, sensitive security deals with them. As he has emphasised to me, and I am in full agreement, all of that will be at risk if we proceed without regard to the serious consequences.'

Volkov again tried to speak. 'Prime Minister, excuse me...' The prime minister again brushed him aside. 'Not now, Arkady. Your turn will come later.' Volkov blanched. The premier continued as if nothing had happened.

'Secondly, we have suffered negative consequences in the past from resorting to assassinations. Not the least of these has been the strong disapproval of the one foreign power whose good will is more important to us than that of anyone else. I refer to our closest ally, the United States, even though they themselves have used precisely that tactic on multiple occasions. Yes, they are hypocrites but so are most countries on the planet. That's a fact of life we have to live with. Third, there is always the risk of collateral damage, including to our own agents. We have bad memories of this from previous operations that—how shall I put it?—were managed in a less than ideal manner. We cannot afford a repeat of such mistakes.'

'Prime Minister, I must again protest,' said Lunenfeld, shaking his head in disbelief. 'This road is sure to lead us to disaster. As I tried to explain…'

'No Moshe, that's enough, you have had your say,' interrupted Adar, making no attempt to conceal his irritation. 'Now it's my turn. Permit me to finish, please.'

Lunenfeld rolled his eyes heavenward and spread his arms in exasperation.

'Thank you. This brings me to my final and most important reservation.'

Always the consummate politician, Adar knew how to generate tension and stretch it to the breaking point for his own benefit. 'Sometimes in public life you have to respond, not to facts and figures nor to experts nor to clever arguments, but to your gut instinct. And my gut instinct tells me that this plan, for all its merits, will fail. Worse, it will backfire. I've seen it happen many times. The bottom line, gentlemen, is this. I don't like it.'

He turned to Lunenfeld. 'The risks are too high. Moshe, I'm sorry. You will not change my mind on the matter. I have decided to cancel *Operation Aleph Bet* with immediate effect. That is an order. This meeting is over.'

[13]

ON HIS JOURNEY BACK TO PARIS, PIERRE CAMBON TRIED TO PUT the ghastly Lake Balaton meeting with Christoph Berg behind him. He failed. He kept hearing that chilling voice reiterating its ominous message like a recording on an endless loop. He just couldn't shut the evil bastard out of his head.

Cambon had been shaken by the encounter for several reasons. First and foremost, Berg had bullied the older man into abject submission—again. This time, the explicit threat of physical violence, usually unspoken but ever-present in the higher echelons of *Destiny*, had been deployed by the operations director to bring Cambon to heel. Perhaps he should have stood up to the intimidation, but Cambon abhorred violence and, in any case, lacked the physical ability to oppose it. The sad fact was that his octogenarian body was simply no match for the muscular Berg.

Second, Berg had revealed to Cambon that the rapid progress of the political bridge-building between *Destiny* and twenty-plus European governments was much further advanced than anyone realised. The populist rulers of Italy, Hungary, Poland and Romania had been the first to sign up to the *Destiny* manifesto, *Our Glorious Birthright*. No one had batted an eyelid at that. The

United Kingdom's approval had followed under their recently elected government, a coalition of left-wing, green and nationalist parties, and that development, too, had generated little comment in the mainstream media. The bigger fish—France, Spain and, above all, Germany, had proved more resistant. Now they too had all but capitulated with scarcely a whimper. How had *Destiny* pulled off this extraordinary stunt? Berg had evaded Cambon's question, tapping the side of his aquiline nose with his bony forefinger. Cambon assumed that this gesture implied that Berg had deployed his favourite twin standbys—blackmail and threats—and he had no desire to learn the unsavoury details.

But it was Berg's third revelation that gave Cambon pause for thought, as it appeared to offer him a possible exit strategy from the whole sorry business. Berg had boasted that his paramilitary intelligence network had made a staggering discovery. The activities of *Destiny* had attracted the close attention of the Israeli secret service, the feared Mossad spy agency. Cambon replayed the scene in as much detail as his failing memory would allow:

'I don't know about you, Berg, but I for one am not prepared to take on the Mossad. It would be suicidal. You must see that, surely?'

Berg responded with a derisive snigger. 'How foolish you are, old man. This is a gift from heaven. Let the verminous Mossad send their best agents. Now that we know their devious plans, we are one step ahead of them. We'll set a neat little trap that they are sure to walk right into. And once they get up close and personal, we'll have a little fun with them.'

Grinning like a child in a sweetie shop, Berg mimed a cut-throat gesture. 'They won't like that, I promise you.' Pulling his chair closer to Cambon, he adopted his most conspiratorial tone. 'You see, Pierre, I have learned much about these people in my life. I have studied them very carefully. I want to let you into a secret. All Jews hate violence, even in self-defence. For all their

US-backed exploits and bravado, they'll run away. They're cowards, every last one of them. My father taught me that a long time ago. They're not like us Volksdeutsche, and it's common knowledge that they're not really Europeans at all. They are orientals through and through. They may try to pull some pathetic little stunt, but when they receive my lesson in the stark realities of power, they will surrender. They won't give up straight away for they are an arrogant, stiff-necked people, as even their own holy book confirms, but it will set them back several weeks or even months, enough time for our people to build an impregnable wall of security around us all. In a way, the Mossad have done us a great favour in exposing a weakness in our defences that we hadn't noticed. Perhaps we should send a letter of thanks to the Israeli government. Wouldn't that be something, eh, old man?'

Berg leaned back in his chair in the smug manner that Cambon had seen many times and heartily loathed. Oblivious to the professor's lack of endorsement of his anti-Jewish sentiments, the Austrian became convulsed in waves of uncontrollable laughter as he savoured the brilliance of his own ironic humour. He didn't seem to mind that Cambon declined to celebrate the joke with him. As his guffaws subsided, he leaned forward. 'Well, Professor, what have you to say to that?'

Cambon's brow furrowed. 'I am not prepared to die on the altar of your recklessness, Berg. Look at me, I'm incapable of defending myself if an Israeli hit-team is sent to slit my throat. And you refused to organise a security detail for me, remember?'

'Aw, the poor professor is afraid of the Jews. But have no fear, old man, those Israeli scum won't touch us. Not now, and not ever. Who do they think they are, these midgets who scheme and plot to obstruct the progress of humanity? No, they will fail in this filthy enterprise as they always have in the past. They've already seriously underestimated us. They are going to learn a bitter lesson.

And I, Christoph Berg, am looking forward to administering it personally. Those Jewish pigs won't know what has hit them.'

As he recalled that conversation, Cambon shuddered. The man was detached from reality—he would lead *Destiny* to certain extinction if he believed his own hate-filled rhetoric. But by far the worst thing about the meeting on the edge of the picturesque Hungarian lake had been Berg's non-verbal language.

Cambon could have sworn that, as Berg reached the climax of his unhinged antisemitic diatribe, the Austrian had licked his lips in anticipation.

[14]

'Do I really have to see her, Tamir? You know she's not my favourite person in the world.'

Although the weather was near perfect and the view from the top of Primrose Hill in north London was spectacular, Sofia was growing agitated. Ever since agreeing to play a supporting role (as yet undefined) in *Operation Aleph Bet*, Sofia had resigned herself to the prospect of having to work in close proximity to Tamir's immediate superior. The two women had met in strained circumstances in the past and Sofia had always found the Israeli psychiatrist-spy intimidating. Keren's striking physical beauty didn't help to endear her to Sofia who, despite her own good looks, was more than a little jealous of the near-symbiotic relationship between the Mossad handler and Tamir. For his part, Tamir dismissed his wife's suspicions as 'ridiculous' and 'paranoid.' That attitude rankled her further and had the opposite effect to the one intended. *Methinks he doth protest too much*, thought Sofia.

'Come on, *ahuvati*. Be reasonable. We've discussed all this before many times. Keren is just doing her job. She happens to be pretty good at it. And she doesn't bite.'

'We both know she's capable of a lot worse than that.'

'What's that supposed to mean?' shot back Tamir, affronted. Sofia shuddered and sat down on the wooden bench next to her husband.

'No, not there, *ahuvati*, leave a space in the middle for our guest.'

'It's fine, stay where you both are.' The familiar accented contralto female voice spoke from behind them. 'Just keep looking straight ahead. It's safer that way. What a wonderful view across London.'

'We didn't see you, Keren, sorry. How long have you been standing there?' asked Tamir, straining to avoid turning his head.

'Long enough. You can be most indiscreet sometimes, Agent Weiss. Sofia, I'm sorry you think of me as a monster. I don't know where you got such an idea.'

'I had no idea you were listening, Keren. I'm sorry.'

'Why? If that's how you feel, you should tell me. All I can say is that you're wrong about me and I'll do my best to prove it to you. But let's not argue. We have more important things to think about.'

'If I'm wrong about you, I apologise.'

'I hear you—and I note your careful choice of words. Anyway, let's forget about it. I'll pretend nothing happened if you will too. Agreed?'

Sofia nodded.

'Good. So how are you? And how is Clara? She must be, what, five now?'

'Six. We're both fine, Keren, thank you. Just about. It's not been an easy time for her, but she's amazing. Children are so resilient, aren't they? Anyway, I didn't think you could be bothered with small talk. Can we get to the point?'

'No problem. I gather that Tamir has explained to you the nature of our current European operation? At least in outline?'

OPERATION ALEPH BET

'Yes, he has. And I wish I'd known about it weeks ago. Everything makes a lot more sense now. And as I keep saying, though nobody seems to listen, I've got skills that could be useful. I'd like to help if I can.'

'Thank you, my dear, but that won't be necessary.'

Tamir sprang to his feet. 'What? I thought we had agreed—'

'Agent Weiss,' said Keren, her voice as cold as steel. 'What do you think you are doing? Resume your seat immediately. That's an order. *Nu?*'

Tamir complied. His face had reddened. 'Keren, what the hell is going on? If Sofia isn't part of the team, why did you drag us out here?'

'Because I wanted to tell both of you this in person. I've just been given fresh instructions from headquarters. They change everything for all of us—not just here in the UK, but across Europe. For reasons I don't yet understand myself, we've been instructed by our government to stand down. *Operation Aleph Bet* has been cancelled until further notice.'

Tamir and Sofia looked at each other in disbelief. Tamir turned to face Keren, whose expression was impassive.

'Eyes ahead, Tamir. Look, you have a good idea how these things work back in Jerusalem. All I can tell you is that we have no say in the matter one way or the other. No one is asking for our opinion. But please, let's not get into the details here.'

'This makes absolutely no sense,' said Sofia. 'You're just going to sit back and let these Nazis take over Europe? How is that possible, Keren? Have you learned nothing from Jewish history?'

'I agree with you, one hundred percent. Yes, we've learned plenty from Jewish history. Most of us, that is. As I said, the decision is not mine. Now, if I may ask of you a favour, Sofia. Please leave us for a few minutes. Just get up and walk away, don't look back at either of us. Behave as if you have no connection to us whatsoever. I'm sorry to do this but I have something highly confidential to discuss with Tamir and I don't have authority to share it with you. Not yet, anyway.'

Sofia clenched her jaw but knew better than to argue. She stood up, stretched out her arms sideways so that they almost touched her companions, and, carefully avoiding even a momentary glance at either of them, ambled slowly down the hill. Once at the bottom of the slope, she doubled back along the park's perimeter path and found a well-concealed spot from where she could observe Tamir and Keren in conversation. It looked heated. Tamir was gesticulating with passion while Keren shook her head every few seconds. Sofia wasn't close enough to hear the words—and wouldn't have understood them if she had—but she was a shrewd analyst of body language. That told her that the argument was intense and bitter. After around three minutes, Tamir threw his hands in the air and stomped off down the hill towards the village.

Sofia headed briskly along the path to meet him. By now, she was more than confused. Abandoning *Operation Aleph Bet* struck her as a monumental blunder. Still, she assumed that there must be a sound rationale for it, albeit one that Tamir was unlikely to share with her even if Keren had disclosed it to him. But there would, at least, be a silver lining to this bizarre development and that realisation lightened her spirits. She might get her husband back at last.

[15]

IT WAS AN ORDINARY ENOUGH SCENE: TWO MIDDLE-AGED MEN sipping long glasses of lemon tea in a verdant Jerusalem garden, chatting in an animated fashion.

Except that the garden was located behind the official residence of the elected leader of the State of Israel. It was under constant electronic and audio-visual surveillance from every conceivable angle and was protected by the tightest cordon of security in the Middle East. The two men were far from ordinary, one being the prime minister of Israel and the other the head of the Mossad intelligence agency. Tensions were running high between them after a bizarre security cabinet meeting at which the prime minister had confounded his colleagues by announcing that *Operation Aleph Bet* was dead in the water.

Today, however, they were back to business as usual. That meant they were discussing matters of life and death.

'Do you mean to tell me, Prime Minister, that you believe, in all seriousness, that cabinet decisions are leaking to *Destiny*? Why didn't you alert me to this sooner?'

'I'm alerting you now, Moshe.'

'So you are, but please, help me understand something. Why did you not inform your cabinet colleagues?'

'I had my reasons, Moshe. Some things are suitable for your ears only. But there's no need to panic. I have everything under control.'

'Excuse me for being so blunt, sir, but in choosing to conceal your knowledge of this leak from your colleagues, you are denying them crucial information. That could be a big mistake, in my opinion.'

'And you are fully entitled to your opinion. But that is all it is. My duty is to take decisions that are, in my judgement, in the best interests of the state.'

'So why not share your judgement with them? They would be supportive.'

'Their support is not the point at issue. As you know, this country is plagued by leaks, even from the highest levels of the security apparatus.'

'Not from the Mossad, I assure you.'

Adar leaned forward and tapped Lunenfeld twice on his knee. 'I believe you, Moshe. In which case, how did *Destiny* discover that Mossad agents were on their case? I can think of only one source.'

'Are you suggesting that the security cabinet has been infiltrated by a *Destiny* informer? That's a serious allegation. Can you give me a name?'

'Unfortunately, I can't, not a definitive one at any rate.' The PM reflexively looked around him in case their conversation was at risk of being overheard. 'But if I had to choose a likely candidate—and I say this with a heavy heart—it would be the defence minister. It's no secret that Volkov has been after my job for years. I hope I'm wrong. He's a competent politician but also an ambitious one. Anyway, whoever it is will be found out soon enough. You see, Moshe, I've taken a leaf out of your book.' He leaned back with a self-satisfied smirk. 'I'm one step ahead of the traitor.'

'Really, Prime Minister? In what way?'

'I decided to try an experiment. By announcing the cancellation of the project in that specific forum, I ensured that all the people in that room have now heard that *Operation Aleph Bet* is no more. If *Destiny* get to hear that news too, as I believe they will, they'll immediately leave our agents in Europe alone and we'll get closer to the source of the leak—close enough to make an arrest at any rate.'

'Are you saying that the little grenade you dropped into the security cabinet meeting was just for show?'

'It was more than that. It was a test of the loyalty of every single one of my most senior government colleagues. One of them, at least, is feeding scraps of information to *Destiny*. I decided to offer that person or persons something more substantial. A main dish rather than a snack. You have to admit that it's a clever plan, eh?' Adar leaned back in a pose of infinite self-approval, his vast chest inflated with such overweening pride, thought Lunenfeld, that it risked exploding out of the constraints of his tight-fitting white shirt.

The Mossad director was speechless. But his brain was in hyperactive mode. How dare this amateur sleuth, this self-serving politician, concoct a smoke-out exercise on his own initiative? There were formal procedures for investigating intelligence leaks to foreign actors and it was the Mossad's job to implement them. His team of professionals were trained and competent in the necessary skills, in contrast to the ham-fisted blundering of this hubristic buffoon. The man's vanity was matched only by his misplaced self-confidence. He was a disgrace to his office and his country.

Lunenfeld was too experienced to permit his emotions to cloud his judgement. He had a job to do. It comprised two immediate tasks: to assess the implications of Adar's disclosure for Israel's security and to undertake a rapid damage-control exercise. The first was straightforward enough. The PM's 'clever plan' was so full of holes that it would fall apart from the outset. By announcing the operation's cancellation to the security cabinet, he had ensured that the decision would rapidly cascade down through the various official security hierarchies across multiple government departments. If any of those were connected to the leak, it would be a near-impossible task to trace it to the source. Meanwhile, *Destiny* would be free to pursue its sinister objectives unfettered and unchallenged. That would place the one million Jews of Europe, along with the nine million citizens of the State of Israel, in existential jeopardy.

The whole idea was not only misguided and ill-conceived, thought Lunenfeld, it was dangerous. It could have endless repercussions—all of them negative—for years to come. It would have to be snuffed out with the minimum of delay before it could inflict serious damage. That much was obvious. His second task was as hard to visualise as it was urgent. Adar's lunacy would have to be reined in and its ruinous impact nullified. But how? He was aware of his reputation for a razor-sharp mind and mental agility. He also understood that he'd have to muster all his intellectual powers to address what he feared was a brewing national security crisis on a scale the country hadn't experienced for decades.

The director closed his eyes and inhaled deeply, as if willing his brain into a higher cognitive gear through a burst of oxygenation.

'Tell me, Moshe, aren't you impressed?' prompted the prime minister impatiently after a too-long silence. 'I'd make a top-notch spook, wouldn't I?'

Lunenfeld clenched his teeth as if afraid that permitting the release of any words from his mouth at that moment could be career-ending mistake. He rose slowly from his seat and ambled over to a nearby rose bush. In an ostentatious gesture, he sniffed at the flower as if savouring its exotic scent. This elaborate mime was designed to disguise his acute anxiety at the turn of events; it also served to create a few precious seconds of thinking time.

By the time he returned to his seat, he had found the solution.

He smiled as benignly as he could at his host. 'If I may say so, Prime Minister, your plan is indeed brilliant. If *Destiny* reveal to us that they have received your message, we'll know, as you say, that the security cabinet is the source of the leak. We can then put each and every one of them through the third degree, including a polygraph test. Rest assured, we'll find our mole within the week.'

The prime minister nodded to himself several times in that triumphalist, self-congratulatory way that his admirers adored and his critics loathed.

'I knew you'd understand, Moshe. *Operation Aleph Bet* is now officially cancelled, and will be in practice too, until we decide to relaunch a more satisfactory version of it in the not-too-distant future.'

'Ah, so you envisage the operation being revived at some point? Could you be more specific about the time scale, Prime Minister?'

'Sorry, Moshe, I can't. Perhaps a few weeks or months from now. I'll reach a decision as soon as I can and inform you, naturally. In the meantime, I am relieved that we won't have to risk a botched assassination attempt and I won't have to have that embarrassing conversation with my Austrian friends and partners.'

He rose, flashed his insincere politician's smile at Lunenfeld and vigorously shook his hand. 'I knew I could rely on you, Moshe. Go and do what you have to do.'

Those were the only meaningful words he had heard all morning, reflected Lunenfeld. He would follow that final instruction of the prime minister to the letter.

[16]

AXEL RUE DIDN'T MUCH CARE FOR BRUSSELS ALTHOUGH IT WAS his hometown. His elderly parents still lived in the city, but he didn't miss the presence in his life of that pair of old washed-out grumps so keeping well out of touch with them was no great hardship. Yet he kept returning to La Grand-Place and its environs against his better judgement. That behaviour pattern was born of an ever-present necessity. He needed to earn a living.

Since his less than honourable discharge from the Belgian army five years earlier, Rue had offered his skills to the highest bidder. He had discovered the existence of a large and lucrative market for ex-soldiers and the security services they could provide. A fitness fanatic all his adult life, in his thirties he remained in good physical shape and was proficient in handling most modern weapons from handguns to smaller calibre mortars. As a peripatetic mercenary, he had earned a small fortune in the last five years and had even toyed with the notion of throwing in the towel, buying a farm in Picardy and putting his feet up for a few decades. The lure of a life of indolent luxury was indeed tempting. That particular pipe dream turned to ashes as he blew his accumulated assets in the casinos and brothels of Europe.

Rue hadn't allowed that temporary setback to defeat him. He was made of far sterner stuff. He'd picked himself up, brushed himself down and embarked on rebuilding his bank balance as rapidly as possible. He had worked out a surefire plan that he was convinced would restore his financial health in a matter of weeks. True, it required the taking of a calculated risk as it involved returning to the roulette wheels and crap tables in each and every one of his favourite haunts across the continent— *just one last time*, as all gambling addicts assure themselves *ad nauseam*. But Rue was confident of his statistical prowess. He had calculated the odds and concluded that they were firmly in his favour, the only uncertain variable being the timescale.

His project started badly and ended in near-disaster. Within a month, he faced destitution and despair. Was it possible that lady luck had finally deserted him? His IOUs were mounting and he could see no escape from a brutal future behind bars—or worse. His last remaining option was to declare himself bankrupt despite the grim implications of such a drastic step. However hard he tried, he couldn't conjure up an alternative solution. Until someone—a saviour? a guardian angel?—made him an offer he couldn't refuse.

That someone was Christoph Berg, his old staff sergeant from his training days in the induction corps of GISS, the Belgian military intelligence service. Rue had disliked the Austrian from the start, a feeling that Berg reciprocated with interest. Still, the two men bore a grudging respect for each other, and the camaraderie of fellow soldiers and veterans tended to trump personality clashes. The fact was that Berg was well connected with the security industry and had tossed in Rue's direction occasional morsels of well-paid work over the years—stewarding political events, screening employees' backgrounds for criminal records, and similar trivia. Those temporary jobs had helped pay Rue's final notice bills, though he had never managed to dislodge the endless burden of crushing debt, let alone savour the pleasure of seeing his headline bank balance in credit over successive months. All that was about to change.

Berg was now dangling before his former protégé a far juicier prize than anything Rue had known in his freelance career. It was a long-term contract running to hundreds of thousands of euros per year. With that kind of salary, he estimated he could clear his debts within six months. Rue was in no position, given his desperate circumstances, to do other than accept Berg's largesse without hesitation. The trouble was that the details of his role were vague. All Berg would reveal was that he needed reliable security for himself and his political organisation, a Europe-wide outfit called *Destiny*. That rang distant alarm bells with Rue, but he didn't let it trouble him. How Berg chose to spend his free time —and his copious funds—was none of Rue's business. Moreover, he was curious to learn what the wily old stoat was up to. When Berg proposed a meeting for a chat in the Belgian capital, Rue promptly agreed.

La Grand-Place was thronging with visitors that afternoon and Rue had to fight his way past a busload of Japanese tourists to squeeze into the cramped basement pub. Once there, he found Berg sitting alone by a window, scanning a local newspaper. Spotting Rue as soon as he entered, Berg smiled broadly and waved him over. 'Bang on time as usual, my friend. I've kept you a seat at my favourite spot in all of Brussels.'

After a perfunctory handshake, Berg ordered two liqueur coffees from a waiter and checked that there were no prying eyes or ears in their vicinity.

'Axel, *mon bon ami*, we have known each other a long time. And I believe we have established a strong bond of trust between us, despite some trifling differences in the past, *n'est-ce pas*?'

Throughout his life, Rue had made a virtue out of eschewing small talk. This didn't seem a good time to deviate from that habit, especially when confronted with humbug. He opted for his preferred method of communication—silence—and waited for Berg to continue.

'That's why I knew you were the right man for this job. It's a big one, perhaps the biggest you will ever have to do. Don't worry, the fee is proportionate to the task.'

'What you mean, Berg, is that there are substantial risks, I assume?'

'Oh, no, I wouldn't go that far. Not for a seasoned professional such as yourself. Everything in life is risky, after all, and especially in your line of work. I really hope you will accept this job, as I know you have all the necessary knowledge and skills for it. But if you do, I must warn you that you will be up against a formidable opponent, one that plays dirty tricks at every turn.'

Rue forced a hollow laugh. 'Don't they all?'

'This is no joke, Axel. These people are devious, cunning, ruthless and highly disciplined. They're no pushover, believe me.'

'That description could apply just as well to me and my boys. Who are we talking about? You're building them up as if they were the Mossad.'

Berg grinned. 'Right first time! They are the Mossad.'

'What? You're kidding, surely? Tell me this is your idea of a joke.'

'Not at all. The Mossad have been dispatched to—what's the technical term—neutralise me and my organisation, *Destiny*.'

'Why would they want to do that?'

'Oh, come on, Axel. You weren't born yesterday. You know what these Jews are like. Paranoid, hysterical, thieving, bloodthirsty. Every single one of them. The Zionist leadership sees me as a threat to their interests. And we all know what those are— power, control, and above all money, money, money.'

Ah, that was it. Rue's heart sank. He'd known of Berg's fanatical antisemitism since their army days and didn't approve of it.

Rue also knew enough about the Mossad to respect their expertise. On the other hand, business was business.

'I see. If I understand you correctly, my job is to neutralise the neutralisers?'

'Exactly so. By all means necessary. It's right up your street and shouldn't pose too big a challenge for you and your guys.'

'Excuse me? Get real, Berg. We're talking Mossad, not the Belgian secret service.'

'That's true, my friend. But we have one major advantage. We know exactly who they are. What's even better is that they don't know that we know.'

Rue nodded slowly. 'If that's true, I'm impressed. I'll need full details—names, ranks, locations. Everything you have on them. Oh, and one more thing. Whatever you had in mind to pay me, you'd better double it.'

Berg grimaced. 'You drive a hard bargain. Still, I expected no less. I want the very best and am prepared to pay for it. You'll have all those requests met in full within the hour. Well now, it looks to me that we have a deal, Axel. Yes? You won't regret it. It's time to go and kick some Jew-ass together, *mon bon ami.*'

[17]

'WHY ARE YOU SO STUBBORN, *AHUVATI*? YOU'RE NOT LISTENING. It's official. *Operation Aleph Bet* is off, *finito*. Forget it.' Tamir, sweating profusely after his morning run across Hampstead Heath, sounded more amused than annoyed. 'We may disagree with that decision, but it's not ours to make. And as you said yourself, the upside is that we're free of that damned project. Isn't that great? We should go out and enjoy London while we can. I'm off to take a shower.'

Sofia frowned as she studied her computer screen. 'I'm tired of arguing. Let's talk about that later. Come and look at this. Have you heard of this man?'

With a resigned sigh, Tamir draped a towel over his shoulders and pulled up a chair next to his wife. 'You are impossible, *motek*. You just shut out what you choose not to hear, don't you? All right, show me. What have you found this time?'

'You need to read the article about this guy. Don't you recognise him? I keep hearing his name. He's the MP for a south London constituency.'

'What of him?'

'He's apparently a rising star of the Labour Party. Tipped as a future leader.'

'I'm very happy for him. Is that it?'

'Hey, Tamir, you accuse me of stubbornness. You're just as bad. Worse, actually. Read the bloody article! Every line.'

With feigned reluctance, Tamir complied with his wife's instruction and scrolled down the pro-Labour Party online tabloid newspaper. The headline read *Man of the Future—Meet Azad Ahmed MP*. A head-and-shoulders photograph of a smiling, slightly balding middle-aged man of South Asian appearance occupied two-thirds of the page. The article offered a potted and sympathetic biography of its subject, starting with his modest childhood in East London where he and his immigrant family lived above his father's grocery shop just off Brick Lane. The young Azad, a devout Muslim, had decided to enter politics after an outbreak of racist violence had ended with his father being hospitalised with a serious head injury. A skinhead thug had hurled a brick through the shop window while screaming anti-Asian obscenities. The old man had survived the attack, but Azad had never forgotten the incident that had traumatised his family and community. With anger in his belly and a determination to 'right historical wrongs,' Azad Ahmed had risen through the ranks of the Labour Party and, after a few false starts, had been elected to parliament. Today, he was known as a radical, a firebrand leftist who was gaining the support of young Muslim and black people, especially. He was also rumoured to be a central figure in a secretive internal pressure group that had come to dominate the grassroots party machinery in his constituency—a rumour he refused to confirm or deny. Ahmed had forged an especially fearsome reputation as an 'enemy of global capitalism' and 'a harsh critic of the policies of the Israeli government.' He was widely respected as a patron of several local charities including one that he had personally founded—the

Orb of Islam, one of the NGOs that had organised several aid flotillas to Gaza.

'All very interesting, *motek*, but why are you making me read this stuff? Because he's a critic of Israel? Most people on the far left are anti-Israeli these days.'

'Do I have to spell it out for you, Tamir? He's a powerful politician on the left of the Labour Party, a longstanding anti-Israeli activist, and a patron of an obscure Muslim charity. I've checked them out, this *Orb of Islam* group. It turns out that they may not be entirely kosher—excuse the expression. The article makes no mention of it, but the Charity Commission are investigating them for possible links to Islamic extremists.'

'That doesn't surprise me. Your point is?'

Sofia sat back in her chair and held her head in her hands. 'Tamir, for an intelligent man who works for the most famous spy agency in the world, you can sometimes be so maddeningly slow. Can't you see the red flags fluttering all the way down the page? This man is terrifying. He's obviously the lynchpin of *Destiny* in the UK.'

'Hold on, now you've lost me, *ahuvati*. That's quite a jump. How did you reach that conclusion?'

'I just used my eyes and ears. And a touch of common sense. You should try it sometimes. In fact, you explained it to me yourself. Isn't *Destiny* so dangerous because it's a coalition of the far left, far right and Islamism?'

'Yes, sure, that's what it's all about, bringing these extremist groups together. All right, for the sake of argument, let me look at your evidence. I can see that this guy ticks two of those boxes. He's on the far left of his party, tick. And this charity may well have Islamist connections, tick. On the other hand, there must be hundreds or even thousands of people in that category in this country. I'm not sure where you're going with this, Sofia. Where's the far-right dimension, and how does *Destiny* fit in?'

Sofia turned and looked directly at her husband. 'You still don't get it, do you?' She wore that mischievous expression that Tamir found both seductive and alarming in equal measure. 'You're going to kick yourself when I tell you, Tamir. Who wrote this puff piece on Ahmed? Who's the sycophantic hack?'

Tamir quickly scrolled up to the top of the article and searched for the byline. He caught his breath. 'My God, I didn't see that. Sofia, you are a genius. They're not even trying to hide it.'

The journalist's name was Christoph Berg.

[18]

MOSHE LUNENFELD WAS ALWAYS ULTRA-CAUTIOUS IN HIS dealings with elected officials. The sensitive nature of his job demanded that of him. A thirty-year career in the Mossad had taught him to tread with extreme care when engaging with politicians, especially those at the highest level of government. However much he might disagree with a policy decision, he never ceased reminding himself that he was a mere civil servant whose central purpose was to support his ministers—up to and including the prime minister of the day.

That at least was the formal, legal position. As in so many aspects of Israeli life, formalities could, in special circumstances, be dispensed with. In the national psyche, there was only one issue that could trump democracy to enable the triggering of such dispensation: security. And if this wasn't a special circumstance, reflected Lunenfeld, what was?

Only twice since the establishment of the state had the intelligence agencies actively sought to overrule the government of the day. The first was shortly after the declaration of independence when political infighting led to an exchange of gunfire and threatened to spill over into all-out civil war. The second was during the ill-fated first Lebanon war in the '80s when a headstrong defence minister had appeared poised to launch a military coup against an unpopular government. Would *Operation Aleph Bet* be number three?

He rehearsed the argument for the umpteenth time. Here was a prime minister who had, with justification in Lunenfeld's view, instructed his intelligence services to draw up urgent measures to counter an existential threat to the nation. A malign and well-organised antisemitic organisation, *Destiny,* had bullied its way to power and influence across Europe and was gearing up to marginalise, disenfranchise, expel and perhaps even destroy Europe's Jews. This was the type of eventuality for which the Zionist pioneers and successive generations of Israelis had sacrificed their blood—to ensure that the Jews of the world were never again left defenceless in the face of persecution and the threat of physical annihilation. Israel would not, could not, turn her back on them now. Yet that was the path the country's current prime minister appeared to have chosen.

On learning of this incomprehensible development, Lunenfeld had understood that he would have to act speedily. *Operation Aleph Bet* had been born after a gestation period of just a few weeks. He had submitted a comprehensive plan to the security cabinet that had approved and activated it under the leadership of one of the agency's most capable officers, Dr Keren Benayoun. Then, just as real, game-changing progress on the ground was in the offing, the PM had backtracked, citing unconvincing concerns about Israel's fragile diplomatic relationship with Austria. The future of the operation, despite its success to date, hung in the balance. That had led quickly to the next decisive and perhaps fatal step: The PM, brooking no dissent, had unilaterally shut down the operation. The security cabinet had acquiesced to their leader's fatuous rationalisation with barely a squeak of protest.

An odd aspect of the debacle was that the Israeli PM had later expressed concern to the Mossad director about possible leaks from the government to *Destiny*. Even odder was Adar's peculiar affect in the face of this admission. Lunenfeld was baffled by the PM's simultaneous insouciance. Adar seemed unfazed by the leak of ultra-sensitive information from the security cabinet to an extremist organisation as dangerous as any terrorist threat that the country had faced in its history. Why had he been so unperturbed by an occurrence that, by any standards, constituted a national emergency? Could he have engineered the crisis to discredit a rival in the cabinet? Or was he attempting to extricate himself from some personal conflict of interest relating to the Austrian leadership? Was it conceivable that the prime minister of Israel had leaked his own country's security secrets to a hostile foreign group to promote his own private agenda, whatever that might be?

Lunenfeld intuitively recoiled from conspiracy theories. In his experience, most of them turned out to be wild overinterpretations of unpleasant events for which a rational explanation existed but had yet to emerge into daylight. Nevertheless, real conspiracies were, on rare occasions, hatched. Was this one of them?

He drew a white linen handkerchief from his pocket and dabbed the beads of sweat that had formed on his forehead. The Mossad director knew where his duty lay. In the face of dysfunctional governance, the state's national security had to be safeguarded by those charged with that responsibility. Lunenfeld contemplated his limited options. None was in the least appealing.

He considered revealing to the PM his suspicions of a high-level conspiracy. That would be a dangerous path: His commander in chief was notoriously impatient with dissenters and there was a risk he might get fired on the spot. Worse, the PM might order the arrest of the Mossad director for sedition. That would be an explosive act that could threaten the integrity of Adar's governing coalition, though the PM would likely rally support from within the security cabinet or even within the ranks of the ruling party in Israel's parliament, the Knesset. It was a safe bet that Adar had ensured that at least two of his senior colleagues would prove rock solid in their support in the event of a leadership challenge. Any number of politicians might even be in on the plot, if that's what it was. And if Lunenfeld somehow persuaded a couple of senior figures to break ranks, it would be easy for the PM to brand the whole exercise an illegitimate and unconstitutional undermining of his authority as head of the elected government—in effect, an attempted *coup d'état*.

As a last resort, Lunenfeld could turn to his senior colleagues within the army, the *Aman* military intelligence service. He enjoyed an excellent working relationship with his opposite number in the IDF, Colonel Yossi Gavron, but there was a complication. Gavron had long coveted the Mossad directorship and was known to have been miffed by the selection committee's choice of Lunenfeld for the top job. In the past, the two men had enjoyed a close and even warm friendship but that had turned chilly following the appointment. Lunenfeld couldn't risk injecting oxygen into the fading embers of that historical rivalry. Were it to spring back to life, the consequences could be unpleasant for both of them.

Lunenfeld was undeterred by the lack of an obvious solution to his quandary. He recognised that sometimes none existed, but that was an insufficient excuse for passivity. This was a national challenge that demanded clearheaded leadership and immediate action. As the political echelon appeared at best paralysed and at worst complicit in the crisis, he, as Mossad director, he would have to act alone. That was no less than the people of Israel would expect of him. But the stakes were sky high. Ordering the implementation of a major and irreversible step could either end his career in ignominy or propel him into the annals of history as the man who saved the country from disaster.

Lunenfeld reviewed his available choices one last time. Since they were all equally unpalatable, his final selection became straightforward. The risks were almost too huge to contemplate but he believed he had no alternative. In such extreme circumstances, the decision almost made itself.

Moshe Lunenfeld had begun to think the unthinkable.

He pressed the intercom on his desk and spoke quietly to his PA, who was surprised by the faint tremor in his voice. 'Get me Doctor Benayoun, please. Urgently.'

[19]

FEW OF THE PEDESTRIANS WANDERING UP AND DOWN THE STEEP slope of Hampstead High Street gave the well-dressed barrel-chested young man wearing stylish Italian sunglasses a second glance. If any had noticed him, they might have assumed he was a local businessman—an entrepreneur, computer salesman or real estate agent perhaps—taking a well-earned coffee break at his favourite pavement café. Most would have doubtless been shocked to discover the true nature of his profession. Axel Rue, a mercenary for all seasons, was planning a murder.

Shielding his tablet device from the sun, Rue studied the map for at least the fifth time. He couldn't make head-nor-tail of the byzantine layout of this part of north London. Most of the pretty streets and lanes curved round on each other and then twisted and turned with a perversity that seem designed to bamboozle the stranger. To add to the confusion, the undulating main thoroughfares were narrow and lined with street furniture of varying dimensions so that clear sightlines were hard to come by.

Were it not for the incessant traffic, thought Rue, Hampstead had the appearance of a quintessential English rural village that had somehow been transplanted to central London. He felt he could live here. Like Brussels, his far smaller hometown, London was blessed with a profusion of greenery that framed many famous vistas throughout the vast conurbation. This topmost point of the northern suburbs of the metropolis was no exception—the rolling hills and dales of Hampstead Heath were visible around almost every corner. The cafes, restaurants and bars may not have been quite up to Belgian standards, yet their quaintness exerted an undeniable appeal even to Rue's jaundiced eye. The populace looked white and middle class by and large though a fair sprinkling of ethnic minorities, some at least of whom were camera-clicking tourists, injected a more cosmopolitan feel to the place.

Rue made a conscious effort to banish these mindless musings. He had to focus on the task in hand. The target's address had been located—it was precisely five hundred metres from where he was sitting. Rue's temporary accomplice, a scruffy looking teenager called Andre, was at that moment cycling in circles around the area delivering free newspapers to a random selection of households while maintaining a watchful eye on the house of interest. The boy was inexperienced and Rue had taken him on with profound reluctance in the absence of alternatives. Never mind, it couldn't be helped. These youngsters had to learn the ropes somehow and reconnaissance was as good a place to start as any. He had given Andre detailed instructions to minimise the risk of a mishap.

Having obtained an extensive analysis of the target from Berg, Rue had wanted to get a closer look at the Israeli to enable a better assessment of his strengths and vulnerabilities. At this stage, that would require meticulous data gathering about the man's appearance, his routines and the opportunities for a decisive strike. 'Today, we're going to keep things simple,' he had instructed his young colleague. 'This guy is no slouch. We'll keep our heads down and monitor him for a while. Then we'll move to the next stage when the time is ripe.'

OPERATION ALEPH BET

So far, all was going to plan. Andre had fulfilled his duties to the letter and was texting Rue brief status update reports every ten minutes as agreed. These messages invariably comprised just three words: *Nothing to see*. This tedious ritual had been repeated several times over the previous hour or so when Rue received the one he had been awaiting. *T leaving flat and coming your way. Yellow sleeveless shirt and blue jeans. Will follow and intervene as instructed.*

At moments like these, Rue switched to professional mode in a flash. Adjusting a concealed mirror flap in his sunglasses that doubled as a camera, he was able to observe, unnoticed, the end of the street from where he expected the target to emerge. The image was remarkably sharp. Rue smiled at the wonders of modern technology. He pressed the video button and started recording. A somewhat harassed mother pushing a pram was the first to turn the corner into the high street.

Just at that moment, a large white van stopped right at the junction, obscuring Rue's view of the street. *Merde*, he muttered under his breath, *get out of the way, you idiot*. The target should have reached the junction by now, but where was he?

Then he saw Andre, cycling unsteadily and then coming to an abrupt halt next to a lamp post, which he grabbed for support. Andre's demeanour was one of utter confusion. Glancing across the street at the café where Rue sat, he dismounted from the bike and started to type on his phone. Meanwhile the white van had moved off. There was no sign of the target. The distraught Andre had texted *Did you see T? I lost him, sorry, boss.*

Rue swore again. How was that possible? All Andre had to do was cycle a short distance behind the Israeli until the latter reached the junction, at which point Andre was supposed to waylay him and ask for directions to the nearest tube station. That was it. The plan was the epitome of elegant simplicity but it had already unravelled. Maybe he had overestimated Andre's abilities. Or underestimated the Israeli's.

What happened next was almost too fast for the human eye to see. A figure in a yellow shirt—that was surely the Mossadnik—was kneeling and performing some sort of physical manoeuvre. Rue thought he heard a male voice emit a shout, then another. A scarlet spray fanned upwards and outwards, glistening as it was caught in a sunbeam. It was only when he spotted a bicycle lying on its side that Rue realised he had to act fast. He leapt out of his seat and sprinted across the road between two slow-moving cars. There was no sign of the yellow-shirted man. Andre was sprawled on the ground whimpering, his face an unrecognisable puffed-up mask of bruised, bleeding tissue.

'Jesus, Andre! What the hell just happened?'

No answer came. Andre appeared to drift in and out of consciousness. A small crowd had started to form a huddle around the junction. The traffic on the high street had come to a halt as drivers craned their necks to see what was going on. Parents were shielding their children's eyes from the scene.

Rue noticed that Andre's whimpering had stopped. 'Stay with me, son. Hang in there.' He snapped open his phone and summoned an ambulance.

[20]

'PACK A COUPLE OF CASES QUICKLY, *AHUVATI*. JUST SOME BASICS. We have to leave in fifteen minutes, maximum. Sorry to do this to you but it's an emergency.' Tamir's voice was soft and measured, which somehow amplified the force of his alarming words.

'What in God's name happened to you?' Sofia was staring at her husband's blood-stained shirt. 'You've been hurt!'

'No, I haven't. Nothing happened to me. But someone else wasn't so lucky. I'll tell you more later, the details don't matter now. Come on, let's get moving. I need to take a shower first but that won't take me long. Grab a few essentials and leave the rest behind. What are you waiting for, *motek*? *Yallah*, hurry.'

'Hold on, Tamir, have you lost your marbles altogether? We can't just leave. What about Clara?'

'Call your mother to collect her from school. Or your sister. Whatever. But do it now. We can't stay here. We're sitting ducks. Please don't argue.' He raced into the bedroom and Sofia followed. He pulled down two suitcases from the top of the wardrobe and flung them open. 'Start packing now, *motek*. I'll explain as much as I can on the way.'

'On the way to where? What's going on? Don't keep me in the dark again, Tamir!'

He turned and placed his hands on her shoulders and locked his earnest eyes on hers. 'All right, listen to me, *ahuvati*. This is serious. They're here. *Destiny*. They know where we live. They're coming after us and we can't sit at home waiting for them. If they find us, they won't hand out cookies. Please believe me, I'm not imagining things. We're in serious danger if we stay. That's all I know right now. Come on, let's get out of here.'

'Okay, I hear you. But something doesn't make sense. Won't they just track us down wherever we run?'

'In theory, yes, but Keren will find us a safe house. She's sending a car now.'

Sofia winced at the mention of Keren's name. 'I might have known that woman had something to do with all this.'

Tamir placed his palms together as if in prayer. 'Please let's not go over that again She's my boss, Sofia, and you know that very well. This problem is not of Keren's making. Quite the opposite, she's helping to keep us safe. Yes, you're right, they will come after us wherever we go, so we have to keep one step ahead of them. Whoever these people are and whatever their motivation, they are capable of anything. I've seen this a dozen times and I'm certain they intend to hurt us. That means they'll be back on our trail very soon whatever happens. Our first priority is to get out of here, *chik chak*.'

'And just abandon our home, our belongings, everything?'

'Once things settle down, we can come back, I promise. Look, I wouldn't do this to us if I thought there was another way. I've been in situations like this before and I know what I'm talking about. You must trust me, Sofia.' He glanced at his watch. '*Nu*? Let's get moving. We have exactly ten minutes.'

'Tamir Weiss, you owe me an apology.' There was anger in Sofia's voice. 'You told me this operation was over. I'm supposed to be a member of the team now, remember? How about treating me like one? I've been patient up till now. So would you please tell me what the fuck is going on?'

They were huddled in the cramped back seat of a sporty Mercedes, surrounded by bulging plastic bags and three small suitcases. As they sped smoothly through the north London streets, the young driver periodically glanced anxiously in the rear-view mirror at his agitated passengers.

Tamir ignored Sofia's question. Not because he hadn't heard it but because he was too busy texting. Sofia had seen that expression before—he was focusing with laser-like attention on his task. She leaned over to try to read the message. Tamir pointedly shielded the screen from his wife's prying eyes. He needn't have bothered, as the exchange was in Hebrew. He pressed the send button and waited. Within thirty seconds the phone rang. Sofia could hear a woman's voice—Keren Benayoun. Who else? Tamir responded mostly in monosyllables. Sofia wished she had learned at least some basic vocabulary of that mysterious language. The conversation lasted under a minute.

'And what does the glamorous doctor order for her patient today?' she asked, her voice strained and unsympathetic. She knew her question was futile even as she posed it. Tamir remained silent as he stared out of the car window, lost in his private thoughts.

Not for the first time, Sofia was forced to ask herself a stark question: *What in God's name am I doing here? I must be out of my mind.*

Later that day, she called her sister to let off steam. Luisa was sympathetic but posed the same question. 'It's a bit late for that sort of soul-searching, isn't it? You must have known what you were getting into, sis. What were you thinking when you got involved with this man?'

The answer she came up with was always a variation on the same theme. 'I wasn't thinking anything, Luisa, it just happened. I didn't choose to fall in love with him. He crashed into my life like a tornado. And do you know the awful truth? If I could turn the clock back, I have the feeling it would just happen all over again.'

[21]

THE JUNCTION OF ROTHSCHILD BOULEVARD AND HERZL STREET, AT the coffee stall, nine sharp.

When the Mossad director issued such a summons, everyone in the organisation who received it held one thought foremost in their mind—don't be late.

Keren Benayoun was early. She loved this quaint corner of Tel Aviv with its boutique hotels, coffee kiosks and striking mix of Bauhaus and modernist architecture. The frantic, noisy bustle of the city centre had failed to encroach on this island of tranquillity. The trees along the scented boulevard were blossoming and the late spring temperature was perfect at this hour of low morning sun. To the untutored eye, the street scene was normal, belying the abnormality of the small country's permanent state of military hypervigilance. The last of the joggers were heading to their homes or offices for a shower and the rush-hour traffic had almost disappeared. A few tourists and dog-walkers were ambling along the green central reservation, dodging bicycles and electric scooters. Keren enjoyed people-watching, not so much out of curiosity but because she felt a sense of responsibility that amounted to a duty of care towards her fellow Israelis, almost none of whom could have the slightest idea that their small country was about to enter yet another full-blown crisis.

She bought a *café hafuch* from the kiosk and wandered over to a vacant table perched near the edge of the walkway. In almost a single action, she put down her paper cup and pulled out her phone to check her inbox. Even before she felt the light touch on her shoulder, she sensed his presence. As usual, the director had arrived one minute ahead of schedule.

'Good morning, doctor. What lovely weather. How are you today?'

Keren declined to respond to Lunenfeld's ritual greeting. Relations between them had chilled since her enforced, though short-lived, 'holiday.' But she had swallowed her pride and was determined to revert to the *status quo ante* as best she could.

Lunenfeld was besuited and tieless, as had become the fashion among senior Israeli officials, as if in subtle tribute to the pointed informality of the early servants of the state. Apparently unaware of his colleague's coolness, he slipped off his jacket, perhaps in an effort to put her at ease, and slung it over the back of a chair. 'I hear there's been an unpleasant incident in London. That's most disturbing, given that *Aleph Bet* has officially been terminated. We need to know what happened and why. What's your theory, doctor?'

'I don't have one, not yet. I'm working on it.' Keren swept her gaze swiftly around them in case of potential eavesdroppers. 'As you say, the order to shut down the operation was issued from the highest level of our country's government. What I don't understand is what *Destiny* are playing at. We're no longer a threat to them, at least on paper. That message should have got through to *Destiny* immediately if the leak channel was open and functioning. It apparently didn't so maybe it's been sealed. Anyway, the couple are safe for the time being. I've found them a comfortable hideaway not far from their home. But that is only a temporary solution. If *Destiny* is determined to hurt them, Berg's thugs will track them down soon enough.'

Lunenfeld removed his spectacles and studied them closely before replacing them. He was smiling at her. 'You are so very perceptive, Keren. Yet again, you have proved your worth to this organisation and justified my faith in you. *Mazal tov.*'

'Excuse me? What did I do?'

'You just found the answer to the puzzle. It's obvious. The leak of the order to terminate *Operation Aleph Bet* should have done the trick but it didn't. Why not? Because that order—on paper, as you rightly pointed out—was countermanded. By me. As you are aware.'

'Yes, I am well aware of that but almost no-one else is. Your counter-order was top secret so it should have been leak-proof.' Keren glanced around them again and lowered her voice. 'Are you saying it leaked from your office? Or from elsewhere within the Mossad?'

'Not necessarily. Look, the people around the PM know me pretty well by now. Someone in a position of influence may have suspected what I was up to and ensured that *Destiny* wasn't fooled by the official line, as it appeared, to quote you, "on paper"'— Lunenfeld mimed the quote marks. 'Whoever it was may have made some enquiries, discovered my counter-order and proceeded to disseminate that information.'

'In that case, who is causing the mischief? I assume you're not suggesting that someone within the government is collaborating with *Destiny*?'

'I'm not suggesting anything. All possibilities have to be considered. I should also tell you, doctor, that I took additional measures to ensure that knowledge of my counter-order was strictly confined to the very highest level of government. Solely and exclusively.'

'I don't follow. Who are you referring to?'

Lunenfeld raised his eyebrows but maintained an eloquent silence.

'My God, you think Adar might be the source!'

Lunenfeld winced at her suggestion. 'I wish I could rule him out, but I can't. He's not my favourite politician but even I would be shocked to discover he was a traitor. But ask yourself this question: isn't it odd that he hasn't summoned me for a dressing down? After all, I defied him. And I informed him that I'd overruled his unambiguous instruction. That's a sacking offence. Yet he did absolutely nothing. Or maybe he confided in someone close to him, someone who passed the information to *Destiny*. Someone who might be trying to frame him, for political reasons.'

'Who might that be? Someone in his office? Or in the security cabinet? Arkady Volkov perhaps? Everyone knows he has his eyes on the top job.'

'The security cabinet wasn't updated on my decision. And Volkov has never been close enough to the PM to receive that sort of confidential information.'

'In which case everything points to Adar alone as the source of the leak. If that's the case, it would mean that he was putting his own intelligence agents at risk. Why on earth would he do such a thing?'

Lunenfeld was no longer smiling. He stood slowly and with exaggerated deliberation, picked up his jacket, brushed it down and slung it over his arm. 'That's what we need to find out, doctor. As soon as possible. And I am confident that your enterprising young couple in London will help us do it.'

[22]

ANY OF CHRISTOPH BERG'S FRIENDS WHO HAPPENED TO SEE HIM that afternoon would have been concerned about his health. With cheeks bright red and nostrils flaring, Berg was incandescent with rage. Pacing around his small office near the Brussels Central Station, he dialled Axel Rue for the third time in five minutes. This time his call was answered.

'You fucking idiot, Rue!' he yelled. 'How could you be so monumentally incompetent? The Weisses got away thanks to you and your pimply sidekick. We'll never find that slippery Jew-boy now. *Mein Gott*, man, what's the point in my paying you all this money? It's a bloody fiasco!'

'Hold your horses, Berg. It's a setback, no question, and I apologise. Shit like this happens in our business. But stay calm. I intend to put it right.'

'Oh, you'll do better than that, Rue. A lot better. I'm implementing an immediate change in our modus operandi. From now on you'll report directly to my man in London. On a daily basis. I'll send you his address. He's waiting for you. I suggest get your fat backside over there right now.'

'If you insist, Herr Berg. But, hey, you'd better change your tone of voice or I'm out. You got that? I won't accept that level of abuse from you or anyone else. Berg, do you understand?' The line was dead.

'*Merde*,' muttered Rue under his breath. He couldn't afford to fall out with Berg. Just as he flipped shut his phone, it vibrated with the arrival of a text message. He reopened it and grimaced. It was the address of his new handler. This had not been part of the deal, but he didn't have much choice if he wanted to save the contract. And the contract was his lifeline. That meant he had no choice but to comply. He squinted along the length of the street and spotted an approaching black cab. He hailed it and climbed in. 'Sancroft Street, Lambeth—quick as you can.'

The *Orb of Islam* office was a modest affair. Located in one of those unremarkable south London backstreets that most residents of the capital would never enter in their lifetimes, the location suited Azad Ahmed MP well. Near enough to Westminster to respond in minutes to the House's division bells, he could walk to a couple of tube stations with ease and even reach Trafalgar Square on foot in about forty minutes. When he wasn't needed at the Commons, he could pursue his real passion—building the *Orb* into the most influential Muslim charity in Europe. He had conceived it originally as an educational NGO for young Muslims who were desperate to hit back at the West for their unforgiveable crimes against their brothers and sisters in Iraq, Afghanistan, Bosnia and, above all, Palestine.

Since its launch just after the start of the imperialistic Iraq war by the American and British Crusader forces, the *Orb* had trebled in size. Income flowed into its coffers from around the world—including Saudi Arabia and, via indirect channels, Iran—and Ahmed could scarcely keep pace with demand for its services. He had taken great care to ensure that the precise nature of many of those services was kept shrouded from public view. The UK regulators, the Charity Commission, had already poked their interfering noses into his office a couple of times, claiming to be acting on complaints that Islamist messages were being disseminated from *Orb* offices. Ahmed understood very well the source of those scurrilous slanders. The UK Jewish community may be small in size, he reflected bitterly, but the multiplier effect of their global connections to their brethren in Europe, the US and Israel was formidable, ensuring access to enormous wealth and unlimited power. These Zionist plotters would have to be stopped, and he was determined to play his part in stopping them.

Thanks be to *Allah, the Beneficent,* he had discovered likeminded allies right across the British political establishment. He had never had much time for the British National Party and other far right groups—all of whom were longstanding persecutors of his Pakistani-origin English-born family—but on the subject of the Jews, he had to acknowledge that these ultranationalists were on the right side of history. Within his own Labour Party, despite a stodgy leadership still stuck in the cul-de-sac of Blairite neoliberalism and fulminating against an imaginary antisemitic tendency on the left of the party, a cadre of bright new stars was ringing in the changes, some in the name of Marxism, others locating themselves in the moderate camp while calling for an attitudinal revolution.

Ahmed was convinced that the Israel-Palestine conflict—and its rebranding as the twenty-first century's anti-apartheid movement—held the key to releasing the world from the Jewish stranglehold. The Greens were already on board. Even old-fashioned centrists, including so-called Liberal Democrats, could be lured into the fold given their passionate sympathy for the Palestinian cause and their opposition to the thieving, racist, apartheid Zionist state of Israel. This was, after all, the one issue that could forge an unprecedented alliance of the political right, left and centre, at least in the UK and perhaps across Europe.

The catalyst of that alliance would be the inspirational vision of the Islamic movement. Ahmed could demonstrate to these disparate groupings that they all supported the same pro-Palestinian objective. To achieve it, they needed to build a coalition of activists that would generate an irresistible momentum towards justice for the most oppressed nation in history. An early priority would be to develop a strike force that would aim its firepower at the heart of the Western imperialist establishment and its international Zionist backers. The weapon to deliver this blow was already in the making: a resurgent Palestine arising like a phoenix between the Jordan and the Mediterranean—from the river to the sea—sweeping away the morally corrupt and politically illegitimate Zionist entity. That victory, in turn, would pave the way for the next stage in the geopolitical *jihad*, the realisation of the greatest dream in all of human history, the revival and re-establishment of the transnational Islamic empire, the Caliphate. *Inshallah*.

The trouble was, understood Ahmed, that all this feverish speculation was nothing more than will-o'-the-wisp. How could his tantalising vision of a glorious future be translated into practical action? That was the million-dollar question.

Allah, the Omnipotent, in his infinite wisdom, gave him the answer. Ahmed would have to forge his own path through the jungle of Jewish obfuscation and treachery, but he now had an inkling of how to find his way. It just needed brighter illumination. Thanks be to God, he had met the man who would provide it. The extraordinary, talented and charismatic Herr Christoph Berg.

Ahmed's reverie was interrupted by a buzz on his intercom. 'A Mr Axel Rue to see you, Mr Ahmed,' announced his secretary.

'Yes, I'm expecting him. Send him in.' Ahmed stood to greet his visitor. The two men shook hands. 'Welcome, Mr Rue. You're younger than I expected. Please take a seat. Thank you so much for coming to see me.'

'Thank you, sir, but I didn't have much choice, as I'm sure you know.' If Rue was discomfited to find himself in the company of this high-powered politician, he didn't show it.

'Ah yes, indeed, our mutual friend Mr Berg has put me in the picture. Can I offer you a cup of tea? Or water, maybe?'

Rue shook his head, remaining hyperalert as the MP eased himself into a high-backed leather chair behind his desk. 'Well now, Mr Rue, I gather from Mr Berg that you've been having a little local difficulty with our Zionist friends, isn't that so?'

'That's one way of putting. But we'll overcome that difficulty, Mr Ahmed.'

'Indeed, you will, my dear chap. If you want my advice, you have to hit those bastards hard, without mercy. Force is the only language they understand, is that not so?'

Rue declined to endorse Ahmed's assertion. 'With the greatest of respect, sir, this is not your area of expertise. Herr Berg has given me a job to do and I intend to do it. I admit that there's been a minor blip but it's a temporary setback. And to be honest, I don't really know why I'm here.'

Ahmed grinned, clasped his hands behind his head and leaned back in his chair. It had one of those swivelling mechanisms that Rue found irritating. Ahmed was an enthusiastic swiveller. 'Not my area of expertise—that's very good, Mr Rue, very good. I must admit, you have already surprised me.'

They were both startled by the loud, continuous ringing of an electric bell. Though it stopped after a few seconds, it seemed to jolt the MP into action. Ahmed leapt from his chair and swept a bunch of papers from his desk into a briefcase. Rue assumed that the strange interview was over, but he was wrong.

'I'm so sorry, Mr Rue, that's the parliamentary division bell. I have to get myself to the House now or else I will be in trouble. One of the burdens of public service. Come with me in the car, please, where we can continue our fascinating conversation.'

The two men descended the staircase together. Only one continued talking.

'Mr Rue, I fully support your efforts to smoke out the Zionist couple. And in the process, they might lead us to their backers. Of which there are many, I assure you. In the City, in the media, in the universities, even in the House of Commons where I am about to cast my vote. But I don't believe we should worry unduly about Mr Weiss. He is just an annoying mosquito. If we succeed in swotting him, others will take his place. No, my friend, our real aim is far more ambitious. It is to drain the swamp that breeds him and his ilk.'

Ahmed could tell that the younger man was puzzled. 'I know what you are thinking. Too much information, am I right? I have to disagree. Information is power. But you are young and you obviously have much to learn, my dear chap. And now is as good a time as any. I don't blame you for your ignorance, it is widespread in this country and indeed all around the world. All I ask is that you hear what I have to say. It will only take a few minutes of your time. Then you can tell me whether you hold to your view that this is, how did you put it, "not my area of expertise."' Ahmed chuckled at his repetition of Rue's words. 'Good, here is our car.'

A polished black limousine drew up in front of them. Ahmed opened the rear door wide for his guest who duly climbed in followed by his host. Once they had buckled up, the MP opened his phone and peered into its lens, using its reverse camera to adjust his tie and comb his thinning hair, all the while continuing to lecture his visitor.

'You see, Mr Rue, so much of the real power that rules our lives is hidden from view. But once you know where to look, you will be astonished at the sheer scale of the deception. It is truly breathtaking. Relax, my good man, and enjoy the ride. This promises to be the most illuminating car journey of your life.'

[23]

BURRARD ROAD IS ONE OF THE SLEEPIEST STREETS IN LONDON. Nestled between two of north London's busiest thoroughfares from where the perpetual hum of traffic is just about audible to its residents day and night, it's as close to an oasis of suburban calm as is to be found anywhere in the metropolis. As a location for a Mossad safe house, it was ideal—an urban backwater that was only seconds from an accessible network of escape routes in all directions. It also happened to be within walking distance of the real Weiss home, now out of bounds to them, in Hampstead Village.

'I suppose it could be worse,' muttered Sofia as she inspected the converted ground floor flat that was to be her new home. 'Someone has spent a pile of cash on this place. All mod cons, and a beautiful garden. Clara won't mind in the slightest. It will just be another big adventure for her.'

'I thought you'd like it,' said Keren. 'The whole place has been refurbished and the furniture is brand new. I know you'd rather be in your own place, but remember this is just a temporary shelter.'

'How temporary?' asked Sofia. Keren shrugged.

'Until we know we're safe,' interjected Tamir. 'That could be any minute now. I just can't understand why they came after us when *Aleph Bet* had been shut down. Maybe they didn't get the memo. It doesn't make any sense. We must be missing something.'

'I agree,' said Keren. 'We're trying to find out what went wrong. Meanwhile, we have to assume that the danger persists. We've thrown a ring of surveillance around you. This is as safe as a safe house gets. Keep your heads down here until further notice.'

'Hold on a sec, I'm not on your payroll, you know,' protested Sofia. 'I can do what I like. Isn't that right, Tamir?'

'Yes, you can do exactly what you like, *ahuvati*—if you care nothing for your life or for the safety of your family.'

Sofia scowled at her husband. 'We'll have to talk about this later.'

'Listen, Sofia,' said Keren. 'I know it's not easy for you. But let's be sensible. I promise you that we'll sort all this out as quickly as we can.'

'Yes, yes, I know. And I suppose I should be grateful. I hate these *Destiny* blackshirts as much as you do. I've already agreed to help you. But I'd also appreciate being allowed to live a semi-normal life with my family.' Sofia wiped away a tear.

Keren placed a hand on Sofia's forearm. 'And you will, Sofia, I guarantee it. Just not now. There are people out there who want to hurt you. All of you. We intend to stop them. You wouldn't want to make our job harder and theirs easier?'

'As if I have a choice.'

'You always have a choice. I just want you to make the right one. I'm late, I must run.' The Israeli picked up her bag and slung it over her shoulder. The two women embraced lightly and briefly, without conviction.

'Oh, one last thing,' said Keren. 'You can leave this house for short periods—if you wear these. Both of you.' She pointed to a plastic bag on the sofa. 'You'll find a couple of wigs and heavy sunglasses in there. Unoriginal but effective disguises. Please use them.'

'I just love fancy dress,' said Sofia sarcastically. 'How thoughtful of you. I can't wait to try them on.'

Keren chose not to respond to the taunt. 'Right, I'll leave you two to get settled. I've posted two guards outside, one each front and back. And that's just the inner layer of security. If you leave the house, we'll tail you. If you see anything suspicious, contact me immediately. Enjoy.'

As she closed the gate of the safe house behind her, Keren paused and stood stock still. One of the Mossad's most experienced officers, this was her standard practice when something felt out of kilter. Her senses were attuned to her environment at all times but more so in circumstances of heightened danger. What had she just heard or seen or felt as she exited the house—a scurrying squirrel, perhaps, or a flapping pigeon, or a gust of wind? Or a more sinister source of disturbance?

There were no obvious visual clues, but she hadn't expected any. She crossed the road and walked briskly a hundred metres towards Fortune Green Road. Having reached the junction at the end of a neat row of whitewashed town houses, she found herself in a busy commercial area. Without missing a step, she slipped into a shady doorway, spun round on her heels and looked back along Burrard Road. There. On the right-hand side of the street, opposite the safe house, an unmarked white van moved at a slow crawl away from her as if the driver was trying to avoid being noticed. If that was his intention, he had failed.

Keren reached for her phone and made the call.

[24]

GENERAL ARKADY VOLKOV HAD BEEN ISRAEL'S MINISTER OF defence for just six months when he experienced what he would later describe as an unpleasant olfactory sensation that seemed to permeate the corridors of power. At first, he thought he detected just a hint of the foul aroma within the higher echelons of the government in which he served. Now he was convinced something more serious was amiss—the stench was becoming overwhelming. His duty was to find the rotting carcass and dispose of it. That was why he had asked to see Mossad director Lunenfeld within the hour.

Volkov was far from the typical Israeli soldier-politician. Following his compulsory service in the Soviet army, he had joined the KGB just before the end of the Cold War and was set on a career path to fame and glory. Then the Berlin Wall—and Volkov's world—came tumbling down around him. The Soviet security forces were thrown into a state of flux verging on panic and Volkov was informed that his services were no longer required. *Perestroika* may have promised liberation for most Russians but for Volkov it was the opposite—a dead end, a Gulag cell with no exit. Apart from domestic spying and a bit of soldiering, he had no skills he could monetise. Close to despair, he faced a future of unemployment and poverty. There was no available escape route—until he met a pretty girl called Galina Lieberman.

The Volkov family could trace their heritage back to minor White Russian aristocracy. Like most of their compatriots, they had never been too keen on Jews, though they knew hardly any (despite rumours of a Jewish ancestor lurking somewhere in their family tree). But they soon took Galina to their hearts. A petite brunette with heartbreakingly beautiful hazel eyes, Galina was a primary school teacher in the lower middle-class Moscow suburb where both families lived. When Arkady announced to his parents that he wanted to marry the girl, they were ultra-sceptical. A Jewess—surely not a suitable match for their Russian prince? But their resistance weakened when they met Galina, her brother Maxime, and the recently widowed Mrs Lieberman. Perhaps the Volkovs decided that the Liebermans, despite external appearances, were in reality 'filthy rich,' as all Jews were said to be, or perhaps they were won over by Arkady's powers of persuasion. Whatever the explanation, the Volkov family's reservations were soon sidelined. Before long, the young couple had received the blessing of both parties and a date was set for a civil wedding ceremony.

Once married, and to Arkady's mild surprise, Galina insisted on kindling Shabbat candles at home each Friday night. Although far from observant, she had always insisted to Arkady that she wanted to preserve her Jewish identity and that any children issuing from the marriage would be raised as Jews. That would be no easy task in Russia where cesspools of anti-semitism always swirled beneath the placid surface of so-called civilised society. Arkady voiced little objection to his wife's aspirations, especially as there was no immediate prospect of starting a family. Galina's modest salary was barely sufficient to meet their most basic needs as a couple, and the arrival of children would stretch their economic capacity well beyond breaking point. In any case, he had a more pressing preoccupation—how to find a job and a regular income. Neither the Volkovs nor the Liebermans were in a position to offer assistance. As their first wedding anniversary approached, Arkady slumped into a deep depression. On the rare occasion when his job applications sufficed to get him an interview, no offer materialised.

'I'm afraid your marriage to a Jew won't have helped your cause,' suggested Galina. 'You know what these people are like, Arkady. Your record should speak for itself, but your personal choices don't play well with them. They'll never appoint you to a senior position in this country's establishment. But don't despair, my darling, I have an idea I want to discuss.'

Galina's idea was straightforward. Emigration. Specifically, *Aliyah*—literally *going up* or immigration to Israel. Arkady's first reaction was horror. Raised in the era of virulent Soviet anti-Zionist propaganda, he viewed the 'Zionist entity' as the epitome of evil. His parents concurred. 'Is she mad? It's dangerous over there. And you're not even a Jew, Arkady, they won't let you in.'

They were wrong. Galina made enquiries and confirmed what she had suspected—that under Israel's Law of Return the spouse of a Jew could acquire instant Israeli citizenship and the full panoply of rights, including interviews with employers, housing assistance and tax breaks. They'd both have to learn Hebrew—Galina already had a smattering—and Arkady would be drafted into the army at officer level given his previous military experience. As time passed, Galina's cajoling paid off and Arkady relented. It was either a life of perpetual struggle and misery in the disintegrating Russian Federation or the start of a new life in Israel. It was a no-brainer. The couple would complete their application forms to be accepted as *olim*, immigrants to the Jewish state. Arkady doubted that they would succeed but his wife sustained him with a relentless optimism. 'This time next year, we'll be Israeli,' she assured him.

And so it transpired. With the agreement of Galina's (though not Arkady's) family, the young couple emigrated from Russia, became Israeli citizens and quickly adopted their new identities in the Jewish homeland. To their surprise, they found Israel to be full of Russians, including many non-Jews. There were Russian shops, newspapers and TV stations. From the start, Arkady felt at home in the country. His Russian Orthodox upbringing proved irrelevant to his new Israeli friends. With Galina's help, he mastered Hebrew at lightning speed. Three strapping Volkov children, *sabras* (native Israelis) every one, entered the world in quick succession.

As for the army, the draft authorities snapped up Arkady without hesitation and assigned him, at his request, to a combat unit where he excelled in all aspects of the rigorous training. Fast-tracked through the ranks at speed, he was soon promoted to the head of the army's southern command where he engineered several successful campaigns against Hamas terrorist cells in the Gaza Strip, in the process of which he demonstrated a highly prized combination of professionalism and creativity that is the hallmark of an outstanding military leader. By now, he was a fully-fledged Israeli and, in the eyes of the troops under his command at least, a heroic figure.

On reaching his mid-forties, and approaching the end of his army contract, he received a surprising message from an ex-army comrade, a fellow Russian (and, like so many of his fellow countrymen, a nationalist firebrand) who had recently been elected to the Knesset. 'We need you in government, Arkady. The sky is the limit for you. Join us. You could even be prime minister someday. Think about it.'

Arkady did think about it, discussed the idea with Galina (now known as Galit) and made his decision.

[25]

'YOU PROBABLY REGARD ME AS AN EXTREMIST, A RELIGIOUS fanatic. Is that not so, Mr Rue?'

Axel Rue shrugged. At the best of times, his appetite for politics was miniscule. Being stuck in a car, even for a few minutes, with this self-absorbed politician—whose arrogant demeanour suggested that he considered himself to be the re-incarnated Winston Churchill—was almost beyond endurance. On the short drive between Lambeth and Westminster, Rue had struggled to concentrate on Ahmed's multiple diatribes—against globalisation, bankers, the media and, above all, *the elite*. He pondered what Ahmed meant by that term.

As if reading his thoughts, Ahmed enlightened him. 'All these threats to the working class are unpleasant. But with determination and sound policies, we can see them all off. Except for one.'

'You mean the global elite, I suppose?' prompted Rue. *Wild guess*.

'Exactly. You are a most perceptive young man. And you know why these people are so elusive?'

'No, I don't.' *But you're going to tell me.*

'Look around you, Mr Rue. What do you see?' They were

approaching the main gate of the Palace of Westminster. The driver pulled into a layby, awaiting instructions.

'I see the Houses of Parliament. And a lot of policemen.'

'Correct. You are very observant, Mr Rue. And what do these two institutions symbolise? Power. The power of the state. My question to you is this. Who runs this powerful state? Not just this one, the United Kingdom, but all the others across the world? Who are the puppet-masters pulling the strings? You don't know? I'll tell you.' He lowered his window and thrust his index finger into the London air. 'They are.' He was pointing to a herd of teenagers milling around outside the gates of parliament, all intent on photographing each other or taking selfies against the backdrop of Big Ben.

'You mean the tourists?' asked Rue, somewhat puzzled at this revelation.

Ahmed laughed. 'No, not these kids. Look over there, just behind them.' He indicated a group of men wearing black suits and hats. They were all facing the same direction and swaying back and forth in a rhythmical manner.

'Ah, you mean the *Chasidim*? At least that's what we call them in Belgium. They're ultra-Orthodox Jews. A bit strange but harmless. They keep themselves to themselves.'

'Mr Rue, you have so much to learn.' Ahmed was shaking his head in exaggerated sadness. 'Whatever you call them, whatever sect they belong to, it makes no difference. They're all involved. Religious, secular, half-Jews, full Jews. They work as a team, a single unit, a well-oiled machine.'

Here we go again. 'I'm sorry, Mr Ahmed, you've lost me there.'

'Oh, for heaven's sake man, wake up and smell the coffee!' Ahmed leaned forward to within inches of Rue's face.

'You think I'm prejudiced, don't you? Let me put you right. I have nothing against Jews. I don't have much time for them, I admit it, but they can do what the hell they like for all I care. However, we can't ignore the fact that they have sworn allegiance to a higher, more dangerous power. And when they do that, they cease being mere Jews and become something else altogether. They become a danger. Do you understand me, Mr Rue?'

'I think I get your meaning, sir.' *I'm beginning to wish I didn't.*

'Israel! The evil Zionist gangster state. That is our enemy.' Ahmed's voice was louder now as he gesticulated wildly as if clearing a path into the depths of his favourite conspiratorial mind-zone. 'Everyone knows that Israel is the number one warmonger in the world. And the Zionists control these people, these *Chasidim* as you call them. You think of them as harmless, do you? My dear chap, you have been misled. They are among the most dangerous foot soldiers of the Zionists. In fact, all Jews everywhere are members of the Zionist army, including the ones who pretend to be just like you and me. As for the Israelis, they are the worst of the worst, the Nazi storm troopers of the global Zionist project. Their so-called state is the head of the octopus that issues a stream of orders, day and night, to its tentacles all around the world. There's even a name for the beast—ZOG. The Zionist Occupation Government. ZOG controls all of us. You didn't know that either, did you?'

'I don't know what to say, Mr Ahmed. I must say it all sounds quite far-fetched to me.' He just wanted to escape from this madman. The driver had switched off the engine, so Rue reached for the door handle and pulled. The door was locked. *Dear God, I'm trapped.*

'Naturally it sounds far-fetched, that's the point.' Ahmed's face was flushed with zealotry. 'It's so unbelievable that people don't believe it. Let me tell you something amazing. I'm about to cast a vote in the House of Commons in the so-called mother of parliaments. Yet it is a completely pointless gesture. The UK parliament is a powerless institution. Whether the vote is about social benefits or a new airport or international aid, it's all irrelevant. Because if the Zionists don't like it, they'll make sure it never happens. Simple as that.'

Rue held his tongue. *I need to get out of this car. Now.*

'Much as I would like to stay and chat, I must go now, Mr Rue, and cast my worthless vote. It has been most interesting talking to you. We will continue your education some other time. I'm sure we will meet again soon.' The doors clicked and Ahmed opened the door on his side. Rue followed suit and almost tumbled out of the limousine into the Westminster street.

'One last thing, Mr Rue. In case you think I'm exaggerating, I assure you that I am not. I can back up everything I have revealed to you today with solid proof.'

'Whatever you say, Mr Ahmed. I must be on my way. I have a job to do and I'll do what I have to do. I'm not really into politics. I'll leave all that to you, if you don't mind.'

Ahmed beamed benignly. 'You are so very naïve, old chap. I don't blame you. Why should you know or care about any of this? These people are cunning, they have hidden the truth from ordinary people like you and me for hundreds of years. The Zionist project is a long-term plan to take control of the entire planet and destroy all non-Jews—the *goyim* as they call us. They will succeed unless we stop them, mark my words. That is why we must take decisive action for our own self-defence. And I know that you, Mr Rue, will help us.'

The two men shook hands and parted. Rue fought to conceal his sense of relief. But Ahmed wasn't quite finished. After walking a few metres towards the entrance to the House, he turned on his heels and called out. 'One last thing, Mr Rue. I must stress that what you are doing for us is not just a job. It's a vocation. A sacred duty. Always remember those words and you will receive your reward in heaven just as surely as here on earth. Farewell, my friend, good luck and be careful.'

'I'll do my best. Thank you, sir.'

'Don't thank me, thank Him.' Ahmed was pointing at the sky. 'We are facing the most dangerous and heartless foe the world has ever seen. Goodbye for now, Mr Rue. And remember, we will be victorious over these treacherous people. Allah is on our side.'

[26]

'THE POINT IS, WE CAN'T STAY HERE, *AHUVATI*.' TAMIR WAS almost whispering as if he feared being overheard. 'The *Destiny* thugs have located us. This safe house is no longer safe. We have to get out of here right now. Take Clara to your sister's and I'll stay here to try to smoke them out. When it's safe for you to return, I'll tell you.'

Sofia was alarmed but she was also angry. Her eyes blazed with indignation. 'I don't know what to say, Tamir. We're trapped like rats in a sack. All right, I'll drop Clara at Luisa's but I'm coming back here for you. That's not up for negotiation, by the way. I'm not running away again. We had a deal. You promised me I'd be on the inside on this one and you'd better keep your word. Don't argue with me, I've made up my mind.'

'This is madness,' muttered Tamir under his breath. But he knew when he was defeated. 'All right. Change of plan. Let's take Clara. I'm coming with you.' As he spoke, he checked his revolver. Sofia made no effort to hide her distaste.

'Jesus, keep that vile thing well hidden from your daughter. I won't have her growing up believing that it's normal to carry a gun. I hope you understand that, at least.'

'Of course I do. But I hope you understand something else too. If I don't carry it, she might not grow up at all.'

'Do you two want to tell me what the hell is going on?' Luisa, Sofia's sister, asked the question with no expectation of receiving an answer. She was holding Clara's hand. 'Go and play in the garden, darling. I'll be out in a minute.'

'Sorry, Luisa. You're such a brick. I don't know what we'd do without you.'

'Maybe you'd live a normal family life for a change,' said Luisa. 'Don't knock it. Children need to have their parents around. And vice versa. You know that.'

Sofia pecked her sister on the cheek, took a final look at her daughter playing on the lawn and headed for the door with her mute husband, his eyes fixed on the floor, following behind her.

On the drive back to the no-longer-safe-house, Sofia sat in the passenger seat, tight-lipped. Tamir glanced anxiously at her every couple of minutes, knowing better than to speak. It was his wife who eventually broke the ice.

'Now that we're colleagues or comrades or whatever you Mossadniks call each other, what do you want me to do, Agent Weiss?'

'What do you mean, *ahuvati*? You're not actually a Mossadnik and I'm certainly not your commanding officer.'

'I should think not. But we are partners in this project, aren't we? More or less?'

Tamir gestured in a way that indicated grudging agreement.

'In which case, use me. Give me something—tangible. I want to contribute.'

'You're already contributing in all kinds of ways. Spotting that article about the Azad Ahmed MP. That was great work. I would never have come across it by chance. Even our intelligence people missed it. They were quite embarrassed about that, I can tell you.'

'Do we know what exactly he's been up to, our cuddly Mr Ahmed?'

'Yes, and it's all bad. His role is twofold. First, he's trying to establish a network of Islamist groups across the UK who will respond to the call for *jihad* at a moment's notice. He's already close to getting that up and running. His second task is more challenging, but the rewards, from his point of view, will be greater. He aims to rally his British hard-left troops to the bigger European cause. That's a tough call. They and *Destiny* are far from natural allies. He's meeting significant resistance.'

Sofia laughed. 'Oh, I've no doubt the bastard will succeed. Extremists may set out in opposite directions but sooner or later they meet in the middle. Communists, fascists and Islamists—what a repulsive combination.'

'One hundred per cent correct, *ahuvati*. But it will take them time. Ahmed is an Islamist to the core, an advocate of violent jihad. But he's also a rising star in the Labour Party, a darling of the hard left, especially their radical fringe. And that's all they are at the moment, a fringe. But they're growing more influential by the day. The leadership of the party is dead against them, but I have no doubt that they'll end up dominating the party sooner or later. That spells big trouble for us. It means that Mr Ahmed will soon be in a position to deliver a large chunk of the British left straight into the arms of his mini-*Fuhrer*, Herr Christoph Berg.'

'It's happened before,' said Sofia. 'Hitler and Stalin pioneered that trick not so long ago. We're lucky their love affair didn't last long. Look where those two ended up—in the dustbin of history. We can take comfort from that, can't we?'

'Maybe, *ahuvati*, but we mustn't be complacent. The fact is that these two dictators dragged millions of innocent people down into the dirt with them. The same thing will happen again. Unless we stop them.'

'How do you propose to do that?'

They were approaching Burrard Road. Tamir slowed down.

'We could start by focusing on Mr Ahmed MP. Somehow, we have to get up close and personal with him. But it won't be easy. He's probably surrounded by tight security round the clock.'

'What's your plan?'

Tamir laughed. 'You ask such great questions, *ahuvati*. But I don't have answers for you. Not yet. And that bothers me. You're right, we need a plan and we don't have one.'

'You mean you don't.'

'No, I don't have a plan. Neither does Keren.'

'I do,' said Sofia.

For a moment, Tamir thought he had misheard his wife. He glanced at her for long enough to notice two things. She was staring at the road ahead, and the faintest trace of a smile was playing on her lips.

[27]

'GENERAL VOLKOV, PLEASE COME IN.' MOSHE LUNENFELD ROSE from his desk and shook his guest's hand with a formality that was devoid of warmth. 'What can I do for you, Minister?'

Volkov removed his jacket and hung it over the back of a chair. A bad sign thought Lunenfeld. The defence minister looked intent on a lengthy consultation—just what his host was hoping to avoid. The two men scarcely knew each other and neither had shown any previous interest in changing that. In any event, a direct approach by a government minister to the head of the Mossad was almost unheard of, a breach of the unwritten protocol that required all such contacts to be mediated via the prime minister's office. In Lunenfeld's view, the quicker this encounter was over, the less embarrassing it would be for all concerned.

'I must thank you for agreeing to see me at such short notice,' said Volkov. 'I realise that my request for this meeting was rather unorthodox. I promise I won't take up too much of your time.'

Lunenfeld smiled. How often had he heard that assurance as a prelude to an interminable discussion? 'I am all ears, General. Please sit down.'

Volkov sat and folded his substantial arms solemnly. 'I don't know how to put this. I come to you with a heavy heart. I am deeply troubled. This is not what I expected when I agreed to accept the defence portfolio.'

'I'm sorry to hear that, General. Please continue.'

'You may know that there are, how shall I put it, certain tensions within the cabinet. That's normal, but matters are now getting out of control.'

'I see.' Lunenfeld glanced at his watch. The last thing he wanted was to get bogged down in the minutiae of personal squabbles between Israeli politicians. They all bickered and fell out with each other on a regular basis, often about the most trivial issues.

Volkov must have sensed he was losing his host's attention. He said, 'I know what you're thinking—what has this got to do with the Mossad? I have a one-word answer for you. Everything. It concerns a major breach of national security. At the highest level.'

Now Lunenfeld was interested. 'Ah, now that could certainly be a matter of concern for the Mossad. I assume you have raised the subject with the prime minister?'

'Naturally. And I am sorry to say that his response disappointed me. It was extremely unsatisfactory. In fact, it was pathetic. And worrying. That is the reason I am here.'

'Please tell me what happened. With as much detail as you can recall.' Lunenfeld withdrew a small notepad and pen from his desk drawer.

Over the ensuing ten minutes, Volkov recounted the hastily arranged security cabinet meeting, at which both men had been present, and the PM's surprise announcement of the abrupt cancellation—without even minimal discussion—of *Operation Aleph Bet*. The ostensible rationale for this decision was that important defence contracts would be jeopardised were an assassination of an Austrian citizen attempted. None of this was new to Lunenfeld. Except for one tiny but crucial detail.

'Mr Lunenfeld, you will recall that the PM informed the security cabinet that he was acting, at least in part, on the advice of his colleague, the minister of defence?'

'Indeed, I do. I confess I was a little surprised to hear that.'

'I am sure you were. So was I. I have to inform you, Mr Lunenfeld, that I gave no such advice. The PM invented that story to give himself cover for the cancellation of the operation. It was entirely his decision and no-one else's.'

'Interesting. Why didn't you say something at the meeting?' asked Lunenfeld, continuing to write without looking up.

'Actually I tried, as you may also recall. He wouldn't let me say a word and then the meeting was over. I was shocked. Frankly, I still am. After that episode, I requested an urgent meeting with the PM. He refused. Can you believe it? I thought of resigning but that may have been his intention. He probably calculated that if I challenged him on his blatant lie, he would deny it and fire me. And who would be believe me? It would be his word against mine. I'm not going to be lured into that trap.'

'Have you discussed this matter with anyone else?'

Volkov shook his head. 'You are the only one. Our PM is a liar, an untrustworthy scoundrel. And yet I am serving under him. As are you. I don't know what we can do but we can't just sit on our hands, can we? Any suggestions?'

Lunenfeld whipped off his spectacles and rubbed his eyes. Then he gazed at the ceiling as though searching for divine guidance. Volkov watched this performance with a detached curiosity. He knew the Mossad director well enough to remain mute while Lunenfeld's cerebral cortex ramped up to top gear. Around a minute later—though it felt far longer to Volkov—Lunenfeld delivered his answer.

'You were right to come to see me, General, and I am glad that you did. And as you've sought my opinion, here it is. Your instinct was right. Here is my opinion. Stay in your post. I need you there. So does the country. Meanwhile, do nothing and say nothing. For now. Just keep in touch. I will need to investigate this serious issue further. There will be further developments, I assure you.'

'That's it?' Volkov's eyes widened.

'Yes, that's it. For now. Leave it with me.' Lunenfeld smiled and stood, prompting his visitor to follow suit though with some reluctance. The two men walked to the door. Lunenfeld turned and limply shook Volkov's hand. His expression was sober. 'Oh, there is just one last thing, General,' said Lunenfeld. 'I need hardly say that this meeting must remain confidential. Strictly between ourselves. In fact, as far as the outside world is concerned, it never happened.'

[28]

'THAT WHICH UNITES US IS FAR MORE IMPORTANT THAN THAT which divides us, *n'est ce pas*, my dear Professor Cambon?'

Christoph Berg was in full flow. The setting was inauspicious —the upstairs function room of a musty old London pub that had seen better days. It did the job though, providing complete privacy for the planners of a new Europe to dream their dreams. Seated around a wooden table were the three key figures in *Destiny*—Pierre Cambon, Azad Ahmed and Berg himself. In a corner near the door sat Axel Rue, who kept a watchful eye on the proceedings while remaining in electronic contact with a couple of heavies in the bustling street outside.

'All I am saying, Herr Berg,' replied Cambon in his heavily accented English, 'is that we should be careful not to get carried away with inflammatory rhetoric. We are sophisticated people, not a bunch of rabble-rousers. We can fulfil our objectives, I believe, without resorting to crude violence.'

'Who said anything about crude violence?' exclaimed Berg, as if hurt by the suggestion. 'First, we will only need to use force if they—our public enemy number one—resist. That's unlikely to happen. These people are cowards as we all know. Second, our response will be fully proportionate to the threat, no more and no less. That means we will stay well within the bounds of the law.'

Cambon persisted. 'I am certain they will resist. Wouldn't you if you were stripped of your rights, fired from your job and told you had no future in your country or anywhere in Europe? And you know something? They're not all bad. I have Jewish friends myself. And, for your information, they're not even all Zionists either.'

Berg blanched, clenching his fists. 'Professor Cambon, you know very well that ninety per cent of them, at least, are self-confessed Zionists. The rest are complicit in Zionist crimes because they refuse to speak out against their murdering brothers and sisters. Even the children are not innocent as they are being trained, as we speak, for future service in the Zionist occupation forces. But let's stop nit-picking, please. They're all evil vermin. Every last one of them. Period. And in case your socialist conscience bothers you, let me remind you what Karl Marx said about these people whose welfare you seem so concerned about. I always carry this aide-memoire with me. These are the words of your great hero.'

He pulled a sheet of paper out of his inside pocket, cleared his throat and started reading aloud, in a mock-heroic theatrical style, *'What is the worldly religion of the Jew? Huckstering. What is his worldly God? Money. Money is the jealous god of Israel, in face of which no other god may exist.'* Berg flashed a cheesy smile at his colleagues, refolded his script and slipped it back into his jacket. 'Gentlemen, I need hardly remind you that Marx was a Jew. That means he had inside knowledge, so he knew what he was talking about. I rest my case.'

Cambon shrugged but said nothing, just as Berg knew he would.

'That's all very interesting,' said Ahmed, 'and no doubt

perfectly valid. But I have a question for you, Herr Berg. How are we going to deal with these people, in practice? Are we talking concentration camps and ghettoes?'

'*Mon Dieu*,' muttered Cambon in exasperation, closing his eyes.

'Don't be ridiculous, Azad,' snapped Berg. 'What are we, old-style Nazis? Not that they were so bad, they just moved too hard and too fast. No, we will be far more refined. Have you forgotten the plan that we all signed up to? Let me remind you. It comprises three stages. First, the Jews will be given ample notice of our intentions to enable them to make the necessary arrangements in an orderly fashion.'

'What arrangements?' asked Cambon.

'Oh, come now, Professor, don't be such a contrarian. You know perfectly well the answer to your question so why do you ask it? To give up their old lives and start new ones somewhere else. Anywhere else so long as it's not on the continent of Europe.'

'One moment, please,' interjected Ahmed. 'Many will opt to go to the Middle East. I am referring to a specific country the Jews call'—he sketched quote marks in the air—"Israel."' Do we want to be recruiting sergeants for the Zionist entity? Do we want to fill the ranks of the Zionist occupation army with a wave of new immigrants who would immediately be sent out to kill Palestinian children? That wouldn't play well in the Muslim community, I must tell you.'

'If they will be stupid enough to go to that gay-infested hellhole they call Tel Aviv, let them go!' shouted Berg, his eyes widening. 'The more the better. Don't you understand? They'd be playing straight into our hands. The Iranian ayatollahs are preparing a surprise for them there, I promise you. Poof! End of story.'

Ahmed looked unconvinced. '*Inshallah*. Let's hope you're

right. But I am unhappy about it. We'll return to this topic later. I have another question. What happens if they refuse to leave Europe?

'Then we activate stage two: our legislative programme. That means they are welcome to stay in Europe but only as temporary residents, with minimal rights—by which I mean no jobs, no benefits, no healthcare, no education, no votes. But no one will starve. We're not monsters. They will be permitted to use any financial resources they may hold. And they hold plenty, believe me. Eventually, when they've spent all their ill-gotten gains, they will change their minds and flee.'

'And if they don't change their minds,' asked Cambon, 'what then, Berg? You think we can just move on without any opposition to stage three?'

'Stage three is a contingency measure only. It is most unlikely we will need to use it. No doubt it will change their minds. They know what's good for them. I expect there will be a few stubborn idiots who will try to hold out. But we will deal with them using the full force of the law.'

'What law?' asked Ahmed.

'The Undesirable Aliens Act. It already exists in most countries as a matter of fact. You should know that, Azad. The UK government passed one in 1979. It just needs, how do you say in English, tweaked—and then extended across the EU. We have assurances from the Commission that it can be done very quickly, as an administrative directive from Brussels. That will permit us to deport the unwilling ones by force, if necessary.'

'Deport them where?' Cambon's voice had risen to falsetto pitch. 'To the North Pole? To the middle of the Atlantic Ocean? Greenland perhaps?'

Berg closed his eyes briefly, then nodded as if in solemn acknowledgement of the Frenchman's suggestion. 'What a brilliant idea, Professor. Yes, indeed. Greenland sounds like a perfect resting place for them. An inspired proposal, thank you. I accept! Let's do it. Gentlemen, this meeting is at an end. It has been most productive. But we've talked enough. Now let's get a move on. We've wasted far too much time already.'

[29]

No matter how hard she tried, Sofia couldn't get used to the perpetual presence of a handful of security guards (albeit in plain clothes) at both the front and back of her temporary home, the no-longer-safe house. Despite their well-intentioned efforts to remain as unobtrusive as possible, these sturdy young men were always in evidence, a constant reminder of the abnormality of her new existence and that of her family. Their necessity was beyond question, but that wasn't the issue for Sofia. More pressing was the unanswerable question that had begun to dominate her every waking moment. *When will this end?*

Tamir, on the other hand, turned that question on its head—how quickly can we destroy *Destiny*? If that objective could be achieved in a day or two, it would have been done. The disruption to the Weiss's family routine was a price they had to pay to ensure the success of the mission. *Destroy the beast and we can all live happily ever after.* Sofia didn't believe that particular fairytale but she bought Tamir's basic premise that they couldn't get their lives back on track until *Destiny* had been decapitated. That was reason enough for her to do all she could to help hasten that outcome.

She flipped open her laptop for the third time that morning. A week earlier, her online research had yielded precious fruit when she had stumbled across Berg's article about Azad Ahmed MP. She was convinced that this man held the key to the future of *Destiny* and the Mossad would have to snatch it from him. On the drive back from Luisa's she had conceived the outline of a plan to achieve that outcome. It was so outrageous that she had decided not to share it with Tamir, fearing he would ridicule the idea. She needed more time to flesh out the details, but time was not in plentiful supply.

By nature, Sofia was intolerant of fatalism and point-blank refused to yield to it. She had glimpsed a way forward, a possible path that would lead them all out of their predicament and their enforced quarantine. But it remained an elusive exit, still shrouded in a fuzzy overgrowth of uncertainty and danger. She'd have to clear all that distracting foliage away—*gardening of the mind* her dear father had called the process of mental hygiene—before she could risk presenting her proposal to Tamir. Pacing around the small living room, she picked up the bag containing the wigs that Keren had instructed them to wear whenever they left the house. Staring at its contents, she bit her lower lip hard as though the self-inflicted pain would, through some mysterious cerebral alchemy, generate a solution.

It seemed to work. The metallic taste of blood on her tongue focused her mind to the point where the answer struck her with the force of a sledgehammer. She slammed shut the lid of her laptop and took several deep breaths. In that instant, she made a decision: Spending endless hours in front of her computer screen was an inefficient use of her time. She would have to step out of cyberspace and re-enter the real world—or at least her deliberately contrived version of it—and that first step would lead to another that would take her straight to the heart of the lion's den within an hour or two.

She couldn't wait to tell her husband. But she'd have to be careful to choose the right moment for her pitch. Even then, he was liable to veto it outright; she could predict his reaction almost word for word: *No way, ahuvati, it's far too dangerous. That guy will eat you alive. I won't let you do it.*

Among her many gifts, Sofia was endowed with one that had served her well over the years: an abundance of patience. Timing was the key. She honed her plan over the next forty-eight hours, rehearsing her responses to the list of killer objections that she knew Tamir would raise. Her opportunity came one evening when they were both lounging on the sofa at home after dinner.

Tamir was in an unusually relaxed mood because he had received orders from Keren to do nothing but wait while a situation assessment was underway in Tel Aviv. He had opened a bottle of their favourite tipple, Pinot Grigio, and they were well on the way to emptying it. Sofia had just spoken to both her sister and her daughter on the phone; she had been reassured about the welfare of both. The atmosphere was as positive as it was ever likely to be, so the moment seemed propitious.

'Tamir, I've been thinking a lot about our friend Ahmed.'

'You poor thing. That's not good for your health.'

'Listen, I have an idea. About how we might get to him. From where we're sitting, he holds the key to unlocking the door to the *Destiny* fortress, right? I think we should use him. And that's where I come in.'

'Oh? Tell me what you mean, *motek*.'

'The thought occurred to me that I could approach him directly.'

'What? Are you out of your mind? Tell me you're joking, *ahuvati*.'

'No, not at all. Just listen for change. I could call his secretary and make an appointment. Wait, don't be so dismissive—I haven't finished. I realise that might not work, I'm not that stupid.

He probably wouldn't give me five minutes of his time without a powerful incentive. I'm just not important enough to him. No woman is. But that's the whole point. We can use that. It's his weak spot. He will underestimate me.'

'Everyone underestimates you, Sofia. I certainly did before I got to know you better. So go on, tell me. I'm listening to every word. Your train of thought is fascinating even when it's a little bit crazy.' Tamir was grinning—a good sign she thought.

'We know he is a vain man, like most politicians. And he's ambitious. That means he's hungry for publicity, lots of it. He gives interviews every other day.'

'What are you driving at? Don't tell me you want to interview him?'

'Clever man—how did you guess?' She took Tamir's hand stroked the back of it. 'I don't see why not. I'm a journalist and that's all he'll care about.'

'A journalist who happens to be married to a Mossad agent?'

'He's unlikely to know that. I doubt if he undertakes a detailed security check on every single hack he speaks to.'

'Don't bank on it. They're already on our trail, remember? That's why we're here.'

'All right, so let's assume his *Destiny* pals have tipped him off about me, that will just enhance the appeal for him. He takes risks in that department, as we saw with the Berg article. Mossad or no Mossad, a woman is a woman and so can be discounted as far as he's concerned. That's intrinsic to his world view.'

Tamir looked sceptical. 'Tell me something. What would you do if you did succeed in getting access to him? Hope that you can persuade him to say something incriminating about *Destiny*? On the record, or even off it? He won't fall for that. He'll just throw you out.'

'That's a risk, I agree. But I think I can minimise it by doing something much more—how shall I put it—daring.'

'Now you've lost me, *ahuvati*.'

Sofia knocked back the remainder of her wine. 'OK, listen, darling. Picture the scene. He's checking himself in the mirror, maybe slapping on some sexy *eau de toilette* that he keeps in his desk drawer for special occasions. He's about to show off his brilliant intellect and unrivalled erudition to the world, yet again, through the medium of yet another sycophantic journo.'

'And into his office sweeps the stunning Ms Lopez or whatever name you choose to call yourself. I hear he's quite a lady's man. He'll fall off his chair when he sees you.'

Sofia smiled wickedly. 'Now you're getting the idea.'

'I am, but I'm not quite there yet. You mean you get the interview, shake hands and leave?'

'Not quite. You can be so naïve at times, Mr Weiss.'

Tamir leaned back and gulped down another mouthful of Pinot. 'Hold on. Please don't tell me you're intending to seduce him?'

'Don't panic. I won't need to. Think about it. Here's this young, know-nothing journalist, an unimportant white Englishwoman, a girl practically. To a man like that, I'm just defenceless prey waiting to be snatched up and devoured. Eaten alive. How could he resist?'

'That's just what bothers me, *ahuvati*. He's liable to make a pass at you. Then what?'

'Then we'll have won, Tamir. Don't worry, you silly man, there's no need to be jealous. Nothing will happen, I'll make sure of that. But I'll give him strong hints that it might. The purpose of the interview will be to trigger his imagination and exploit it for our benefit. My role will be to dangle the bait in front of his nose. When he jumps at it, as I predict he will, we can reel him in at any time and place of our choosing. He'll be my prey, darling, not the other way round.'

Tamir opened his mouth to protest. His wife stopped him in his tracks.

'Enough! There's something I need to do, Agent Weiss. Right now.'

Sofia leaned across to her anxious husband and delivered a long, sensuous kiss to his grateful lips.

[30]

WE ARE SORRY, THE PRIME MINISTER IS UNAVAILABLE TODAY. We are unable to provide any further details. Please leave a message and we will get back to you as soon as possible.

The same pre-recorded message was being relayed, over and over, by all the staff in the prime minister's office, the Knesset, the civil service and the military. Some of the enquiries were coming from the PM's own family. Most worrying for senior government officials was that the phalanx of security guards who were, of necessity, always wrapped around the most powerful man in the country, were themselves baffled. The PM's spokesperson's unit, usually adept at spinning a convincing yarn based on the established *line to take*, had fallen silent. Frantic efforts to locate their boss had drawn a complete blank. Even the premier's closest advisors appeared bemused by the sudden and unexplained disappearance of the man who was supposed to be running the country.

For the previous nine to twelve hours—nobody was certain the precise length of time—the Israeli prime minister had vanished from the face of the earth. By default, the country's leadership had been transferred into the reluctant hands of

Avraham Sassoon, the deputy prime minister, who also happened to be the minister of the interior and therefore responsible for homeland security.

The rumours took a few hours to gain traction, partly thanks to the start of Shabbat, the Jewish day of rest and (for the devout) spirituality and prayer. From around midday on Friday, almost all government departments, public services and the media were reduced to a skeleton staff whose triaging skills were tested to the limit in their attempts to ensure that nothing of importance happened until the end of the weekend on Saturday night. Three sectors were exempt from this weekly national shutdown: all emergency services (including first responders), the military, and the top layer of government. In practice, the widely held assumption was that healthcare workers, soldiers and ministers of state were either at work or accessible by telephone. It was a pragmatic system that had served the country well. Until the current prime minister went AWOL.

Matters came to a head around midday on Saturday. Almost as one, the burgeoning media pack, swirling around the exterior of the PM's residence in Jerusalem, became seized of a collective conviction that was well-founded—that neither deputy PM Sassoon nor anyone else in government had the faintest idea where their chief was or what he was up to. By early Saturday afternoon, the incident had become public knowledge. Across all the broadcast media, children's cartoons and sports commentaries were being interrupted by frequent news flashes announcing, with appropriate solemnity, that the whereabouts of the PM had become 'a matter of intense concern.' Among the wilder rumours flying around were that he had been taken ill, had suffered a nervous breakdown, had been kidnapped or had been assassinated. These sprouted wings on the major Israeli social media platforms. It was only a matter of time before such sensational speculation would be internationalised. Someone would have to act fast to calm the nation's nerves.

That task fell to the hapless Sassoon. A silvery-haired, mild-mannered and somewhat colourless man who hailed from an immigrant Iraqi Jewish family, he generally attracted little interest among the Israeli public. All that had changed overnight. He now found himself thrust into the epicentre of an unprecedented storm. A party loyalist who had been in government most of his adult life, he was viewed by his colleagues as a competent if uninspiring politician who could always be relied upon to say and do nothing out of the ordinary. Sassoon was, however, blessed with an unusual talent—he could command grudging respect right across the political spectrum. He had established for himself a precious reputation for integrity in the chaotic world of politics. In short, he was widely regarded as a safe pair of hands. In times of crisis, his reassuring presence was often in demand to douse the flames of incipient mass hysteria.

Sassoon had never relished being thrust into the limelight, but he recognised its political value. It gave him the opportunity to raise his profile and communicate directly with the public on whose steadfast support his future career depended. Today was different. He knew he wouldn't panic, but he felt well out of his comfort zone. Never in the history of Israel had a sitting prime minister disappeared without trace. There had been several instances of senior Israeli politicians undertaking secret meetings with foreign dignitaries under cover of darkness, often to avoid embarrassment to Arab leaders who couldn't risk being caught red-handed negotiating with the hated 'Zionist entity.' In such cases, a handful of key officials understood the nature of the mission and issued periodic bland statements to the press while maintaining a tight grip on the truth. This was not one of them for an astonishing reason: no one knew what the truth was.

By late afternoon, Sassoon was exhausted. He'd had more

than enough. All of his senior government colleagues were angry and alarmed. They demanded answers and he could offer none. The opposition was already initiating the procedure for the immediate recall of the Knesset. The ambassadors of eleven countries, among them the United States, Israel's closest ally, had submitted formal requests for urgent clarification. Both the domestic and foreign media were in meltdown, clamouring for a public statement. Breaking-news updates, while largely devoid of content, were verging on the bizarre. In the absence of hard facts, journalists were filling the gaps with fantastic tales of scandal, revolution and death. Conspiracy theorists were having a field day.

Sassoon didn't baulk from the harsh reality. The buck stopped with him. He'd have to act. Not tomorrow, not in an hour, but now. Mopping beads of perspiration from his brow, he picked up his phone and dialled the five-digit secret number that was known only to a select group of senior ministers and officials. He was calling the one man whom he trusted to extricate him—and the government—from the ballooning crisis.

'Lunenfeld, I'm sure you know why I'm contacting you. We're losing control. It's a complete fiasco, a *fashla*. I need your help. We all do.'

The Mossad chief was his usual unruffled self. 'I was expecting to hear from you, Minister. I will help you to the best of my ability. That's what I'm here for. Stay where you are, I'm coming over now.'

[31]

SITTING IN HIS MODEST BEDSIT IN ISLINGTON, AXEL RUE SIPPED his lukewarm coffee without pleasure. The bracken-coloured English brew was almost undrinkable. How many more days must he fester in this soul-destroying dump? He had held out for a luxury or even four-star hotel, but Berg had vetoed that idea outright. So here he was, waiting for action, confined to his makeshift barracks and hating every second of it. Even the weather was dire, at least as damp and gloomy as Brussels. *Patience, Axel*, he chided himself, *you can't rush this—everything passes eventually. Meanwhile think of the money...*

The trouble was that his current predicament was to some extent of his own making. He'd fluffed his opening lines in the drama he was supposed to direct. There could be no repeat performance of that embarrassing farce. Nor would there be. One of Rue's secrets of success was his ability to learn fast from mistakes. In his business, that was a mandatory skill. Second chances were rare, third chances unheard of. Rue knew that he was on probation. One more slip like the Hampstead fiasco would mean the immediate termination of his contract.

This time would be different for two reasons. First, he had

handpicked an accomplice in whom he had complete confidence. Zoltan, a Hungarian odd-job man always on the lookout for an opportunity to earn an extra crust or two, was the perfect sidekick. Rue had worked with him on three previous UK assignments and Zoltan had always delivered without fuss or complaint. Built like a wrestler, he perhaps wasn't the brightest lightbulb in the room, but he was strong, reliable and ruthless—the diametric opposite of Andre, the stupid kid on the bike who had just been discharged from the facial surgery unit of the Royal Free Hospital having suffered an encounter with the rock-hard fist of Mossad Agent Weiss. Second, Rue would take his time and keep his distance from his quarry until he was sure of completing the task to his employer's satisfaction.

The Israelis believed, for now, that they were well protected and with reason: penetrating their multi-layered security cordon posed a formidable challenge. Rue was confident he could overcome it given sufficient time. While Berg was pressing for instant action, Rue was answerable to Azad Ahmed now. The MP, preoccupied as he was with his own multiple problems, was content to cut the Belgian some slack. Zoltan would keep the so-called safe house under surveillance for a few days and work out how to neutralise the two external guards—one each at front and rear—while Rue formulated a plan to get access to the Weisses.

To Rue's surprise, Ahmed had insisted on a minimum of violence. The targets were to be kept alive and well until they could be delivered into the hands of the psychopathic Christoph Berg and his team of 'expert interrogators.' Rue didn't rate the chances of the couple surviving longer than twenty-four hours in the hands of these sadists, but by then they would no longer be his responsibility.

Rue had always prided himself in being a pragmatist as well as a man of action; he had no time for endless agonising over the pros and cons of multiple theoretical options. But this nut was proving harder to crack than most. As if acting out the metaphor, he clenched and unclenched his right fist in frustration. If all problems in the world of security were soluble, and Rue felt in the depths of his gut that they were, he was irritated that couldn't see how to solve this one.

As always when facing such conundrums, Rue resorted to first principles. *Don't overcomplicate*, was his motto. The assignment was straightforward enough. Bottom line: Weiss—with or without his wife—would have to be abducted from (or near) the safe house. End of story. It would need to be done without a shot being fired or any kind of untoward disturbance that might excite the attention of curious neighbours lurking behind twitching net curtains. That meant somehow getting close enough to the front door to grab the targets, bundle them into a van and dissolve the whole shebang into the ether, out of sight of the Mossad guards, in a matter of seconds. It sounded easy enough, but Rue had enough experience to recognise the potential pitfalls. He needed a flash of inspiration, a key to the puzzle, a big idea.

He was grappling with that thought when he was startled by a loud noise—the clatter of the letterbox in the hallway downstairs. The postal service had just delivered a parcel, a heavy one by the sound of it. Rue wandered over to the window and looked down. A uniformed postman was locking up the rear doors of his parked red minivan. He was a youngish man, sporting a pair of tropical shorts despite the showery weather. Rue was struck by his jaunty air, reinforced by his incessant tuneless whistling. Perhaps he was looking forward to the imminent end of his shift. Or maybe he was just rejoicing, along with his fellow-Londoners, in the fact that it had stopped raining.

Lucky chap, thought Rue as he gulped down the remains of the brown liquid. *There's a man at ease with the world* a*nd he probably doesn't even realise what a privilege that is.* A glint of sunlight emerged from behind a dark cloud and illuminated the mundane street scene below like a giant stage set. The little postal vehicle spluttered to life, scuttled down the street and was out of sight in seconds.

Since his early childhood, Rue had exhibited a talent for lateral thinking, making connections between sets of phenomena that look, at first sight, quite unrelated. It was an ability of which he himself was scarcely aware, except on those occasions where his brain cells sparked to life and led him to that eureka moment when he cracked a conundrum that had proved resistant to conventional problem-solving. The process was as mysterious to him as it was productive, but when the cellular chemistry slid into action and delivered that flash of insight, the experience was revelatory and exhilarating.

A van, the postman, a parcel delivery, a routine disturbance, a mundane event, nothing to see here in this everyday occurrence.

The molecules collided, the synapses crackled and there it was —the flash.

For the first time in weeks, Axel Rue smiled.

[32]

'What do you think?' Sofia swept into the living room and curtsied with a coy smile as though greeting royalty.

Tamir stared at his wife in disbelief. He had never seen such an extraordinary apparition. Before him stood a vision of Hollywood glamour that screamed a single name. Marilyn Monroe. 'My God, *ahuvati*, I wouldn't have recognised you! How did you do that?'

'It's not that difficult, actually. Blonde wig, red lipstick, a body-hugging little red dress and a pair of heels is all it takes. I hope you approve of your new colleague, the amazing Diana Candy, journalist extraordinaire.'

'You look sensational. Not sure that the brown eyes match the blondie look, though I doubt that he'll notice. Isn't that neckline a bit—low? Your boobs are almost shaking hands with me.'

'That's the whole point,' she laughed. 'Don't be so prudish, Tamir. A push-up bra is a waste of time unless I'm *décolleté*. I have to exploit my assets to the fullest.'

'You're doing that all right. Ahmed will be foaming at the mouth by the time you've finished with him. Are you sure you don't want a wire?'

'No need,' smiled Sofia coquettishly. 'You'll be able to hear the whole interview when I get home.' She pulled her phone out of her handbag. 'I'll be recording every word from the start. He's already agreed to that. It won't faze him—it's standard journalistic practice these days. Even if he changes his mind, I'll pretend to switch it off and he'll be none the wiser.' She picked up her lightweight overcoat and slipped it over her shoulders.

'I'm still not sure about this. Who knows what he'll do? You'll be at his mercy, Sofia. There must be another way to get to him without exposing you to such high risk.'

'Stop worrying, Mr Weiss. You didn't marry a shrinking violet, or hadn't you noticed? Listen, I know exactly what I'm doing and I can look after myself. Let me remind you that I'm an honorary Mossadnik. Have a little faith in your fellow spooks.'

Tamir frowned. He had run out of objections. Sofia stretched up and pecked him on the cheek, leaving a scarlet lipstick mark.

Tamir took her hand in his. 'Promise you'll call me immediately if you feel you're in the slightest danger?'

'Yes, I promise. But enough already—to coin one of your favourite Israeli phrases. My taxi will be waiting outside. Wish me luck, Agent Weiss.'

———

'Welcome to the *Orb of Islam*, Miss Candy. Please come in and sit down.'

'You can call me Diana. I'm not a fan of formality.'

'Oh, nor am I, not at all—Diana. Call me Azad, please.'

As Azad Ahmed MP ushered his glamorous guest to the most comfortable armchair in the room, Sofia noticed that he stole a brief glance at himself in the tall wall mirror as if to reassure himself that he was presenting his best face to the world. He had donned a smart three-piece suit for the occasion, complete with matching green silk tie and breast pocket handkerchief. Sofia flashed him an encouraging smile, as though to endorse his excellent sartorial taste.

'What would you like to drink, Diana?'

'Nothing for now, thank you, Mr Ahmed.'

'Maybe later. Now, I am placing myself entirely at your disposal,' purred the MP.

Sofia gingerly lowered herself into the seat, ineffectually tugging downwards at the hem of her miniscule skirt. She slowly crossed and uncrossed her long legs a couple of times, ensuring that a generous display of shapely thigh remained on display at all times, and placed her phone horizontally on the low coffee table in front of her. She looked up, eyebrows raised quizzically at her host, who was momentarily nonplussed.

'Ah, I see you wish to record our conversation? That's not a problem, go ahead.'

'Thank you, Mr—Azad.' She touched the phone's screen. 'May we start?'

'We may. Ask me anything you like, my dear. I have nothing to hide.'

Sofia forced another smile. 'Wonderful. You are the perfect subject, Azad. There's so much I'd like to ask you. I doubt we'll cover everything in one session. And I know you're a very busy man, so I'll be as quick as I can.'

'There is no hurry, my dear. Have no fear. For you, I will always make time.'

'Thank you, I appreciate it. Look, I won't beat about the bush.' She fixed her gaze on her interviewee—and, as a bonus, offered him another heart-stopping smile. While he was lapping up that treat, she said, 'Give me one moment, please, Azad, I just need to find something…' She leaned forward to rummage in her handbag, ensuring in the process that the MP received a long, unhindered view of her generous cleavage. Ahmed, she noticed, made no effort to avert his eyes. Retrieving a notepad and biro pen, Sofia sat back and continued in a matter-of-fact tone. 'Tell me honestly, Azad, does *Orb of Islam* have direct or indirect links to terrorist groups?'

Ahmed thrust his head backwards as if he had been shot, the colour draining from his cheeks. He gripped the sides of his chair and hauled himself to his feet. He eyes bulged as though they were about to explode.

'Damn your impertinence, woman! What kind of a question is that?'

Sofia pouted in mock concern. 'Oh dear, I've offended you, I'm so sorry,' she simpered. 'I just took you at your word, Azad. You said I could ask anything I liked. And my readers will be most interested to hear your answer. After all, it's common knowledge that the Charity Commission is investigating your organisation's possible links to jihadists. I'm giving you a chance to set the record straight once and for all. You should welcome that opportunity, I would have thought—unless you would prefer to offer my readers the standard "no comment"?' That would be perfectly fine, though I must admit they'll be hugely disappointed. She beamed another extra-warm smile at him.

Partially mollified and straining to recover his composure, Ahmed slowly sank back into his seat. He nodded. 'Yes, you're right, my dear. You're just doing your job. I apologise for my over-hasty reaction.' He removed the silk handkerchief from his jacket's breast pocket and mopped his brow. 'My answer to your somewhat provocative question, Diana, is categorical. No, we have no links to terrorist groups. None whatsoever. We never have and never will. The Charity Commission are wasting their time and taxpayers' money. The people putting about such an idea are malicious rumour-mongers. They are defending their own narrow political interests by attempting to smear me and my organisation.'

'Ah, that's an interesting observation. Tell me, please, who are these people who are trying to smear you? And what are their narrow political interests?'

Ahmed laughed in a manner that sounded to Sofia's ears, like gallows humour. 'Oh, I think you know very well who they are, my dear. The establishment, the global capitalist elite. They are terrified of losing their grip on their fabulous wealth. They will stop at nothing to prevent us coming to power and seizing all the assets they have stolen from the people we represent. That's what it's all about.'

'Hold on, I don't understand.' Sofia furrowed her brow. 'When you talk of the elite, do you mean the British government?'

'Not just them, but they are part of it. I'm referring to the whole lot of them—the media, the banks, foreign governments…'

'Really? Which foreign governments? The United States?'

'Yes, and many others too. They are all more or less in cahoots. And then there's the one behind the scenes pulling the strings.' Ahmed mimed the actions of a puppet-master.

'You mean the Americans? Or perhaps you are referring to someone else?'

Ahmed appeared on the verge of answering when he hesitated, studying Sofia's face as though searching for a clue. Suddenly, he pulled up his left sleeve and examined his watch.

'Good heavens, how time flies. And I've just remembered something—so stupid of me. I'm afraid duty calls. I have to be in the House of Commons to hear a ministerial statement. We must finish the interview now, I'm so sorry.'

'I quite understand. Thank you so much for your time, Azad. I appreciate it very much. Again, I apologise if I took you aback by my—directness. That's just the way I am.'

'Not at all, nothing happened. As I said, you were just doing your job. Again, I apologise for biting your head off. But perhaps we can complete the interview on another occasion? If you are agreeable?' He stood and Sofia followed suit.

'Of course.' She held out a slim, elegant hand. Ahmed lightly took it and chivalrously kissed the tips of her fingers, leaving his lips in contact with her skin just a moment longer than necessary. 'We should certainly meet again, Azad. I'd like that very much. Anywhere, any time. We have so much more to talk about. Perhaps we can find a more relaxed setting next time? I'll let you choose the time and place. You can call me on this private number.' She held out a card that he almost snatched out of her hand.

'Rest assured, I most certainly will. It was a great pleasure and privilege to meet you, Diana. I am so looking forward to our next meeting.'

[33]

WHEN DEPUTY PRIME MINISTER SASSOON OPENED THE DOOR TO his office, he was surprised to see two men in suits enter—Mossad director Lunenfeld and defence minister Volkov. Both wore funereal expressions.

Sassoon attempted to puncture the gloom with a smile and a touch of ritual bonhomie. 'Come in, gentlemen. How are you both? Enjoying the delightful weather, I hope?'

It was obvious that neither visitor was in the mood for even the most minimal small talk. After an awkward interregnum, Lunenfeld spoke first.

'Minister, General Volkov has some information that may be relevant to this meeting. I thought it important that he should be here.'

'Yes, you are quite right. We need all the information we can get about this sorry situation. Please sit down. I've ordered a large pot of mint tea. Though I must admit,' Sassoon chuckled, 'I suspect we could all do with something a lot stronger in the circumstances.'

His two visitors exchanged glances but remained stony-faced as they took their seats.

'Mr Sassoon,' continued Lunenfeld, 'You are acting prime minister now. Accordingly, whatever decisions are taken in this room are yours and yours alone. Nevertheless, we want to assure you that we are here to offer you our full and unstinting support for you in these difficult times.'

Sassoon winced. If ever a political sentence sounded the death knell of a promising career, it was the one that the Mossad director had just uttered. 'Thank you, Moshe, I appreciate that. I'll need all the help you can give me. This whole thing is a nightmare. Never in my wildest fantasies did I imagine I would have to face such an extraordinary scenario. Can you throw any light on our missing leader's behaviour?'

'Perhaps. That's why General Volkov is here. Minister?' Lunenfeld turned to Volkov and gestured to him to open the discussion.

Volkov spoke quietly but with authority in his customary deep baritone. 'Deputy Prime Minister, what I am about to tell you is highly confidential and must remain within these four walls. Not even our closest cabinet colleagues should hear of it. Not under any circumstances. Do I make myself clear?'

'Hold on a second, Arkady. I thought I was in charge now. Is that not so?'

'Indeed, you are, Avraham, I don't dispute that....'

'In which case,' interrupted Sassoon, jettisoning any lingering pretence of conviviality, 'who are you to tell me what is confidential and what is not?'

The general was unfazed by Sassoon's petulance. He had grown so accustomed to sharp gear-changes in mood from his senior political colleagues that he almost expected them. He shrugged and spread his enormous palms, smiling disingenuously. 'Hey, my friend, don't be so touchy! I'm here to help you, remember? Do you want to hear what I have to say or not? Get off your high horse, Avraham, it doesn't suit you.'

'Gentlemen, please!' interjected Lunenfeld. 'We're all in this together. The nation of Israel is in jeopardy and you two are bickering like spoilt children. It's disgraceful. Enough!'

His stern words had the desired effect. The two politicians blinked sheepishly at him but held their tongues.

'Good. Let's move on,' said Lunenfeld, 'We all understand that every word spoken in this room remains in this room. Now I suggest we focus on the task in hand and get down to *tachles*. General, please. You have something significant to tell us, have you not?'

Volkov swallowed hard and, still glowering at Sassoon, pulled a sheaf of papers out of his inside jacket pocket. 'It's all here, in black and white.'

Consulting his notes, at times reading from them as if for the first time, Volkov then proceeded to outline the recent series of events, starting with the embarrassing security cabinet meeting at which the prime minister had announced his unexpected decision to cancel *Operation Aleph Bet*, and the mysterious 'failed leak' of that instruction to *Destiny* following Lunenfeld's countermanding of the cancellation.

After five minutes of his factual monologue, Volkov stopped and awaited his listeners' reaction. When none ensued, he asked, '*Nu*, gentlemen? What shall we do? Our prime minister lied to us at the security cabinet meeting, behaved irresponsibly in cancelling a counter-terrorist operation that has placed our people at risk, and has now disappeared without trace. That leads me to one conclusion. Do I need to spell it out?'

'Yes, you do,' prompted Lunenfeld softly. Go on, General.'

'This man is not fit for the highest office in the land. He has to go.'

'What are you suggesting?' said Sassoon. 'Some kind of impeachment?'

'That would be a serious step,' said Lunenfeld. 'It would also be, to put it mildly, premature at this point. And dangerous. First things first. Our priority is to establish where the PM is and why. We don't even know whether he's alive or dead or something in-between. Even assuming he's in the best of heath, the political shenanigans can come later.'

'I disagree completely, Moshe,' retorted Volkov. 'This is a major crisis that requires urgent action…'

Lunenfeld held up his hand. 'One moment, please.' A phone was buzzing. It was Lunenfeld's. 'Excuse me, gentlemen, I have to answer this.'

He picked up the device and walked to the far end of the room. With his back to the ministers, he listened intently and nodded once. Without responding to the caller, he clicked his phone shut and returned to the conference table. As usual, his facial expression gave nothing away. By contrast, his words astonished his listeners.

'Gentlemen, I have important breaking news for you. News that directly impacts on this discussion. Our dear leader is, it seems, back in the land of the living. And he is safe and well, to all external appearances.'

'What? Where is he?' cried Sassoon, rising to his feet.

'He's addressing the Israel public from his office in Jerusalem. Right now.'

'We'd better get over there fast,' said Volkov. 'Come on, guys, let's move. We need to find out what the scoundrel has to say.'

'No need, my friends. All we have to do is switch on the TV.'

[34]

AXEL RUE WAS GROWING TIRED OF THE CONVERSATION WITH HIS London handler. He was tempted to hang up but knew that such a reckless act of defiance would likely backfire.

'I'm sorry, Mr Ahmed, please listen to me. You don't seem to understand what I'm telling you. It can't be done today. We're not ready. The risks are far too high. We could be entering a minefield. This is my professional opinion.' Rue was adamant. So was his employer.

'Now listen to me very carefully, Mr Rue,' intoned Azad Ahmed, injecting more than a hint of menace into his voice. 'You are being paid a handsome fee to undertake an important task for us. I have been delegated the dubious pleasure of ensuring that you do your work as required. That means that you do what I say and not the other way around—unless you wish to incur unpleasant consequences. Do I make myself clear?'

'Perfectly,' said Rue. 'But the fact of the matter...'

'The fact of the matter,' interrupted Ahmed, almost shouting, 'is that you have twenty-four hours to complete your mission. If you fail, your contract will be terminated forthwith. And you will be punished severely, I promise you. Just do it.' There was a click and the line was dead.

'Have it your way,' muttered Rue into the unresponsive phone. He speed-dialled and his call was answered instantly. 'Zoltan, there's been a change of plan.'

Two hours later, a nondescript white van drew up outside an equally nondescript house in Burrard Road, West Hampstead. Two well-built men in light blue overalls got out and looked up and down the street. One of the workers, clutching an oblong cardboard box, opened a metal gate and strode up to the front door; he pressed the buzzer. The other remained at the rear of the van, holding open the door.

This unremarkable event was nevertheless attracting interest. There was a shout from across the road. A shaven-headed, athletic-looking youth in a track suit, apparently in the midst of his morning jog, crossed the empty road and sidled up to the van.

'Hey, what's up, you guys?' said the young man with a hint of a foreign accent.

'We're just delivering a parcel, mate. What's it to you anyway?'

'You must have the wrong address. There are no deliveries to this house.'

'Have a look for yourself. I have the order right here in black and white. See?' The jogger glanced at the slip of paper he was being proffered but looked unconvinced. He approached the rear of the van warily, trying to peer inside. As he slipped his right hand into a hip pocket, there was sharp, cracking sound, like a loud peel of thunder. Had the young man remained conscious for long enough, he might have recognised it as the sound of metal striking bone. Five seconds later, his crumpled body lay on the van floor.

The front door of the town house opened gingerly. That was the only invitation the delivery men needed. They crashed into the hallway, causing a commotion that could be heard halfway down the street. One of the intruders grabbed Tamir around the neck while the other stabbed him in the arm with a syringe. At lightning speed, the Israeli head-butted one of his assailants, breaking the bridge of his nose, and thrust his knee hard into the groin of the second. But it was all in vain—heavy-duty tranquillisers work fast. After a few seconds writhing, the Mossadnik was motionless. Half-a-minute later, the white van drove off with its newly acquired human cargo of two unconscious Israelis.

'Mission accomplished, sir,' spoke Rue into his phone. 'Unfortunately, there were a couple of problems. That's what comes of a rushed job.'

'What problems?' asked Ahmed.

'We got Weiss but not his missus. She was either hiding out or had gone walkabout. Should we go back for her?'

'That's not good, not good at all. No. don't go back. They'll have triple security there by now or they'll have whisked her away to another location. Never mind, Mr Rue, Weiss is the real prize. We'll deal with the woman later if she causes any trouble, which I doubt she will.'

'Thank you, Mr Ahmed, I appreciate your understanding. We are heading for the channel crossing now, to the usual place.'

'You did well enough in the circumstances, though not perfectly,' said the MP. 'But I'm sure Mr Berg will be a very happy man when he receives your little gift. Did you say there was another problem?'

'We had to take out a Mossad agent who came sniffing around. I know you said we should avoid violence and we tried but he was reaching for his weapon. He was threatening the success of the entire mission. We had no choice.'

'And you stopped him. That's fair enough. You did what was necessary. Is he badly injured?'

'Zoltan got a little bit carried away, I'm afraid. He hit the Israeli pretty hard on his head. Zoltan's a strong guy but he can be hot-headed. That's his nature.'

'What are you trying to tell me, Mr Rue. What's the state of the piece of Israeli scum that Zoltan took out?'

'That's the second problem, Mr Ahmed. He's dead.'

[35]

'Sorry, love,' said the cab driver, 'but this is as close as I can get.'

They had arrived at the junction of Finchley Road and Burrard Street where some sort of incident was in progress. Sofia felt her stomach knot. Two police cars, at least, were blocking all movement in or out of the street.

'I can walk from here, thank you.' She stepped out of the cab, paid the driver and, steadying herself on her high heels, approached a uniformed policewoman.

'Excuse me, officer. What's going on? Can you let me through, please?'

'And who might you be, madam?' asked the policewoman unsmilingly.

'I'm Sofia Weiss and I live here. This is my home. What happened? Can I speak to my husband?' She took a couple of steps forward but was stopped by the officer.

'One moment, madam. You can't just walk into a crime scene. Stay here while I consult with my boss.' She turned away and started speaking into her crackling radio.

Five minutes later, Sofia was sitting in her living room sipping a mug of pale, sweet tea. Her hands were trembling, and her heart was pounding so hard she was convinced it could be heard across the street.

'And that's all we know at this point, I'm afraid, Mrs Weiss.' The Scotland Yard detective was a plump, besuited middle-aged man with surprisingly long hair and old-fashioned greying sideburns. He clutched a small white booklet into which he scribbled occasional notes. His manner was friendly, yet formal. 'According to at least two witnesses, your husband was taken, with some degree of violence, by persons unknown.'

'Violence? My God, was he hurt?'

'We don't know, I'm afraid. As far as we can ascertain, he was manhandled into a delivery van by two burly characters who took him by surprise right at the front door. They also grabbed a passerby, but we don't yet know anything about him or his identity except that he was jogging. It all happened very quickly. We're checking CCTV footage, but we've found nothing helpful so far.'

Conscious that her Hollywood-style attire and was attracting unwanted attention from the other two policemen in the room, she demurely adjusted the hem of her skirt.

'Who were these people? Do you have any idea?'

The inspector shrugged. 'We were rather hoping you might enlighten us. Have you or your husband been threatened by anyone, madam?'

In the course of ten seconds, Sofia grappled with the implications of that question and how she should answer it. The last thing she and Tamir needed was for the Met to get involved in a Mossad operation. But the policeman would need an answer.

'Madam? Did you understand my question?'

'Yes. I'm really sorry, inspector, I don't mean to be unhelpful, but I can't think straight right now.'

'That's quite understandable, Mrs Weiss. You've had a major shock. Let me ask you a different question. I gather your husband is attached to the Israeli Embassy?'

'Yes, in a way.' She hesitated, unsure what she should reveal to her interrogator. Did he know about Tamir's Mossad connection? Maybe she should tell him so that he could transfer the case to more competent authorities? What would Tamir want her to do?

She made a decision. 'Inspector, there is something you should know.'

'Oh? Please, go on. The more you can tell me, the more I can help.'

'The thing is, it's a rather delicate matter...' Just then, a phone buzzed. It was the inspector's.

'Excuse me one moment.' He hastily left the room, leaving Sofia in the company of the two young officers. She looked up at their faces and smiled nervously. The younger man blushed. The door opened and the inspector strode back in, buttoning up his suit jacket.

'I've just received some surprising news. This case is no longer the responsibility of the Metropolitan Police. We have to go. Sorry about this, madam, but we've been instructed to wrap up immediately and leave you to your own devices.'

'I beg your pardon?' Sofia was flabbergasted. 'What on earth do you mean? Have you found my husband? Am I safe here?'

'I can't speculate about any of that, sorry. The Israeli Embassy are now involved, and they'll ensure your security, I'm told. I'm afraid I can't discuss the matter any further with you, Mrs Weiss. We're off the case with immediate effect. Apparently national security considerations demand it. Both the home secretary and foreign secretary have been informed and the Met's commissioner

—that's our big chief—is in full agreement. He's signed it off, so it's not up for discussion.'

'Wait, you're just going to leave me here?' There was a fine tremor in Sofia's voice.

'I'm sorry, but it's out of our hands. If I were you, I'd lock all your doors and windows until the Embassy people arrive. Goodbye, Mrs Weiss. And good luck. Looks like you'll need it.'

[36]

MOSSAD DIRECTOR LUNENFELD, ALONG WITH GOVERNMENT ministers Volkov and Sassoon, stood transfixed in front of the large television screen in the agency's nerve centre as their prime minister, newly risen from the dead yet appearing none the worse for wear, explained to the Israeli public the significance—and triumphant conclusion, as he put it—of his twenty-four-hour disappearing act. His demeanour was calm and almost statesmanlike.

'My dear friends, I am sorry to have caused you all needless anxiety. That was not my intention, but it became an unfortunate necessity, as you will shortly learn. Over the past few hours, I and I alone have been working ceaselessly, tirelessly, to protect our national interests and those of the one million Jews who currently live within the borders of the European Union. And I am very happy to report to you that those efforts have borne fruit. In fact, that is the understatement of the century.

'As we all know, in recent years recent political developments in Europe have cast a long shadow across that continent to the point where our Jewish brothers and sisters have felt themselves increasingly isolated and vulnerable. None of us imagined, in our worst nightmares, that we would witness a return, in the twenty-first century, of lethal, murderous Jew-hatred to the streets of Paris or London or Vienna. How could a region whose soil became soaked in the blood of our forebears within living memory once again revert to the barbarism of fascism and anti-Jewish bigotry on a vast and terrifying scale? Sadly, I have to tell you that's exactly what is happening again before our eyes.

'The crisis our people are confronting in Europe today is no less than an existential one. An extremist, hate-filled and potentially genocidal movement is sweeping away the multiple checks and balances that were so painstakingly constructed after the Second World War to prevent the horrors of the Third Reich from ever revisiting the continent. I'm sorry to have to report that these mechanisms have failed. One by one, the European democracies have proved incapable of resisting the onward rush of violence, a tsunami of terror. A terror that threatens all the peoples of Europe, especially ethnic and religious minorities, but that is specifically targeting one group of people above all others: the Jewish people.

'This is not merely a frightening state of affairs, it is a wholly intolerable one. We will not look away from those who seek to destroy us even if the so-called international community, in its all-too-familiar cowardly fashion, tries to ignore them. We cannot sit idly by while another enormous tragedy befalls our people. And we will not, for we have the means to prevent it. Indeed, that is why the State of Israel, the sovereign nation of the Jewish people, was reborn in 1948, despite ceaseless and often violent opposition to our existence. As your prime minister, I concluded that we had to act. And we have done so. Or to be more precise, I have done so, acting on your behalf.'

In what appeared to be a rehearsed move, the TV director chose that moment to zoom in on the PM's face. With a half-smile, Adar looked directly into the camera's lens and projected to the public his favoured expression of empathetic sincerity. It was an artifice that fooled few viewers, least of all the trio of officials who were watching the performance a few metres from the Mossad director's office.

'Friends, sometimes it is necessary to take difficult decisions in the national interest. Sometimes we have to negotiate with people with whom we profoundly disagree and whose values are not our values. Sometimes we have to sup with the devil in order to thwart his plans. Sometimes we have to choose, not between good and bad, but between bad and worse. We have experienced this agonising dilemma many times in our history and we have usually made the right choices. Today, we are forced, yet again, to face that choice. Running away from it to preserve our sense of moral purity is not an option.

The close-up switched back to a head-and-shoulders shot.

'You know, Judaism has many fine ethical principles. One stands out, for me, above all—*pikuach nefesh*, the saving of life. Our rabbis and sages have taught us to value human life above all other divine gifts. During these last dark hours, I have drawn great solace from this remarkable, life-affirming principle. That is what has motivated me to risk everything—my career, my reputation, my future—in order to achieve this overriding goal of *pikuach nefesh*. I believe that my close engagement with the leaders of the antisemitic *Destiny* movement represents a fulfilment of that goal.

'Accordingly, I took the decision to sit down with the leaders of our enemies and negotiate a deal. Yes, I know what you are thinking—but don't rush to judgement, I beg you. After many long hours of bitter haggling, we reached an agreement. The main components of this deal are outlined in a document that I will shortly make public. In essence, what will happen is this: Every last Jew who is currently stranded within the confines of the prison that the European Union has become for them will be handed a key. That key will unlock the cell doors and permit our people to escape from who knows what grim fate would otherwise await them.

'How has this positive outcome been achieved? I can't reveal all the details, for reasons that I am sure you appreciate, but I can tell you this. We have paid a heavy price for that key in political and diplomatic currency. On the other hand, the outcome will be the rescue of close to a million innocent souls—men, women and children—who will be able, after an initial but temporary phase of resettlement, to look forward to a future of peace and safety and prosperity in their safe and welcoming homeland, Israel.'

The TV director switched to a second more lateral camera. Adar turned to face it, banishing the smile and summoning all the gravitas he could muster.

'Now, I am handing over to you, the citizens of this great country, another key—the key to my fate. You will decide whether or not you continue to invest in me that precious trust that all democratic political leaders require. I am dissolving my government with immediate effect. We go to elections within weeks. Thank you. The people of Israel live—*Am Yisrael Chai.*'

[37]

'THIS IS MADNESS! IT CAN'T BE DONE!' PIERRE CAMBON, RED-faced and perspiring, was shouting and thumping his walking stick on the concrete floor to amplify his anger.

'*Calmons-nous*, Professor,' pleaded Christoph Berg quietly, placing an emollient palm on the older man's forearm 'Let's not argue over a misunderstanding. You are wrong on this as on so many things. It can be done, and it will be done. Everything is under control. My control. The necessary instructions have been printed and will soon be ready for delivery. I estimate that the deportations to Greenland can start within a month.'

The two men were seated around a small folding wooden table in the basement of a shabby, dimly lit office in central Brussels. The air was dank and the atmosphere toxic.

'Berg, you are either a fool or a madman. How in God's name do you think you can get away with deporting close to a million people, full citizens of the European Union, in the twenty-first century?'

'This is not about me, Pierre, it's about us, about the future. And please don't try to distance yourself from the flagship policy of *Destiny*. You've known all along what we intended to do about our Zionist problem, and you signed up to it. No, don't deny it! You voiced some reservations, we heard you out respectfully and you were overruled.'

'You are a fiend, Berg, I wish I'd never met you and got tangled up in your crazy schemes. You make me sick to the depths of my stomach.'

'But you're still here, Pierre, aren't you? I'm not forcing you to agree to anything. Just say the word, and you can walk away right now.' Berg pulled up his left sleeve to expose his watch. 'No hurry, you old fool, but you have thirty seconds to decide. That's ample time, isn't it? That's because I'm feeling in an unusually generous mood today. Actually, you have—let's see—only twenty seconds now. This is it, comrade. What's your decision? Think very carefully before you answer.'

Berg placed his right hand in the inside breast pocket of his corduroy jacket. Cambon knew what was lodged in there and what the menacing gesture was intended to accomplish. It succeeded. The two men stared at each other. Neither moved. Cambon broke the tension by looking up at the low ceiling and sighing audibly.

'Just as I thought, old man,' sneered Berg. 'You're all talk, no action. Deep down, I know you agree with me. You need to swallow your scruples and stop behaving like a spoilt teenager. We have work to do.'

'I keep thinking about all these poor people and how they will react.'

'What poor people? They're Jews, Pierre, and they are the opposite of poor. What is more, they'll do what they're told, just like last time. Your soft heart really puzzles me. Why should you feel sorry for them? We both know that they've had it coming. Look what they're doing to the Palestinians—their cruel policies of apartheid, colonialism, ethnic cleansing, genocide. The poor Arabs are the ones you should feel sorry for. Do I have to remind you that Zionists are today's Nazis? We're doing Europe a favour by getting rid of them. Look, don't think of it as a mass deportation but rather as the constructive relocation of highly undesirable aliens. Of terrorists, in effect. Everyone knows that they are undermining the moral fabric of Europe for their own benefit. What we're doing is an act of self-defence. Under the UN Charter, it's completely legal, moral and necessary.'

'And you really think the rest of the world will buy that argument and allow this to go ahead without anyone raising a murmur of protest?'

'I don't think it, I know it. The European Council have already nodded it through, and individual member states won't raise any serious objections.'

'How can you possibly predict that?' cried Cambon. 'All hell will be let loose when the European Parliament convenes next week. They've taken a strong stand against antisemitism over many years.'

Berg shook his head slowly and smiled as if amused at the naivety of a small child. 'The Parliament won't be involved. We're bypassing them altogether using a special legislative device called the Passerelle Clause of the Lisbon Treaty. Don't worry, old chap, it's all been taken care of.'

'So it seems. What about the Danes? They are responsible for the foreign affairs of Greenland. There's no way they'll allow this to happen.'

'They've raised no objections. On the contrary, they are delighted. Greenland is an underpopulated wasteland that could do with an injection of personnel and money, and the Jews will have, as usual, plenty of cash in their pockets when they arrive. They'll flourish there, I guarantee it. Anyway, it seems that matters of immigration have been devolved to the autonomous Greenland government and they are totally on our side, rest assured of that. The allure of all that Jewish gold has turned their

heads. Just stop fretting. These are exciting times. Savour them.'
Berg stood. 'Have we finished? Let's go. We have an appointment with the Mossad. It would be impolite to keep them waiting.'

Cambon, remaining seated, said 'Just one moment, what about the Israelis? They won't roll over and accept this. And if they start squealing, so will Washington.'

Berg smiled, resumed his seat and leaned forward to within a few centimetres of Cambon's face. 'Ah, my dear Pierre, your sharp mind misses nothing. I should have told you, how remiss of me. The Israelis have been taken care of. Let me rephrase that—they have changed their minds and withdrawn their previous objections to our plans. We even killed one of their agents in London and they didn't make a song and dance about it. Not the tiniest squeak. That proves that they're fully on board with the programme. And naturally that means the Americans are also. You know how these things work. The words "puppets and strings" come to mind.'

'What in heaven's name are you talking about, Berg?'

Berg drew a sheet of printed paper out of his jacket pocket. 'I can see that you are sceptical. Have no fear. I have just pulled off one of the greatest diplomatic achievements in history. You see, I'm not just a pretty face. I can operate the levers of power when I have to. I decided to negotiate with our mortal enemies. And as I expected, they caved. *Voila, mon ami!* I signed this agreement with the Israeli prime minister this morning. Read it. I think you'll be most impressed. He has given us the green light to proceed. Your fears have proved groundless, old man. There will be no Jewish or Israeli resistance, just as I predicted. And that means that the US and other countries will accept our policy as a *fait accompli*. This is a great day for our movement. We're pushing full steam ahead. *Destiny* is on the road to greatness. Nothing will stop us now.'

[38]

'WHAT AM I SUPPOSED TO DO NOW, KEREN?' SOFIA'S VOICE began to crack as she fought to hold back tears. 'We can't live here, obviously, unless you scale up your pathetically inadequate security tenfold. And we have to find Tamir. He could be dead by now, for all we know. And one of the security guards is missing—he's probably had his throat cut.' She sprang to her feet. 'But why are we even having this conversation? We should be out there looking for them right now!'

'One thing at a time, my dear,' said the Mossad officer, adopting her most soothing bedside manner. 'Please sit down, it's not helpful to panic.' Sofia returned to the armchair.

'Now listen to me,' continued Keren. 'You are right. Tamir is in danger, I won't hide that from you. But he can look after himself. He's exceptionally resourceful, as we both know, and he has survival skills that you can't even imagine. But I'm also concerned about him. There's no sense in denying the possibility that he could be in great danger.'

'Thanks for nothing. You're contradicting yourself now—oh, don't worry, he'll be fine, except that he might be murdered any minute.'

Keren shook her head. 'Don't put words in my mouth; I didn't say that. Maybe I expressed myself badly. And we have reason to believe that he is still alive.'

'What do you mean? Have you heard from the kidnappers?'

'Not directly. But we did receive a message of sorts. The young security guard who was taken with Tamir was carrying it. He's dead I'm afraid. Just turned twenty-one and barely three weeks with the agency. We found his body this morning. They had just dumped it at the roadside a few miles from here.'

'Jesus, that's awful. Poor guy. And his poor family, I suppose that means Tamir is alive or they would have dumped him too?'

'Correct, that's our assumption, too. These people have shown their true colours. As we suspected, they are cold-blooded killers and we will have to respond appropriately. Look, Tamir is in a horrible situation but having a meltdown won't help him. We have to stay calm and think logically. We'll discuss what's to be done about Tamir in a moment. The first priority is your safety and that of your daughter.'

'Clara's fine. She's with my sister and is used to being shunted between us. It's so unfair on her. She'll probably grow up hating me.'

'I'm really sorry that you've had to be separated from your daughter,' said Keren. 'But she won't hate you. Children are adaptable. You can take my word for it. I've researched this subject in depth.'

'You're a child psychiatrist, aren't you? I'd forgotten that.' Sofia sighed and gazed into the middle distance for a few moments, as if distracted by a disturbing thought. Keren watched the younger woman and waited for her to restore her focus on the conversation.

'This is hard for you, Sofia, I appreciate that, but I am confident that Clara will be fine. She knows you love her and will always return to her sooner or later. Just thank your lucky stars that you have such an obliging sister.'

'You're right, I am lucky to have Luisa. I suppose I just need reassurance that I'm not the world's worst mother. But what about me? This place gives me the creeps.'

'I completely understand. We failed to keep you and Tamir safe and you are right to be angry. On the other hand, wherever you go, you'll be in a degree of danger. We shouldn't underestimate these people.'

'Meaning what? I just have to sit here until they come back and kidnap me, too?' Sofia made no attempt to conceal her exasperation.

'We won't let that happen. But I must be honest with you. They are much more competent than we gave them credit for. I'm afraid that means there is a chance they will find you wherever you go. Running away isn't the answer. We have to take the initiative.' Keren stretched forward and grasped both of Sofia's hands. 'Don't despair. I have an idea. More than that, I'm working with some colleagues on a plan. I will put it to you as soon as I can. It will achieve two objectives—it will get you out of immediate danger and will bring us closer to locating and rescuing Tamir from his captors. Don't ask, I'll explain everything to you as soon as I can. Give us a little time to work out the details.'

'What sort of thing you have in mind? Can you at least tell me that?'

'Patience, Sofia. First, I want you to go and change out of those ridiculous clothes. Then pack them in a suitcase along with a few necessities. We're going to be on the move very soon.'

'Where are we going? And why do you want me to bring the Marilyn outfit?'

'We're going to Brussels. To the *Destiny* headquarters, or to somewhere nearby where we they are holding Tamir. With luck, the people involved in the kidnapping will lead us straight to him.

As for these clothes, they will be extremely useful, believe me. We're going to set a trap for the leader of their movement.

'What kind of trap? Are we talking bees and honey again?'

Keren smiled. 'The kind that you have already shown yourself so skilled at.'

'You mean with the MP? You want me to repeat that stunt?'

'It worked with Azad Ahmed and I can't see any reason why it wouldn't work with the other leaders of *Destiny*. Extremists thrive on attention and they crave that more than anything. What is more, these are all men. And men will be men—you're an attractive woman so I don't need to tell you that. In my experience, that's especially true of fringe politicians. Something about being in unaccustomed proximity to power seems to induce many of them to behave like adolescent boys. They just can't help themselves however hard they try.'

Sofia had to laugh at that. 'Too true, Keren. They're pathetic, aren't they?' Within seconds, her expression clouded again. 'Let me think about it. Supposing it works and we get up close and personal with these monsters. What happens then?'

'Two things, mainly. We'll get valuable information—about the state of their organisation and about Tamir's welfare. And then we'll do whatever is necessary to neutralise them.'

'Excuse me? Does that mean what I think it means?'

'It may be the only way to save Tamir. And to stop *Destiny* in its tracks. We underestimated them in the past and we can't afford to make that mistake again. They've already murdered one of our agents and we can't let them repeat that stunt. The hard truth is that you can't reason with a poisonous snake. We'll do what always has to be done when we're faced with one. We'll cut off its head.'

[39]

AS THE CABINET WAS ASSEMBLING IN THE MAIN CONFERENCE chamber, two men in grey suits were sitting in the adjacent waiting room studying an official-looking document that each had spread on his lap. Defence minister Volkov gathered up his papers and casually threw them onto the coffee table. He took a few sips from the glass of orange juice that he had contrived, by a practised sleight of hand, to lace with his favourite brand of vodka. He studied the face of his boss, searching for a sign of weakness. The Israeli prime minister, Yoav Adar, sat opposite him and looked as relaxed, fit and well-groomed as ever.

'Lighten up, Arkady, it's not the end of the world. I'm still here, the government hasn't fallen and you are still my trusted defence minister. When the next polls come out, you'll see how our popularity will have soared as a direct result of this piece of paper. The public will understand that we have taken care of this crisis in the best possible manner—by rescuing hundreds of thousands of our fellow Jews. We'll be swept back to power with a landslide majority in the Knesset. That will give us four more years to pass our legislative programme. So why the gloomy face?'

Volkov drained his glass and slammed it down noisily on the table. 'Prime Minister, I have a question. Why am I here?'

The PM grinned and spread his arms as if he were about to embrace his colleague. 'Because I love you, Arkady,' he cried. 'We are kindred spirits, you and I, are we not? You understand better than most the value of *realpolitik*.' Suddenly, the smile was gone. 'All right, let me put my cards on the table. I'm not a fool, despite what some of you think. I've taken a huge risk and I know very well that I'm going to struggle to get the support of the cabinet for this deal. But with your backing, I can win them round. *We* can win them round. I need to know that I can rely on you, my friend.'

Volkov picked up his copy of the memorandum and squinted at it in silence for a few moments. When he spoke, he pointedly avoided eye contact with the PM.

'I'm afraid I don't share your sense of optimism about this document, Yoav. In fact, I have to tell you that I am deeply worried about it. It goes without saying that we're all thrilled that you have returned to us in good health and in such high spirits. We were concerned about you, as was the entire nation. But that strange episode is behind us now. We have to look to the future. And that means facing up to the implications of this extraordinary memorandum you have signed with our mortal enemies.'

'I think you mean our ex-enemies.'

'I'm not at all sure about that and neither should you be,' growled Volkov, his eyes darting around the room. 'They've already killed a young Mossad agent and they will probably try to repeat that trick if they get the chance. How will you look into the eyes of his parents and tell them you've made a deal with his murderers?'

'I'll have no problem doing that,' said Adar, 'because I'll explain to them that their son's sacrifice has saved many more lives. Sometimes you have to take a step backwards to take two steps forward. You know that better than anyone, Arkady.'

Volkov closed his eyes for a moment. 'This is madness, Yoav. Look, I don't doubt your intentions. But just because you are the prime minister doesn't mean you're infallible. The results of your gamble may be far more dangerous than you realise. Unless I'm missing something, this document is full of holes. Some of them are bigger than the Negev desert. These people are racists and fascists, Yoav. The worst of the worst. They will lie through their teeth in the morning sell their grandmother at the market in the afternoon. Believe me, I know their type, I used to work with them in the old Soviet days. That means they are unreliable partners. What makes you think they'll stand by any agreement they sign?'

Adar was about to answer but Arkady's question was rhetorical. His diatribe had turned into an unstoppable verbal torrent. 'I wouldn't trust them a centimetre. Think about it, Yoav, this is a magnificent *coup* for them. They will trumpet this agreement to the whole world as evidence of their brilliant diplomacy. And who is going to oppose them? If the government of Israel is willing to shake hands with them, why shouldn't the rest of the democratic world? The Jews can't be in such danger after all if the Jewish state itself is willing to deal with them. Their next move will be to open negotiations with the Americans. The global media will be summoned to witness a ceremonial handshake between the US president and Pierre Cambon on the White House lawn. *Destiny* will be tipped for a Nobel Peace Prize. They will become the undisputed, internationally recognised rulers of Europe.'

'And in the meantime, I will have saved the Jewish people from disaster!' shouted the PM unable to conceal his anger. 'Does that count for nothing?'

'Listen to yourself, Yoav—doesn't something sound familiar? You have just handed these bastards their victory on a plate. All for the sake of some empty promises. You will go down in history as Israel's Neville Chamberlain. Is that what you want?'

The PM rose to his feet. He spoke softly but the tremor in his voice betrayed his emotion. 'What I want, and so should you, Arkady, is to safeguard the security of our people, not just here in Israel but around the world. That's what this agreement has achieved. Can't you see that?'

Now Volkov stood, picked up his empty glass and held it up to the light. 'What I see is this little object. Look at it. It's pretty, isn't it? But don't be deceived, it's a fragile piece of glitter. You can see right through it. That should be a clue. And it can't carry the burden you are about to place on it. Watch.' He raised his arm and, with one continuous movement, swung it in an arc like a baseball pitcher. The glass flew out of his hand and smashed noisily against the wall.

Two security guards rushed into the room but the PM, without looking at them, raised his hand and said, 'Everything is fine. Leave us, please.'

'That's what will happen to your precious memorandum, Prime Minister,' continued Volkov. 'It's the likely fate awaiting the Jews of Europe, including the majority who will be sent to Iceland.'

'Greenland,' Adar corrected him.

'Oh, Greenland, is it? That paradise on earth. Are you out of your mind? What will happen to them there? No, I'm sorry, it won't wash. As your defence minister, I can't approve your crazy scheme. You are playing silly games with the security of the State of Israel and the Jewish people, and probably the entire democratic world as well. I will not be associated with this act of absolute folly.'

The PM was visibly shaken. 'What exactly are you saying, Arkady?'

'I'm sorry, Prime Minister. We have been friends and

colleagues for many years, but you leave me no choice. Please inform the rest of the cabinet that I have just submitted my resignation, effective immediately. As of now, the State of Israel has no minister of defence. I will issue a full statement to the media within the hour. You're on your own, Yoav, and you have no-one to blame but yourself.'

Hands trembling, Volkov gathered up his papers along with his phone and, without a glance backwards, left the room.

[40]

WHEN TAMIR AWOKE, HE BECAME AWARE OF TWO POWERFUL sensations, neither of which was pleasant. First, he had a headache. It wasn't the kind of knife-like pain that follows a blow but rather a diffuse, unfocused discomfort that seemed to encase his entire skull in a vice. Second, he couldn't move his arms or legs—they had been strapped to the sides of the upright chair on which he was sitting and they hurt like hell. With a supreme physical effort, he could just about extend his wrists and ankles a couple of inches, but no further movement was possible. That was when the penny dropped—he was being held prisoner. His top priority was to get his bearings.

Where was he? He squinted at his surroundings but could see little due to the miserly light. The combination of a damp chill in the air and the absence of furnishings suggested that he was in some sort of basement or warehouse. Beneath his feet was a cold and unyielding concrete floor. Ahead of him was a single shuttered window. At the far end of the room, up against the wall, lay a grimy mattress next to which sat a metal bucket. That latter item must be his *en suite* bathroom, he surmised, though he wondered how he was supposed to use it in his current immobilised state.

He tried to piece together the sequence of events. He reviewed in his mind his last moments in the West Hampstead house. After the doorbell had rung, he had glanced through the peephole and had been reassured sufficiently by what he saw to open the door. That had been his first blunder—how could he have been so witless? What happened to all his years of training and experience? It was an unforgiveable lapse and his superiors would be unimpressed. Especially the doctor—what was her name? The good-looking one. Now, he'd lost his train of thought…

He reran the memory tape. He'd opened the door. What then? A uniformed delivery man was holding a parcel. Another guy had appeared from somewhere and they had grabbed him by the neck.

Why hadn't he fought back? He must have attempted to beat them off, surely? He recalled experiencing a sharp pain in his arm, then blankness. He had been injected with some sort of powerful tranquilliser, ketamine perhaps. That would explain the headache. Or perhaps that was due to dehydration—he had a raging thirst. But he had to focus on the one key question that was his main preoccupation. Who were these people and why had they brought him here to this dank, airless cellar?

A key rattled in the door and someone entered. Seconds later, the room was filled with a bright light. As Tamir's eyes adjusted, he glimpsed the outlines of two visitors standing at his side. They were conversing in an undertone. One was a youngish man of medium height and solidly built. The other, he thought he recognised: a balding, wiry middle-aged character with frameless spectacles, a goatee beard and thinning red hair. The latter spoke first in a strong German accent.

'Mr Weiss, welcome to Brussels. My apologies for this temporary inconvenience. We owe you an explanation, which you will receive shortly. First, the introductions. My name is Christoph Berg and this is my colleague, Axel Rue. We represent a wonderful organisation called *Destiny* that is sweeping Europe and will transform the entire world. I have no doubt that you have heard about us.'

So that was it. His brain fog was clearing. He had been abducted by *Destiny*. Berg was its leader and potential mass murderer. If he was to survive this ordeal, he would have to focus on his predicament, and quickly.

'I know exactly who you are,' said Tamir, 'and wonderful isn't the adjective that comes to mind when I think of a repulsive bunch of racist thugs.'

Berg grinned, displaying a set of perfectly chiselled white teeth. 'Ah, so our Israeli friend has a sense of humour. Excellent —you will need it. Would you like something to drink? Mr Rue, please.' Berg snapped his fingers and Rue produced a plastic bottle from his pocket. Berg grabbed it and unscrewed the top. He offered the water to Tamir. 'Perhaps you would like me to help you as you are unfortunately indisposed?' Tamir nodded.

'With pleasure, my Zionist friend.' Still grinning, Berg raised the bottle above Tamir's head and poured its contents over him. Tamir shuddered under the cold deluge and strained to extract a few drops of the dripping moisture with his protruding tongue.

'Listen to me, Mr Weiss,' said Berg, no longer smiling, 'I have some advice for you. You will have to change your tone. We clearly dislike each other. That is to be expected. We come from very different cultures and hold very different values. But I am sure we are both rational men. If you are rude to me, I will be rude to you in return. By contrast, if you are cooperative, you will find in me a willing partner. Do you follow me? Good. Now, shall we start again? Mr Rue, untie our friend, give him a proper drink and let's get down to business.'

Two hours later, unshackled and partially rehydrated, Tamir was more confused than ever. Berg had subjected him to a bizarre 'history lesson' that erased Europe's dark past and exonerated extremist governments of both right and left of any wrongdoing in the twentieth century. He portrayed Hitler as a prophetic, misunderstood visionary who had been forced, against his will, into adopting repressive measures against spies, dissidents, and that all-powerful and well-funded fifth column that had sought to frustrate him at every turn—the Jews. It was only natural that the people of Europe should now wish to deal with this unfinished business and seek to solve the Jewish problem once and for all.

'You mean, by implementing another Final Solution?' Tamir had interjected. That comment had provoked a further diatribe against Jews, gays, Roma and 'all the fellow travellers who have been bribed by Soros and the Rothschilds.' Berg insisted that he himself bore no ill-will towards anyone but that the stubbornness of 'certain people' had left him with no choice but to adopt firm action. He was sure Tamir, despite his own Jewish background, would come reconsider his views and work with *Destiny* to ensure that Europe was rid of its Jews in the most orderly manner possible. 'After all, your prime minister agrees with us.'

'Excuse me? What did you just say about my prime minister?' Tamir had long lost all interest in Berg's ramblings and had felt no inclination to contradict him. That last sentence had startled him back into the conversation.

'Ah, so you didn't know about this diplomatic breakthrough? No, why should you, it all happened within the last twenty-four hours or so while you were having a little snooze. Yes, your boss, the prime minister of Israel, has signed a memorandum of understanding with our President Cambon. Look, it's on the front of *The Times* of London—and every other major newspaper around the world.' Berg handed Tamir a newspaper. The headline read: *Israel signs deal with Destiny.* Scanning the first paragraph, Tamir tried to absorb the key points of the agreement—that ten percent of the Jews of Europe would be permitted to emigrate to Israel immediately in exchange for that country's recognition of *Destiny*. The rest would be relocated to Greenland.

'This can't be right. It's fake news,' protested Tamir.

'On the contrary,' said Berg, 'I can confirm that it's the gospel truth because I was there when the agreement was signed. It's actually a fantastic bargain for you people. Not one of your precious Jewish brothers and sisters will come to any harm. We are being unbelievably generous. In exchange for the release of one hundred thousand Jews into the hands of the Zionists, the remaining nine hundred thousand or so will be resettled in new homes in the wonderful island of Greenland. Your little escapade —what do you call it, *Operation Aleph Bet*?—is now redundant. I expect it has been called off by now. You just haven't been at home to receive your new orders.'

Tamir was struggling to process Berg's stream of mind-boggling announcements. If true, Berg had a point—the operation was indeed pointless. Yet something didn't add up, apart from the absurdity of the whole idea. Lunenfeld must have known this deal was in the works, in which case why hadn't he informed his agents on the ground?

'If what you say is true, then yes, I admit that I'm surprised,' said Tamir. 'And shocked. But let's suppose I believe every word you are telling me. What was the point of bringing me here?'

'That's a good question, Mr Weiss. We thought long and hard about it. The easiest course of action would have been to leave you and your beautiful wife in peace in the suburbs of London. But then we came up with a much better idea. Allow me to put a proposition to you. I think you'll find it most appealing. Believe me, it will be in your best interests to accept it. If you reject it, I fear there will be grave consequences. Not just for you but for your delightful family.'

'What sort of proposition?'

'All in good time, Mr Weiss. Meanwhile, I would like you to become intimately acquainted with my esteemed colleague Mr Rue. His interpersonal skills are legendary. As you are about to discover.'

[41]

SOFIA FORCED HERSELF TO TAKE SLOW DEEP BREATHS. TAMIR HAD warned her of the dangers of anxiety-induced hyperventilation, and the way it causes your stomach to contract and your muscles to tighten; her symptoms followed his script to the letter. *There's only one cure*, he had stressed—*stop exhaling so much carbon dioxide from your lungs. That means slowing the ventilatory cycle down as much as you can tolerate.*

Christoph Berg had agreed with remarkable alacrity to meet Sofia, aka Diana Candy. He must have known about her fraught interview with his *Destiny* point-man in London, Azad Ahmed. Did Berg know that she was working for the Mossad? Sofia guessed that he did but she also agreed with Keren's view that Berg's political instincts would trump his suspicions about the English journalist's motives. Wasn't any publicity good publicity? Yet she couldn't dispel the fear that she might be walking into a trap set for her by Berg and his coterie of gangsters. Either way, she had made her decision; it was too late to retreat now.

Having switched trains at Brussels Midi, where the Eurostar from London had arrived bang on time, Sofia conducted a final mirror check in the cramped carriage toilet. To the accompaniment of a prolonged brake squeal, she had to smile at the dazzling (if anxious) blonde bombshell peering back at her. *Come on Diana, you've done it before and you can do it again. Marilyn would have been proud of you.*

The rendezvous was convenient enough; the prestigious hotel was only a dozen metres across the road from the station. Sofia announced her presence to the receptionist, settled down in a comfortable lobby armchair, crossed her well-toned legs as provocatively as she dared, and waited. On a side table within reach, a glossy magazine, *Vogue International,* beckoned. Perfect. She picked it up and began to rifle through its pages.

'Excuse me, madam.' A young, broad-shouldered man in a dark suit was standing over her. 'Mr Berg will see you now. Please follow me.'

She nodded and forced a smile that the young man ignored. They headed for the lift. Sofia's heart was pounding. *Deep, slow breaths, Sofia,* Tamir would say. *That's it, you'll be fine, ahuvati.*

Her escort knocked lightly on the door. It opened immediately and she entered. That was all she remembered of most of the rest of the afternoon.

―――

Tamir Weiss was having a bad day. He feared it was about to get worse. His head was throbbing and he felt groggy. He'd been unconscious again for an indefinite period of time. At least he'd been moved out of that dank dungeon. He was now in a new, brighter environment that might have been a hotel room. Was that a positive development? He took nothing for granted.

Unpleasant memories of recent events intruded, one by one, on his consciousness. After Berg's revelation of the Israeli pact with *Destiny*, Berg's accomplice, Axel Rue, had bound him again to an upright wooden chair. The Belgian had deployed a thick leather belt to whack him repeatedly—and with apparent relish—across his thighs, shoulders, and even face. The purpose of this unsavoury ritual had not been, as Tamir had initially assumed, to extract information but to demonstrate the imbalance of power between Tamir and his tormentors. Further unwelcome details flashed before him like blinding firecrackers. They comprised hazy images and sensations of sustained physical assault, including a cascade of stinging blows to sensitive areas of his anatomy that generated intermittent spasms of acute pain around his pelvic region.

Tamir sought comfort from the thought that he had survived up to this point. That mild reassurance was offset by another realisation—he was again shackled to his chair with heavy duty ropes digging deep into his wrists and ankles. In the paradoxical way the human brain works, that discovery seemed to clear his mind. He had been trained for this type of abuse and knew he could endure still more severe mistreatment. More challenging were the psychological methods his abusers had deployed—the unquenched thirst, the sleep deprivation and, above all, the ceaseless threats to his family.

'Mr Weiss, we are impressed,' pronounced Berg, placing a patronising hand on Tamir's bruised shoulder. 'You have a defiant spirit and have demonstrated great physical courage. So unlike a Jew. But now we have a special little surprise for you, one that includes a young lady who is rather close to your heart.'

Berg's unnerving announcement cut through the knot of Tamir's jangling emotions. 'Axel, bring in Miss Candy. Or should I say Mrs Weiss? Don't be alarmed, my friend, she's just taking a little afternoon nap.'

Tamir stopped breathing. It took some seconds before he recognised the figure that Rue placed on the floor a few feet away from his chair. Sofia, in her journalistic disguise, was partially covered by a grubby grey blanket.

'Sofia, it's me, Tamir, can you hear me?'

The figure stirred. She was semiconscious but alive. Tamir was disinclined to express gratitude to his captors for this small mercy. Then Sofia raised her head a few inches and the blonde wig slipped, partially revealing her pale, drawn face. She managed to offer Tamir a half-smile of recognition before lapsing back into unconsciousness.

'My God, Berg, what the hell have you done to her?'

'You mean apart from administering a small dose of chloroform? Absolutely nothing. She'll be fit as a fiddle in no time. Meanwhile, you and I must talk.'

Keeping his eyes on his wife, Tamir asked, 'What is there to talk about? I thought you'd got your deal with Israel?'

'Ah yes, so we have. But that's the problem, you see. On reflection, I've concluded that we've been far too generous. We need to renegotiate it. Now, this minute.'

So that was it. The torture he had endured had been a prelude to the real business of the day. If Berg's purpose had been to soften him up, he was in for a disappointment. Except that he now held a possible trump card—Sofia.

'You've lost me, Berg. I can't negotiate on behalf of my government. You must know that.'

'True. But you can put my proposed minor amendment to them and I'm sure they will listen to you with great interest.'

'What amendment?' Tamir turned to face the Austrian.

'The little matter of the hundred thousand Jews that will become Israelis. It seems that our Palestinian friends are unhappy with it. They want that number reduced to zero. And I can see their point. Those thieving Jews will simply steal more Arab land. Those who are fit enough will be drafted into your Zionist occupation army to indulge their favourite pastime of killing innocent little Arab children.'

'That's nonsense, Berg, and you know it. In any case you've

already signed the deal. You're bound by its terms. You can't just tear it up.'

'Quite right, Mr Weiss. That's why I am offering a reasonable compromise. The hundred thousand will go to Israel as promised —just as soon as we're sure the rest have arrived and are settled in Greenland. It's just a matter of establishing an orderly sequence of events. I think that's fair, don't you?'

'Fair? You're out of your mind, Berg. There's no way your crazy scheme will work. You're talking about relocating a million people against their will. It won't work.'

'My concern exactly. That's why the relocation must be concluded first to ensure that your Israeli masters comply with the agreement. I don't trust them a centimetre and neither do the Arabs. We both know why. They're Jews after all. No offence.'

'And why should the Israeli government trust you and your Jew-hating followers to keep your side of the bargain? How will we know that the Greenland Jews will be safe and that the hundred thousand will get safely to Israel?'

Berg frowned in a mock clownish manner for a few seconds before displaying a fake, toothy grin. 'Really, Weiss, you are so cynical. You can trust me because I'm a man who keeps his word. How could you possibly doubt me?'

'Because you're an unhinged, psychopathic, lying, Nazi piece of shit, that's why.'

'Ah, such typical Jew exaggeration. Just as I expected. But come now, we're wasting time. Look, Weiss, this is no big deal. Nothing will change, just the order of events.'

Tamir shifted in his chair, trying without success to loosen the ropes binding his wrists and ankles. Berg started pacing the room.

'But why are we even having this discussion, Mr Weiss? You have zero choice about anything. Unless you agree, you and your missus won't leave this building alive. Then what use will you be to your Zionist friends? I'm doing you a favour by offering you and your pretty wife the chance to see your child again.'

'You bastard, Berg. Lay a finger on my wife or child and you'll regret it.'

'Come now, be realistic, Weiss. Look at you. You are in no position to threaten me. You can't even empty your bladder without my permission. All I'm asking is that you convey my proposal to your government with a strong personal recommendation from yourself that they accept it and, *Achtung*, we are in business. While you're doing that, we will hold on to your darling little wife as—what's the word?—surety. Just to give you a little incentive. Once your task has been completed, we can all go home to our families and everyone will be happy, *jah*? Given your predicament, it's a good solution, is it not? What do you say?'

Tamir muttered something under his breath. Berg crouched before him and pushed his face close to that of the Israeli's. 'Say again, I didn't catch that.'

'Oh, my apologies, Berg,' said Tamir, 'I should have made myself clearer. Catch this.' The violent headbutt caused a crack that echoed around the room. Berg tottered and fell to the floor. Axel Rue, who had maintained a respectful distance throughout the conversation, leapt forward and struck Tamir hard across his face. Berg's forehead was bleeding, but he managed to stand upright.

'Give him some more of your medicine, Rue. He needs to calm down. You can rough him up a bit, but don't kill him just yet. It's time for us to have some fun.'

A groan distracted the attention of all three men. Sofia was stirring again.

'Good, the girl's coming round,' said Berg with satisfaction. 'What perfect timing. After this uppity Jew-boy has suffered a tenth of the punishment he deserves, he will watch what we do to English Zionist whores.'

[42]

AS THE SCARLET-TINGED MIST BEGAN TO DISSIPATE AROUND HIM, Tamir became aware of the pulsating agony that bore deep into his cheeks and jaw. The taste of blood in his mouth was a further indication that he'd been beaten up again, but he struggled to recall any of the details of this round of abuse and perhaps that was just as well. If the worst of his ordeal had been buried in his unconscious, that was where it should remain.

Once more, Tamir forced himself to focus on his surroundings. The immediate threats to his wellbeing were Berg and Rue, who were engrossed in an animated conversation by the window. A third, somewhat rotund, elderly man who seemed familiar to Tamir was sitting on the bed conversing with a woman lying on her side, partially clothed, close to the edge of the mattress. She was conscious, but seemed unresponsive to the man's gentle interrogation. Who were these people?

Then the curtain lifted and he found his answer all too quickly.

'Oh no, Sofia, *ahuvati*,' he croaked. The woman raised her head.

'Tamir, darling, what have they done to you? You're bleeding.'

'I'll live. I've been in a couple of boxing matches with these guys, but I was at a slight disadvantage as they tied me to this chair first. What about you? Are you hurt?'

Sofia shook her head unconvincingly. Before she could reply, the obese figure rose unsteadily with the help of a walking stick and addressed them both with a Gallic bow.

'Permit me to introduce myself. I am Professor Pierre Cambon, president of *Destiny*. You may have heard of me. I must apologise for my colleagues' atrocious behaviour towards you both. Mr Weiss, I assure that your wife has not been harmed or,' he paused searching for the English word, 'defiled in any way. Fortunately, I was able to prevent such an outrage from taking place.'

'It's true, Tamir,' said Sofia, 'he arrived just in time and stopped them.'

'Good for him. But if he's such a great guy, why am I still tied to this chair?'

Cambon hobbled across the room. 'Quite right, Mr Weiss. Allow me to put that right at once.'

Rue and Berg, suddenly aware of this unwelcome turn of events, rushed in tandem towards the old man. 'Hey, professor,' shouted Berg, 'What the hell are you doing?'

Tamir's view was partially obstructed by Cambon who was fiddling with the leather bindings on his captive's wrists. He sensed the danger before he saw it.

'Watch out, professor—look behind you.'

Cambon seemed deaf to Tamir's warning. He had just released Tamir from his bondage when Berg's fist struck Cambon on the back of the neck. In slow motion, the elderly academic crumpled to the floor. Tamir, now liberated, launched himself at Berg and grabbed him by the throat. Berg thrust his knee upwards into

Tamir's groin, winding the Israeli and forcing him to release his grip. As Tamir fought for breath, he watched helplessly as Axel Rue ambled almost casually across the room to join the fray. His *sang froid* was more than justified; he was pointing a gun straight at Tamir.

'On the floor, Weiss, face down!' shouted Rue. 'Now!'

As Tamir dropped to his knees, he became aware of a faint rustling sound. Then a husky woman's voice, almost unrecognisable.

'Drop your weapon, Rue, or you're a dead man,' said Sofia.

Rue froze. 'Ah, the beautiful sleeper awakes. But you've forgotten something, madame. You are unarmed. I know that because I searched you myself. I know you are bluffing.'

'Maybe she is unarmed, but I'm not.' Cambon's baritone voice was querulous but determined. 'Mrs Weiss, step away please.'

Sofia obliged, after helping the Frenchman to his feet.

'Drop your gun, Rue,' continued Cambon, sounding more confident now.

'Ignore him, Rue,' yelled Berg, who was standing behind his thuggish employee. 'He won't shoot. He's a coward. I think he may even be a secret Jew.'

'Let's find out, shall we?' said the Belgian as he swivelled, pointing his weapon directly at the elderly professor. 'It seems you're brave enough to hold a gun, *mon ami*. You have my respect for that. But you won't dare to use it, will you? Give it to me, there's a good chap.' Rue reached out his free hand, palm upwards. Nothing happened.

Cambon and Rue stood motionless in their dangerous confrontation. The two men were face to face, each with his gun pointed at the other's chest, neither showing any sign of conceding. But the gap in credibility was a yawning one. Cambon's face was drawn, perspiring and anxious, and his gun was visibly shaking. By contrast, Rue's demeanour was calm and confident.

'Oh, stop this charade,' said Berg, stepping forward to grab Cambon's pistol. 'We're wasting time. Come on, old man, hand over your little toy, the game's up.'

The bang was deafening. Who had fired? For a few seconds, nobody moved. Then the Austrian uttered an eerie gasp and collapsed, gurgling, onto the floor. Only then did Tamir see the spreading patch of bright red blood on his chest. Within seconds, Berg lay immobile.

There was a clattering sound as Cambon dropped the smoking weapon. Tamir leapt forward and seized it. He pointed it at the Belgian bodyguard. 'You're next, Rue, unless you do exactly what I say. Drop your weapon. Now!'

Rue obliged. Sofia rushed forward and retrieved the shiny object.

'*Kol hakavod, motek,*' said Tamir as he slammed Rue into the chair that he had recently vacated. 'Great work, Sofia. Let's make sure our friend here learns what it feels like to be tied up and helpless for a few hours. Hand me that rope. Professor, thank you. You just saved our lives. I suggest you call the police immediately and explain to them that you acted in self-defence.'

Cambon, now shaking like a leaf, mopped his brow. '*Mon Dieu.* I've never killed anyone before. I didn't intend it.'

'No, you didn't,' agreed Tamir. 'Berg rushed you and you reacted instinctively, as anyone would. Just tell the police the truth. Don't worry, you have a witness to back you up. If he doesn't, he'll be the main suspect in the murder, given his background. Isn't that right, Monsieur Rue? Incidentally, they will be most interested to learn that you're wanted in Britain for the murder of a young Israeli jogger in London. How many homicide charges do you want to face? You decide.'

Rue glowered at Tamir but said nothing as the Israeli applied the finishing touches to the knots—pulled tighter around his wrists and ankles than strictly necessary—that rendered the Belgian helpless.

'Come on, *ahuvati*, let's get out of here.'

Among her many skills, Keren was an expert driver. They seemed to be eating up the kilometres in a race with unseen competitors. Sofia rested her head on Tamir's shoulder. The car was heading out of town, tearing through the featureless outer suburbs of Brussels.

'Let me tell you,' said Keren, 'I was very worried about you both. Falling into the hands of *Destiny* was a bad idea. But in the end, you did well, much better than I expected.'

'Wow,' said Tamir, 'that's a rarity. A compliment from Dr Benayoun. Thank you, boss. That's a collector's item. I'll treasure it.'

'Who says I was talking about you, Agent Weiss?'

Tamir laughed. 'I should have known. Yes, I'm proud of my wife too.'

'I should think so!' said Sofia. 'I appreciate the praise, Keren, but we got lucky. Let's not forget it was the poor old professor who came to our rescue. Who would have believed he would turn out to be a friend?'

'Cambon?' Keren spoke his name with more than a hint of contempt. 'He's no friend of ours, I assure you. But he never liked Berg and he was disgusted at the way they treated you, Sofia. But I agree, he turned out to be a *mensch* when it mattered.'

'A what?' asked Sofia.

'A *mensch*. It's a Yiddish word. It means a real gentleman,' said Keren. 'That's what Cambon is, at least when it comes to treating women with respect. And he certainly helped us when we needed him. Let's give him a bit of credit, *nachon*, Tamir?'

'I agree. And I can't see *Destiny* recovering from the loss of Berg,' said Tamir. 'He was their driving force. We'll keep an eye on them in case a new leader emerges, but they are as good as finished. Job done.'

'Maybe or maybe not,' said Keren. 'Let's not get too carried away. Mr Ahmed may try to take over and keep the organisation going. Though he's been tainted by the Charity Commission's investigation that hasn't been completed after several months. That's a bad sign for the charity being scrutinised. But the death of *Destiny*'s leader has dealt them a severe blow, there's no doubt about that.'

'What happens now?' asked Sofia. 'Where are we going?'

'To a safe house just outside of the city. Yes, I know, another one. But only for a few hours. First, we have to get you two cleaned up, fed and watered and looking human again. At the moment you both look like something out of a zombie horror movie.'

'Then what—back to dear old London town?'

'Eventually, yes. But before that we have to take a four-hour flight from Brussels airport and stop off somewhere. Don't ask for more details because I won't tell you. But I think you will get quite a surprise. Don't look so worried—it's a pleasant one this time.'

Sofia wasn't worried about the trip. She was concerned about weightier matters—the future of the Weiss family and the additional responsibilities that were coming their way.

She patted her lower abdomen as if to reassure the tiny bunch of cells that would soon enough make their presence felt.

[43]

MOSHE LUNENFELD HAD DEALT WITH MANY ISRAELI PRIME ministers. All had strengths and weaknesses. None had betrayed their country. Until this one.

He reread the status report from European operations commander, Dr Keren Benayoun. She had confirmed his worst fears. The *Destiny* leadership had struck an agreement with his prime minister, behind his back and without seeking the approval, even in principle, of his cabinet colleagues, let alone the Knesset. The deal comprised a terrible bargain whereby nine out of ten European Jews would be abandoned to the mercy of the extremist Christoph Berg while the remaining hundred thousand would be granted safe passage to Israel. As if that weren't shocking enough, Keren had just informed her boss that Berg had reneged on even that tawdry agreement and had threatened to murder the Weiss couple unless the PM agreed to rewrite its terms. What was Berg's key demand? That the release of the hundred thousand Jews destined for Israel would be delayed until the Greenland transports had been completed. That would expose the entire Jewish population of Europe to whatever fate Berg decreed for them.

Through a stroke of luck—with a little help from the Mossad—the *Destiny* leadership had turned on itself; Berg was dead and Cambon had resigned. In the short-term, at least, *Destiny* was finished. And so was Israeli prime minister Yoav Adar.

Lunenfeld was thankful that he didn't have to break the news to Adar himself. Volkov, the former defence minister (and now minister without portfolio) had called an emergency meeting of the cabinet—as he was permitted to do under government guidelines—and would give the floor to the Mossad director who would read a brief statement and then issue an even briefer order.

Yallah, let's get this over, he exhorted himself.

Sofia was riveted to the giant TV screen in their five-star hotel room. To her English eyes, the Israeli media in overdrive was a wondrous sight even if she could barely understand a word—Tamir did his best to translate for her. All the radio and TV stations interrupted their schedules to announce the dramatic news: the prime minister had resigned and was under arrest. Confusion reigned as to which had come first, the arrest or the resignation, but the end result was the same. The country's elected leader had gone. Yoav Adar was led away from the cabinet office in handcuffs under suspicion of breaking multiple laws—leaking confidential government decisions, negotiating in secret with Israel's enemies, and jeopardising the lives of up to a million European Jews. The levers of power had been passed, for the second time in a week, to Avraham Sassoon, the deputy prime minister, pending the dissolution of the Knesset and a snap general election.

At his arraignment, Adar's final public statement to the Israeli people was an anaemic affair: *I acted in good faith out of a desire to achieve the best possible outcome for Europe's Jews, but I recognised, in retrospect, that I may have made an error of judgement for which I apologise.* An endless stream of reporters and analysts issued their far harsher and near-unanimous verdict: Adar was a traitor. The Israeli public, long used to political scandals, was stunned. How could this have happened? Why had the democratic system failed so dismally? Was Adar aided by accomplices? How had the Mossad uncovered the plot? What would happen to Europe's Jews now, and how many would head for Israel? All of these questions were answered in the customary feverish but speculative style—in the near-complete absence of hard evidence—by excited commentators across the political spectrum.

By now Tamir was bored with the story. He knew that Israel's pre-eminence as the lead item in the international media wouldn't last more than a few days. The truth was unlikely to emerge in the short-term and foreign correspondents based in the country were as baffled as their Israeli colleagues. All the media had identified the villains of the story—Adar and *Destiny*. But they struggled to untangle the complex and ultimately successful machinations of the two central whistle-blowers—the Mossad director and the former defence minister. Both had declined to comment. Eventually the cacophony subsided and the media circus packed its bags to head off in pursuit of the next front-page story.

Even in frenetic Israel, headlines changed and life moved on. The Adar Affair, as it became known, was just another colourful footnote in Israel's endless political drama over which historians of the future would argue, analyse and hypothesise without ever reaching a definitive conclusion about the true sequence of events. For now, editors were inclined to dump the story in the 'too difficult' drawer.

But for one young couple—Tamir and Sofia Weiss—the story was far from over.

When Keren announced her 'surprise' to the Weisses following their ordeal in Brussels, Sofia had a feeling they were headed for Tel Aviv. That was fine by her, provided it was a couple of days' recuperation—and presumably a session or two of intensive interrogation at Mossad HQ—at most. What she hadn't realised was that Keren had arranged for Luisa to drop off little Clara at the airport to join her parents. The reunion had been emotional. Clara displayed her usual resilience, expressing no hint of resentment or confusion at the unexpected reappearance of her parents.

Sofia was so overjoyed at the reconstitution of her family that she didn't care how long the diversion to Israel lasted—a week, a month, a year—it mattered little. The Weisses were whole again and everything else would fall into place. Including a new addition to the family that would arrive, Sofia estimated, around seven months later. She hadn't told Tamir her news yet and he hadn't noticed her changing shape. But delaying the inevitable wasn't an option. All she had to do was find the right moment...

Otherwise, everything turned out even better than expected. Keren completed their formal debriefing at the poolside of their luxury hotel in an hour and left them in peace thereafter. After three days of pampering, Tamir proposed that they relocate to his small flat in Tel Aviv's chic Yemenite quarter where they could rehearse being a normal family again in preparation for their ultimate return to London. 'We're not tourists in this country, after all, are we, *ahuvati*? Let's enjoy the authentic Tel Aviv lifestyle for a while.'

Sofia didn't argue. She settled easily into Tamir's comfortable pad that was a mere ten-minute stroll to the nearest beach. She was in no hurry to reacquaint herself with the grey skies of London and neither was Clara, whose young skin had turned a gorgeous hue of golden brown. All three were happy and Sofia saw no reason to disrupt their hard-earned tranquillity. This idyllic phase of their lives had been bestowed on them like a gift from the gods and she was determined to savour every moment.

[44]

THREE WEEKS HAD ELAPSED SINCE THEIR BRUSSELS TRAUMA. After their debriefing session with Keren, the Weisses were told they were free to go wherever they wished—for a while. Unlike Sofia, Tamir was a paid Mossad employee after all. He was bound to receive new orders sooner or later.

They had just dropped off Clara at her summer camp where her Hebrew was progressing by leaps and bounds. Sitting in a shady spot at an outside table of their favourite café in Dizengoff Street, Tamir leaned forward and placed both hands on his wife's forearm. That was an uncharacteristic gesture. Sofia knew that something was up.

'You look stressed, Tamir. What's wrong?'

'Nothing's wrong but yes, you're right, I am stressed. I'm not sure I should tell you, but I heard something that's really freaking me out. From Keren.'

Sofia no longer winced at the mention of the name since the psychiatrist had reunited their small family. 'I suppose you mean something that involves your next task?'

'I wasn't going to mention it to you, *ahuvati*. But I think that was a mistake.'

'You bet it was. Tell me about it now and I'll give you my opinion, if you want it.'

'Of course, I want it.' Tamir's eyes followed a passing motorised scooter mounted by a *haredi* rabbi. 'We think *Destiny* may be planning a big operation. I mean a mega-operation. To prove they're still in business after Berg's death.'

'What kind of operation?'

'An attack of some kind. I don't know the details—terrorism, I suppose.'

'You mean against Israeli targets? Where?'

'Not just Israelis. Jews. In Paris, Berlin and London—maybe other places too. Keren didn't divulge the details. Cities with big Jewish communities. Where Jews congregate in synagogues or community centres or bar mitzvah parties—that sort of thing.'

'Wow. This is important, Tamir. It sounds like *Destiny* isn't finished yet. Presumably our friend Azad Ahmed is involved. When did Keren tell you this?'

'About a week ago. Maybe ten days.'

'Why on earth didn't mention this to me before now?' Sofia's eyes flashed anger at her husband.

'Because I was afraid it would disrupt our plans to go back to England. As I said, it was a mistake, I'm sorry. I should have said something earlier, a*huvati.*'

'Yes, you should. Jesus, Tamir, this changes everything.'

Tamir knew how to read Sofia's ever-changing facial expressions. This one signalled an impending announcement of substance that could cause friction. He braced himself.

'Tamir, darling, let's not rush back to London. I have another idea.'

'We can live anywhere you like, *ahuvati*. I did a lot of thinking while we lounged by that pool. And I owe you, big time. You got me out of that Belgian hellhole. I was lucky to avoid being hospitalised—or worse.'

'Hey, you repaid that debt—and more—when you brought me on board your *Destiny* project. That means we're quits. Now we have to decide where we're going to live.'

'Where would you like to live? London, I suppose?'

'I always think of London as home. But let's stay in Israel for a while, at least. Clara is so happy here.'

'If that's what you want, I'll be delighted. But Israel isn't the safest place in the world right now. If the Iranians launch a major attack on Tel Aviv...'

'Is that likely? Or have you heard something?'

Tamir didn't answer. Sofia had learned how to interpret those silences.

'God, I sometimes hate this bloody country! Is there no end to the violence here? All right, here's a suggestion. We'll compromise. Let's get out of Tel Aviv. We could go south to the Negev. What's the name of that city—Beer Sheva? It must be safer there, surely?'

'Probably, though not necessarily. It's all relative. But we can move there if that's what you want. Let me talk to Keren first. She has to know about our change of plan.'

―――

The early morning train from Tel Aviv's Savidor station to Beer Sheva was surprisingly fast and comfortable. Most of the passengers were young exhausted soldiers heading back to their bases after a brief weekend at home. Sofia had never become reconciled to the ubiquitous sight of these weapon-bearing teenagers but she had come to recognise the necessity for the security of the most militarily vulnerable country on earth.

Over the course of an hour, Sofia had watched the landscape changing colour from green to yellow to brown. The bleak, undulating desert scenery was at first alarming then awe-inspiring and finally soothing—it reminded her of the work of a Scottish artist called Bet Low whom she'd discovered in a tiny art gallery in Glasgow—but it lapsed into a dusty monotone that was too soporific for her taste. The capital city of the Negev was another matter. Sprawling low-rise housing quickly gave way to a forest of dizzyingly high commercial towers that wouldn't have looked out of place in Manhattan or Melbourne. The jarring contrast between this concrete extravaganza and her child's eye fantasy of a little biblical village was startling. Could she make her home in this alien habitat?

They alighted at Beer Sheva's university station and climbed into a taxi. Tamir gave the driver an address. After about thirty seconds, Sofia spotted a comical statue in the middle of a roundabout; a stout little man standing on his head.

'How odd. Who is that? Does he have some sort of religious significance?'

'In a way it does, I suppose. That's Israel's first prime minister, David Ben Gurion—the university of the Negev that you can see all around you is named after him. In his later years he dabbled in Buddhism and practised yoga. He used to spend hours meditating upside down on the Tel Aviv beach.'

Fifteen minutes later they were in a pretty, verdant suburb laid out in a symmetrical grid pattern of immaculately manicured streets lined with detached red-roofed cottages.

Sofia was intrigued. 'What is this place? It looks quite wealthy.'

'There is quite a bit of money here but it's also where many academics and artists live. I think you'll like it here. It's a beautiful little oasis in the desert. Welcome to Omer.'

Sofia appeared underwhelmed at the prospect.

'What's wrong, *ahuvati*? I can tell something's bothering you.'

'Tamir, I have to be honest with you. This is no good. I don't think I can live here.'

'What do you mean? You haven't even given it a chance.'

They had arrived. The taxi unloaded them at a small villa with a wooden front gate festooned with bougainvillea. Beyond the entrance lay a lawn and flowerbeds replete with seasonal flowers and plants.

The interior didn't disappoint. The couple deposited their luggage in the hallway and slumped into a well-upholstered sofa in the salon. Sofia shook her head in paradoxical approval of the house and its stunning view of the desert. Tamir took his wife's hand into his own. 'Talk to me, Sofia.'

'It's lovely. It's not the location, it's not the desert and it's not Israel. I just don't want to be alone in this place.' *Tell him now.* The thing is, Tamir, I have news for you. I'm pregnant.'

Tamir was dumbstruck, but only for about five seconds. He took her in his arms kissed her on the forehead. 'Well that's wonderful, *ahuvati*. When did you find out?'

'A few weeks ago. I didn't want to tell you till I'd had time to think. And I've made a decision. I want to have this baby in Tel Aviv, not out here in the sticks. Then we can move to the desert. I know I'm being a nuisance and should have told you all this ages ago. Please don't try to talk me out of it. It's not up for discussion. We have to go back. Now.'

Seven months later, the Weiss family had cause to celebrate another great milestone.

'*Mazal tov abba ve-imah. Yesh lachem tinok bari.*'

'What did the nurse just say, Tamir? Is the baby OK?'

'The baby is fine, *ahuvati*. She said congratulations to mum and dad, you have a healthy baby boy.'

'I knew it would be a boy. He was kicking me like a maniac these last few weeks.'

'Maybe he'll be a footballer,' said Tamir with a smile. 'He'll play for Israel and we'll sure need him.'

'Or England!' exclaimed Sofia. 'We'll need him too, I promise you. You know what? Let him decide.'

Twenty-four hours later they were on their way to their new desert home (courtesy of the Israeli government)—this time in kibbutz Sde Boker and planning baby Leo's *brit milah*—the circumcision ceremony that Sofia had insisted on, to Tamir's bemusement.

The kibbutz was a stunning oasis of greenery and multicoloured flora in the most desolate pale-brown landscape Sofia had ever seen. Its tranquillity was appealing but how could they bring up a family in this oven-baked desert environment? The nearest decent-sized town was an hour away and that was no metropolis. Suddenly Hampstead seemed a distant planet and all the more alluring for it.

'This was your idea, remember?' Tamir reminded her. 'You wanted to take the kids well away from Tel Aviv or London or anywhere else that Iranians or neo-Nazis might decide to vaporise.'

'I must have been off my head. Though I suppose that's preferable to being dead.'

'Can I make a suggestion, *ahuvati*? Let's give it six months. If we're all still alive and well by then, let's review. If you're still uncomfortable here, we can move. Deal?'

'Deal. And I'll hold you to it, trust me.'

'Believe me, *motek*, I do. I expect no less. In the meantime, I have to pack. I have a job to do in London. It's connected to this *Destiny* plot to attack Jewish targets in Europe.'

Sofia couldn't conceal her disappointment 'Shit! I can't believe *Destiny* hasn't disintegrated by now. How long will you be away?'

'A week, maybe less.'

'Would it be pointless asking what the job is?'

'Yes, *motek*. Not because I'm keeping it a secret but because I don't know what it is myself. I'll get my orders when I arrive.'

'From Keren, you mean?'

'You know how it is. She's my commanding officer after all.'

'Maybe we'll come with you.'

'No, I don't want you in London, at least until this latest *Destiny* threat is over. I'll go on my own and get back as soon as I can. And our new baby needs you here, after his little operation the other day.'

'Be careful, Tamir. After all we've been through, it would be such a waste to throw it away now.'

[45]

AZAD AHMED MP WAS A WORRIED MAN. FOLLOWING THE DEATH of Berg (whom he'd never much liked anyway) and the resignation of Cambon (whom he despised for his intellectualism), he'd floated on a cloud of euphoria. That was because there had been no obvious successor as leader of *Destiny*—other than his good self. He would have a heaven-sent opportunity to realise the dream he had nurtured since boyhood—the revival of the caliphate, first across Europe and Asia and then worldwide. He couldn't wait to get started on what would be the greatest project of his life. He would be hailed as a hero across the Islamic world, including both Iran and Saudi Arabia. And he would be credited with healing the Sunni-Shia divide that had blighted Islam for far too long.

Life was so unfair. Through no fault of his own, events had conspired against him and both those countries—as well as the devious Zionists—were causing him a headache. The crisis in *Destiny* had annoyed the Saudis and they had given him notice that their support for the organisation was 'under review.' Worse, his connection to the Kingdom's secret service, the General Intelligence Presidency, had been leaked to the Arab press (deliberately?) and the Iranians were displeased, to put it mildly. He would have to be patient or his dreams would turn to dust. Or so he had believed. Suddenly he had a new priority, one that trumped all else—to stay alive.

When he got the call from a local imam (whom he knew vaguely) requesting a meeting to discuss a charitable campaign that the *Orb of Islam* was about to launch, he offered a couple of dates around a fortnight hence. When the imam insisted that the matter was urgent and that they would have to meet within days rather than weeks, Ahmed was thrown into a panic. The imam was known to be close to the Saudi royal family and was rumoured to be an active member of his country's secret service. That meant he was also more than likely under constant Iranian surveillance. He couldn't risk Iranian wrath at such a sensitive time for his political career. But the imam was persistent and the appointment was made. That turned out to be a near-fatal error.

Within two hours of that conversation, a text message arrived from an unknown source offering to arrange a 'substantial donation to the *Orb of Islam* subject to the closure of the Charity Commission investigation.' Ahmed expressed his appreciation and added an assurance that the *Orb* would shortly be cleared by the Commission. But he smelt a rodent when a further SMS arrived within minutes. The second message was ominous. It indicated that the donor would like to visit the NGO's offices in person and meet Ahmed alone 'for a confidential discussion.' It also said that he should expect his visitor two days hence in the late afternoon when he would receive his well-earned reward. The double meaning was not lost on Ahmed. This kind of gallows humour was a hallmark of the dreaded Islamic Revolutionary Guard Corps.

As he stared at his phone, he broke out in a cold sweat. The IRGC were unforgiving of double agents, and the Saudis were equally vengeful. The Charity Commission review was piling on additional pressure that he could do without. If the *Orb*'s funds were frozen, both countries would demand a refund of their substantial donations. And both would be nervous that the MP's knowledge of the money trail could help the UK counterterrorism agency trace it all the way back to Tehran and Riyadh, respectively. That would be sufficient reason for both countries to deploy an execution squad to south London. As the Saudi secret service had been badly burned by the Khashoggi affair, they were unlikely to strike first. The immediate threat would come from the mullahs.

Ahmed was not a sensitive man except when his own welfare was threatened. This was such a time. He was a politician, not a fighter. Would the Saudis save him from an IRGC killer? Their track record was poor; once they decided an asset was of little further value to them, it would be tossed on the scrapheap. No, they would be unlikely to concern themselves with his safety and might even have tipped off the Iranians that he had been covertly working for the Kingdom. He was trapped between two equal and opposite forces of unbridled brutality. Who else would help him in his hour of desperate need? That was the moment he found himself thinking the unthinkable.

He slipped his hand into his inside jacket pocket and pulled out the card that the blonde bombshell journalist had given him. He read the words *Diana Candy* and smiled. He had been preoccupied by that woman ever since her whirlwind visit to his office —even after he had learned from his Destiny colleagues that she was a Mossad agent who had probably wished him harm. Yet here was a delicious irony—the Zionists were the only people who would be motivated to save his skin as they were currently in the throes of attempting to improve their on-off relations with Riyadh. If they were to spirit him out of London to safety, that would elevate them is Saudi eyes perhaps cement relations between Israel and the Kingdom. Could this wheeze work? It would be a huge risk, but he had run out of options. He dialled her number.

Tamir had just settled himself down in a small café in Kennington Road—a mere ten minutes' walk from his quarry in Sancroft Street—when his phone rang. It was Sofia and she was using the doubly encrypted network. This would be a business call.

'You won't believe who just called me, Tamir.'

'Try me, *ahuvati*.'

'Mr Ahmed. Remember I gave him my card? The fake journalist, Diana? It turns out he knows who I am and who I was working for.'

'I'm sorry to hear that but I'm not surprised. What did he want?'

'This sounds weird, I know, but he wants our help. He's in acute danger from the IRGC and he says only Israel can save him.'

'That's rich coming from one of Europe's most prominent antisemites. It sounds like a trap to me.'

'Wait, there's more. He said that if we help him, he'll help us.'

'Meaning what exactly?'

'Meaning internationally. Diplomatically, I suppose. He said he could strengthen links between Israel and the most important Arab state.'

Tamir whistled. 'That's a big claim. He's talking about the Kingdom. How does he think he can do that?'

'Because he's their man in Europe.'

'Say that again?'

'Oh, wake up, darling. Because he's been working for the Saudis. He's GIP's man in *Destiny*. Or was. Now that *Destiny* has gone belly up, they've told him to get out of London before the Iranians get to him.'

'Why should the Saudis care any more about him than the Iranians?'

'Because they've invested a ton of money in his so-called charity and they want it back. They don't have agents in London since the Khashoggi affair, but they know that we do. If we rescue Ahmed and smuggle him out of the UK, they'll show their gratitude to the Jewish state in a tangible way—not just a cold peace treaty along Egyptian lines but trade, tourism, technology, education. The works. He used those actual words. This is it, Tamir. I hooked Ahmed, remember? Now it's paying off for us, big time. This could pave the way for a big breakthrough for Israel's relationship with the Arab and Muslim world. I know it seems weird, but I think we'd be mad not to help him.'

'I'm not sure that we can. I don't have the authority to set the wheels in motion.'

'You will soon.'

'What do you mean?'

'I've just spoken to Keren and she agrees. She's already setting those wheels in motion. Mossad HQ are checking the Saudi offer to ensure it's genuine. If it is, you'll get the authority you need in a matter of hours.'

When Keren Benayoun received the call from Sofia, she was both pleased and alarmed. The pleasure was twofold—that the young Englishwoman had set aside her fears and jealousy of the older woman whom she had once regarded as a threat to her marriage, and that she was behaving at last as a true Mossadnik whose prime responsibility was the welfare of Israel. The alarm arose from the professional dilemma that Keren faced. Sofia's message conveyed more than a cry for help from a dangerous fanatic whom the agency had identified as a danger to the Jewish people; it demanded rapid action that could cause reverberations, good and bad, for the agency, Keren's career, and the international standing of Israel.

Keren knew she should get rapid clearance from her boss once the agency had confirmed the authenticity of the Saudi offer, but she feared that Lunenfeld would wish to tread carefully and consult with his political masters. All that would take time—especially given Israel's non-functioning government in the wake of the Adar affair—and time wasn't a resource Keren had the luxury of enjoying. No, involving Lunenfeld at this stage wasn't an option. This was an emergency. To deal with it, she would have to act on her own initiative and pray that the train of events she was about to trigger would yield success rather than disaster.

She made two quick calls. The first was to Agent Weiss, modifying the orders he'd received just a few days earlier. The second was to a governmental contact she rarely used but trusted implicitly. He was located in a mundane-looking building in central Jerusalem, the Ministry of Foreign Affairs, A Section. The A stood for Arab Affairs.

For the first time in his life, Azad Ahmed MP was petrified. With the implosion of *Destiny*, the mantle of leadership—his rightful inheritance in his eyes—had been snatched from his grasp. Worse, the vision of the global caliphate had turned to dust. The opportunity to resurrect the project, in accordance with the will of Allah, would be unlikely to arise again for a generation. The result was that his conservative Saudi backers had pulled the plug on their financial support for the *Orb*—and that, in turn, had caused the GIP to renege on their promise to ensure his security on foreign soil. Their half-hearted promise to grant him political asylum in Riyadh in exchange for a hefty cash refund had been a non-starter given two unfortunate realities: most of the Saudi donations to the *Orb* had been transferred to the private account of the late Christoph Berg, and London had become a death trap from which he had no practical means of escape. GIP had abandoned their London operation and withdrawn all the agents following Saudi Arabia's rift with the UK in the wake of the Khashoggi fiasco. That left the field open for the Kingdom's arch rival for the leadership of the world's Muslims—the Islamic Republic of Iran—to step in and deliver their judgement on Ahmed's performance, a judgement that the MP understood was near-certain to be terminal.

After packing his wife and children off to longsuffering relatives in Pakistan, Ahmed prepared to fight for his life. It was a fight he was bound to lose—unless the unlikeliest of saviours were to rescue him. His call to Ms Candy, the beautiful young English journalist whom the late Christoph Berg had (on a tip-off from an undisclosed source) exposed as an agent of Mossad, had not gone well. After several hours of silence, she had sent him a text message with a curt instruction: *Stay in your office and wait.* Wait for what? For his execution? That must now be imminent. He had little doubt that the Mossad wanted him dead as he was the most likely next political leader of radical Islam in Europe. But in offering to act as the catalyst for an Israeli-Saudi peace pact, the Israelis would surely be tempted to give the roulette wheel a spin. If they didn't, he was facing his final hours.

Having sent his puzzled secretary home early, he was now alone in the building and tried to focus on his overriding priority —survival. Never in his life had he imagined that he would one day have to face such an existential threat. He was woefully ill-prepared to handle it. Why had he paid so little attention to his personal security? Too late, that was water under the bridge; he had to make the best of his limited skills in that department. He rushed from floor to floor in a frantic search for potential weak spots that an unwelcome visitor might exploit to gain access. He bolted the two entrances to the building and shuttered all the windows, grabbed a bottle of mineral water from the fridge, and headed back upstairs to his top-floor office.

He wandered over to his office window and surveyed the scene. The sun was setting behind a thick cloud that cast an ominous blood-red streak across the early evening London skyline. It would soon be nightfall and he would be more vulnerable than ever. He could try to make a run for it, but London was swarming with IRGC agents and he was bound to be spotted. With no sign of a last-minute Mossad intervention, there was only one course of action left to him—to pray for divine mercy.

He recalled that GIP, the Saudi intelligence agency, had offered him a weapon shortly after his recruitment—he had refused. How could he have been so pig-headed? If he had just swallowed his scruples, he would be holding a gun in his hand right now. That would at least have given him the option of suicide. Too late, he would have to prepare to use his bare fists against a putative Iranian murderer. Exhausted from a succession of sleepless nights and the chronic anxiety that recent events had generated, he slumped into his leatherbound swivel chair. Within minutes, he had dozed off.

Half an hour later, he awoke with a start. What had disturbed him? The office was dark and silent. He picked up his phone and hauled himself to his feet. Then he froze. He could hear footsteps in the corridor outside his office. Their soft tread was almost drowned out by the thumping of his chest. He had locked down the entire building including his office door, but he knew it was hardly likely to hinder a trained assassin for long.

The blood drained from his face and the room began to spin. It was over. His legs gave way and he crumpled to the floor, shaking from head to foot, to await the imminent launch of his journey to meet his maker.

―――

While Azad Ahmed was suffering his nervous breakdown, agent Tamir Weiss was just a few metres away, crouching among the bushes of a mini-park across the road. His cramped posture was painful, but Tamir hadn't joined the Mossad to indulge his creature comforts. His operational objective, as conveyed to him by Keren, and for reasons that she had not explained, was to keep the three-storey Lambeth office block that housed the *Orb of Islam* under close surveillance and take 'any necessary action' to protect the charity's founder and driving force. As the sun began to set, he flipped the switch on his binoculars to night-vision mode; they penetrated with ease the enveloping gloom of the London dusk.

An hour earlier, he had caught sight of a profile he recognised —that of Azad Ahmed MP—near a top floor window. He was the only member of the charity's staff left in the building and appeared, on the scant available evidence, to be in a state of extreme agitation. That was hardly a surprise given the gravity of his plight. The Iranians were coming for him and the MP knew it. Having sent out a distress call via Sofia (aka Diana Candy) to his former enemy, the Mossad, Ahmed must have been wondering whether and how the Israelis would try to save him and, if they did, what their chances of success were. As the gloom descended on Lambeth, Tamir was pondering the same questions when he became aware of a third party in his field of vision.

About fifteen minutes earlier, Tamir had spotted a figure in a black hooded jacket wandering along Sancroft Street towards Kennington Road and had decided he was just a local teenager waiting to meet his friends. He had ignored him. Bad mistake. Now that the same character was loitering directly in front of

Ahmed's building, the Israeli decided he'd better pay him much closer attention. The youth was scanning his environment with the practised wariness of a professional burglar. Or spy. Or killer.

Tamir was only twenty metres away and well concealed in the shadows, but he reflexively held his breath, sensing that some sort of action was about to kick off. His instinctive awareness of impending danger was, as always, sound. The hooded man had extracted an implement from the folds of his clothing and was using it to prise open the door that would lead him, within seconds, to the beleaguered MP. A high-pitched whine produced by an electronic drill, Tamir presumed, was followed seconds later by sharp metallic clunk. That was the signal Tamir had awaited. It was time to move.

He donned his black woollen balaclava, checked that his revolver was ready to fire, and sprinted across the road. When he reached the entrance, the intruder was already inside, unaware that he was being followed. Tamir pushed against the open door, slipped into the hallway and listened hard. The tell-tale creaking of the wooden stairs to the upper floors revealed the approximate location of the visitor, but then stopped. The presumptive killer had reached his destination on the top floor and must have paused outside Ahmed's office. Two seconds later, an explosive crashing sound was followed by shouting. Tamir leapt up the staircase, gun in hand, and rushed towards the source of the mayhem at the end of the landing. A door had been smashed open and was hanging askew on its hinges. Inside the room, Tamir witnessed a pitiful sight.

Ahmed was on his knees, wailing and begging for his life. The hooded man, oblivious to his victim's pleas, was in the process of fitting a silencer to a long-barrelled pistol when Ahmed fell silent, his gaze now transfixed on this second armed interloper. The assassin whirled round and pointed his weapon directly at Tamir, who was the first to react. Two shots resonated and the

Iranian dropped to the floor, blood seeping from the corner of his mouth. Tamir moved with extreme caution towards the body and kicked the weapon away from its late owner. He pulled off his balaclava and looked at the trembling politician who appeared to be praying.

'Mr Ahmed, are you all right?'

'*Allahu Akbar*, yes, yes. I am more than all right, I am alive. Thanks to you, sir. You are from the Mossad, I assume? Ms Candy sent you?'

Tamir declined to answer that question. As he checked Ahmed for any sign of injury, he said, 'I am following specific orders from my superiors. I'll explain the details to you later. First, we have to get rid of this body and get out of this place without attracting too much attention. That could be difficult as it's more than likely that someone in the neighbourhood has heard those gunshots. The London police have an armed response unit just around the corner. And the Iranians will want to know what has happened to their man. We have very little time. Please listen carefully to my instructions and follow them to the letter. Both of our lives may depend on it. Mr Ahmed, are you with me?'

Mr Ahmed wasn't. He had passed clean out.

[46]

THE NEW ISRAELI PRIME MINISTER, ARKADY VOLKOV, HAD MANY talents. Communicating with world's mass media was not one of them. But he knew he had no option—he had to face them. The future of Israel depended on him giving, at a minimum, a competent performance.

When news broke of the arrest of his disgraced predecessor, Yoav Adar, the chattering classes both in Israel and abroad worked themselves into a collective frenzy. As always, that response had consequences, and most of them were negative. Across the globe, anti-Israel demonstrators were exploiting the opportunity to demand sanctions against the country that—in their minds—had perpetrated a war crime by signing the short-lived agreement with *Destiny*. The UN General Assembly was gearing up to issue a new raft of condemnations of Israel that would, as usual, gain the automatic support of the Arab League and assorted dictatorships.

Against this background of turmoil in the Middle East, London's Metropolitan Police were investigating an apparently unrelated event—the sudden disappearance of a prominent personality of Asian heritage, a hard-left politician suspected of having links with Islamic fundamentalists. Azad Ahmed MP had vanished from the face of the earth.

Nothing excites the great British public more than a juicy political scandal. When news of the disappearance of the politician hit the headlines, editors rushed to judgement, competing with each other in a race to promote the most outlandish conspiracy theories. Not since the Stonehouse affair of 1974, when a Labour MP tried to fake his own death, were the media so engulfed in such a ferment of speculation and hysteria. The Israeli embassy in London monitored the outpouring of bizarre hypotheses and noted a curious fact: not one commentator alluded either to Ahmed's antisemitism or to *Destiny*, not to mention the possible role of a foreign intelligence service in his disappearance. That blind spot suited Mossad—and, by extension, their political masters in Jerusalem—to a tee. To the consternation of his party colleagues, the British media quickly lost interest in Ahmed's fate. Persistent journalistic questioning of the Met proved unproductive. An urgent request under the Freedom of Information Act revealed that the first page of the Ahmed police file was headed with three words: *Missing Presumed Dead*.

The local coroner's verdict would remain an open one for the foreseeable future for a good reason: a body was never found.

Tamir met Keren for his debriefing on the steps of St Paul's Cathedral. It was a popular spot for London office workers to grab a snack on their lunch break and unload onto colleagues or acquaintances a litany of complaints about their bosses. The two

Israelis, merging seamlessly with the crowd, were preoccupied with less mundane matters.

Keren was in a business-like mood. 'You've done your job well, Tamir, and Lunenfeld is delighted. He sends his congratulations. But he wants more data. A lot more. For a start, what exactly happened to Ahmed?'

'I'd rather not go into details. I'm still coming to terms with the whole thing myself.'

'What are you talking about? You're still coming to terms with it, are you? Listen, I have news for you, young man. That's not our way. You're an employee of the agency. That's a fact you have to come to terms with this minute. We have no secrets from each other and you know it.'

'I promise I'll write my report very soon. Both you and Lunenfeld will get the whole story. Just give me a little breathing space, please. I'm asking you as a friend, not my commanding officer. And as a psychiatrist.'

'Meaning what? Are you saying you have PTSD?'

'I don't have enough knowledge of psychology to put a label on it. That's your area of expertise, isn't it? All I know is that I can't talk about it right now. Sorry.'

'Now listen carefully, Weiss. When you joined the agency, you knew you'd be faced with difficult and even traumatic situations. But this is unprofessional behaviour. We need to know the facts before we can evaluate the status of this operation. And you are the only one who has them. So do your job and write that report, even as a draft, if not today, then tomorrow. We'll sort out your emotions later. This is not up for discussion. Got that?'

Tamir didn't reply—it wouldn't have mattered anyway. Keren had made the position clear. And she wasn't finished with her recalcitrant agent. 'Right, this meeting is over. We'll meet here again in forty-eight hours. You will give me your report then—or you will be relieved of your duties. That's an order.'

Director Lunenfeld could scarcely believe his eyes. In his long years of service to Mossad, he had never encountered a scenario as extraordinary as this one. Recent events in London had demonstrated the prowess of the agency's finest but the brief operational report he held in his hands, written by his most resourceful agent Tamir Weiss, along with a brief commentary by Dr Benayoun, defied gravity. A high-profile English politician had, according to British official sources, vanished into thin air without leaving the slightest clue as to his fate. The nature of that fate, and how it had been inflicted, was the subject of the text in which Lunenfeld was now immersed.

When he reached the final sentence, he poured himself a glass of mineral water, flipped back the pages to the beginning and started to read the astonishing document again.

Field Report
by
Agent E19-TW

Mission Aim: To decapitate the Transnational European Political Movement *Destiny,* thereby rendering it ineffective.

Mission Objective: To neutralise, by whatever means necessary, current *Destiny* Director Azad Ahmed, MP, London, UK.

Mission Method: I travelled to London where the Target was easily located in his office. He was working alone, and so I presented to him, under duress, the limited options available to him. He offered no resistance.

Here is the verbatim account of the 'offer' I presented to him:
You have a choice Mr Ahmed. Either you forfeit your life now or you flee, under my supervision, to a major Islamic country of my choosing that will grant you asylum, a new identity, citizenship, safe lodgings, and employment. This latter course may be available to you on the clear understanding that you will fulfil two conditions: 1. That you will not, under any circumstances, return to any country on the continent of Europe for the remainder of your natural life; 2. That you will wear an electronic tag (supplied with charger) that we will provide. You will henceforth wear this tag on your person on a permanent basis.

Mission Outcome: The Target accepted the latter course (with reservations) and his exit from the UK was arranged within twelve hours. The country in question is a major Islamic power in the Middle East with whom the State of Israel has minimal relations but with whom high-level inter-governmental relations are generally held to be good. Covert informal cooperation between branches of the two countries' security services is believed to be ongoing (to be confirmed). I have contacted, via the agency, our assets in that country who have verified the Target's arrival and settlement in the capital, a large metropolitan centre. HQ in TA will confirm that the electronic tag is functioning efficiently and locatable 24/7.

Conclusion: The mission aim and objective have both been successfully fulfilled.

Follow-up: The removal of the current acting head of *Destiny* is no guarantee that a substitute leader will not be appointed. It appears, however, that there is no obvious successor. I therefore recommend careful ongoing monitoring of a) Mr Ahmed's whereabouts and status, and; b) the activities (if any) of activists associated with *Destiny*, with a view to ensuring that the organisation (or any successor entity) will never again pose a threat to the wellbeing of the Jews of Europe and/or the State of Israel.

Signed: Agent Tamir Weiss
Countersigned: Operations Commanding Officer for Europe Keren Benayoun

Lunenfeld was perplexed. The report didn't add up—numerous internal contradictions rendered the whole narrative suspect. On the one hand, the Weiss couple and Benayoun had shown an extraordinary degree of competence and creativity in achieving the mission's aim; on the other, they had exceeded their remit by their foray into the murky world of international Israeli diplomacy while apparently evading the watchful eye of the IRGC that was known to have a strong presence in London. How had they achieved all this on their own initiative? And how should Lunenfeld react to the report? Challenge his agents on its veracity? Congratulate them while rapping them across the knuckles for their chutzpah? Such a response would elevate the concept of the mixed message to a whole new level. Something was amiss and Lunenfeld was determined to find it.

He pressed the intercom button on his desk. 'Contact Dr Benayoun and the Weisses, please, as soon as they are all back in the country. I want to meet the agents first and then all of them together. It's urgent.'

Tamir always enjoyed the El Al flight from London to Tel Aviv. It gave him time to relax, clear his head and ponder the future. Above all, he looked forward to going home. He had conducted an unusually demanding and distasteful field operation. All he craved now was a period of domestic normality to restore his peace of mind.

The fly in the ointment was a large one: he and Keren had been summoned to Lunenfeld's office. He'd expected that; it was routine practice. But, the Mossad director had, for the first time, included Sofia on the invitation list. Why did he want to involve her? Was that a good or bad sign? Keren seemed taken aback, too, and claimed to be as baffled as Tamir. No point in fretting, they'd all find out soon enough. Tamir closed his eyes and tried to snatch some sleep as the plane's engines modulated into their close-harmony melody that indicated the start of their final descent to Ben Gurion airport.

Sofia was overjoyed that Tamir had returned from London to his family in the Negev sooner than expected.

'Hey, that was quick,' cooed Sofia as she wrapped her arms around her husband. 'Is everything OK? You look worn out, darling.'

'I'm tired, but I did what I had to do. Everything went like clockwork.'

'Maybe you'd like to enlighten me about what you were up to over there?'

'Sorry, *ahuvati*, I'd rather not do that—not yet. You'll hear about it soon enough. The bottom line is that the London operation was a success. Thanks in large part to your intervention. And I have more good news.'

'You're on a roll, Agent Weiss. Go on, don't keep me in suspense.'

'*Destiny* has folded now that Berg is dead, Cambon has resigned and Ahmed is out of the picture. No successors have been appointed. They are leaderless and demoralised. In effect, the organisation has been disbanded. Including all the national branches across Europe. They're no longer a functioning outfit.'

'That's worth a special celebration. And the Jews of Europe are safe?'

'It seems that way, for now. Until the next lunatic comes along. As far as we can tell, there's little prospect of that happening in the short term now that *Destiny* is no more. That can change and we'll have to remain alert to any new risks on the horizon, but the immediate danger has passed.'

'What happens now?'

'I'm not sure. We have to pay a visit to Lunenfeld tomorrow.'

'By "we" you mean you and Keren?'

'And you. He was insistent that you should be there too, at midday sharp. Keren and I have to be there earlier to finalise our report. They'll send a car for you.'

'Wow, that's a first. I supposed I should be flattered. Any idea why?'

'Not really. Except that you played a key part in this operation and Lunenfeld knows that. But it's unusual for anyone from outside the agency to meet the director in person. Anyway, you're right, you should take it as a compliment. A very big one.'

Prime minister Volkov was euphoric. Within weeks of his appointment, he was on the verge of pulling off one of the greatest political achievements in Israel's history—the establishment of full diplomatic, commercial and cultural relations with the Kingdom of Saudi Arabia, the birthplace of Islam and a long-standing opponent of peace with the Jewish state.

Not that Volkov could take the credit for the bizarre chain of events that had led to the breakthrough. That accolade belonged to the security services and, above all, to the Mossad director and his small team of elite European agents. Volkov wouldn't hesitate to accept the bouquets that would be showered on him, but he also believed in the old-school mantra of credit-where-credit-is-due. He'd have to signal his appreciation to Lunenfeld and the agency in some tangible way that the public would recognise, while maintaining the necessary discretion over the identities of the personalities involved.

The germ of an idea was forming in his mind. Could it work? He pressed the intercom on his desk and asked his secretary to make two calls. The first was to the president's office. The second was to the director of the Mossad.

[47]

SOFIA WAS IN A PANIC. AN OFFICIAL CAR WAS ABOUT TO ARRIVE and transport her from her Negev home to meet the Mossad chief and she had no idea what to do with her children. Tamir had left before dawn and she had exhausted all her potential sources of child care. Kindly neighbours had volunteered to step into the breach but Sofia was reluctant to entrust her family to the care of complete strangers. There was only one solution—to take them with her. Israel was a child-oriented country, but this was stretching the concept *ad absurdum*. No matter, she had no choice. She texted Tamir, *All three of us are on our way*.

In the event, she needn't have worried. As soon as she and the children had negotiated the stringent security checks just inside the spacious lobby of the glass-and-concrete government building in north-eastern Tel Aviv, two good-humoured uniformed female soldiers rushed to her aid and took control of the children. They assured Sofia—in a mixture of Hebrew and English—that the little ones would be well looked-after during her meeting. After a brief interlude of hesitation, during which she assessed these enthusiastic young Israeli women to be trustworthy and competent, Sofia complied and handed them over along with the bulging shoulder bag of childcare accoutrements. The children complied after the briefest of protests.

A smart young man in a suit and tieless white shirt materialised from nowhere and said, 'Please come this way, Mrs Weiss. The director is ready to receive you now.'

Could this really be Mossad headquarters? The ordinariness of her surroundings clashed with the awesome reputation of this near-mythical organisation. Sofia had never met Lunenfeld, though she felt she knew him almost as well as she did Tamir. She wished she had dressed in more formal attire for what was turning into a momentous occasion.

Keren and Tamir were already in the conference room, both looking tired and ashen-faced. Tamir rushed over to embrace his wife, while Keren pretended to study her phone.

'I hear the kids are being looked after somewhere in this building,' said Tamir. 'Don't worry, they're in good hands. Sorry I had to leave home so early this morning. I seem to have got into a spot of bother with my employers. How are you all doing?'

'We're doing fine, better than you, it seems. What's going on?'

At that moment, the door swung open. It was Lunenfeld. 'Tell you later,' muttered Tamir. 'Let me introduce you to the director.'

'No need, I can do it myself,' said Lunenfeld in his nearly flawless English. He strode across the room, hand outstretched. 'What a pleasure to meet you finally, Mrs Weiss. I hear nothing but good things about you.'

What an absolute charmer, thought Sofia. She couldn't help blushing at the unexpected flattery. 'They're probably all undeserved,' she said.

'I will be the judge of that,' said the director, adopting the uber-convivial expression that he reserved for outsiders but fooled no one inside the agency. 'Please sit, all of you. Mrs Weiss, thank you for coming. I wanted you to be here because I have some interesting news for you and your husband. But let's get the formalities out of the way first.' He turned to Keren. 'Dr Benayoun, may I ask you to read to us all the field report you received from Agent Weiss and then approved? In English, of course. Please proceed.'

Keren opened her file and cleared her throat. Before she could begin, Lunenfeld spoke again. 'On second thoughts, don't bother with that piece of half-baked fiction the two of you cooked up for me this morning. Give it to me, please.'

Keren handed the A4 sheets to Lunenfeld who, with an exaggerated theatrical gesture, tore them in two and tossed them into the bin. He removed his spectacles and smiled at Keren, who displayed no surprise at this development. 'Ah, that's better, isn't it? Having studied your so-called report in great detail, I have come to realise that there is only one suitable place to file it. Now, doctor, please tell me what really happened in London.'

After a mutual affirmatory nod to Tamir, Keren said, 'You are correct, sir. The report Agent Weiss and I gave you was not entirely accurate. This is unacceptable behaviour on our part—we understand that—and you will have to decide what sanctions to implement against us. Despite that, we are confident that our actions were justified—if not in keeping with Mossad regulations—and that our belief in their necessity has been vindicated by subsequent events.'

She paused in expectation of a reaction. As there was none, she continued. 'We also admit that we had no doubt that you would discover the truth once the consequences of our actions became clear. We knew that we were taking a risk with our future careers. Why did we do it? Because we concluded that the benefits to our country far outweighed personal considerations. If I may, sir, I would like to invite Agent Weiss to continue our presentation of the facts of this complex operation.'

Lunenfeld nodded and turned to Tamir, who pulled out a sheaf of papers from his briefcase. 'If you have no objection, sir, I will refer to my notes. They are an accurate and complete account of my actions. I give you my word on that.'

'Good,' said Lunenfeld, leaning back in his chair with obvious satisfaction. 'Better late than never. Please proceed, Agent Weiss.'

Tamir began to read in a monotone. He described the chain of events that had unfolded in London—including how a panic-stricken Ahmed had been confronted by both Tamir and an Iranian assassin almost simultaneously. How had that happened? Ahmed had contacted Sofia—having been tipped off by his Iranian masters that the English 'journalist' was working for Mossad—and had pleaded for her help in saving his life, which he believed to be in imminent danger from the IRGC.

'Wait,' said Lunenfeld. 'At this point, I would like to hear from Mrs Weiss the nature of her conversation with Mr Ahmed. Mrs Weiss, please take up the story.'

'Yes, of course, and thank you for giving me the opportunity to explain how I got involved.' Sofia spoke softly but with an eloquence that impressed everyone in the room. 'I was amazed to get the call from Mr Ahmed, as you can imagine. He claimed to be in possession of important information that he wished to communicate to Mossad, since it concerned what he called Israel's geopolitical status—he wouldn't expand on that phrase other than to hint that he was (or at least had been) also on the payroll of the Saudi secret service, but that the Kingdom had abandoned him following the collapse of *Destiny*. He feared that the Iranians were planning to kill him for what they regarded as his treasonous relationship with their longstanding arch enemies, the Saudis. When I heard this, I concluded that his predicament was real and that his information could be of vital interest to Israel. I decided to contact Dr Benayoun immediately.'

'Thank you, Mrs Weiss, that was most helpful.' He turned to Keren. 'Doctor?'

'After receiving Sofia's call, I requested an intelligence assessment from within the agency and other governmental branches. They confirmed that Ahmed's fears were valid. I contacted Agent Weiss with this new information and stressed to him the opportunity it presented for improving Israeli-Saudi relations. I instructed him to keep Ahmed under close surveillance and to use his judgement regarding any necessary intervention to protect the MP.' Keren turned to Tamir. 'Perhaps Agent Weiss will continue?' Lunenfeld nodded.

'Within a few hours of commencing the surveillance,' said Tamir, 'I identified a visitor lurking in the vicinity of the *Orb* premises. The behaviour of this unidentified individual suggested to me that he was a hostile actor, presumably an IRGC agent who intended to threaten or even inflict harm on the politician. My concern was heightened when the visitor forcibly entered the building. I followed closely behind the intruder who shortly thereafter tried to kill both myself and Ahmed.'

Sofia gasped and covered her mouth with the palm of her hand. 'Oh my God, Tamir.'

Without looking at his wife, Tamir continued his account. 'As you can see, he failed. I prevailed and killed the Iranian. Then I made my offer to the MP—although we actually dreamed it up together. Mr Ahmed exchanged his clothes with those of the deceased assailant. We took Ahmed's passport and placed it inside a plastic folder—the type often used by frequent travellers. We then disposed of the corpse, along with the MP's ID, in the river Thames knowing that if the UK police ever found the body, they would confirm Ahmed's death and close the case. That's it.'

There was a prolonged silence that was marred only by the screeching of a police siren in the middle distance.

Lunenfeld stood and fixed his unnerving stare on all three of them. He shook his head and said, without raising his voice, 'You all deserve the severest possible reprimand in deviating from your orders in the most reckless manner. You could have caused an international incident that might have endangered Israel's diplomatic relations as well as the lives of many of our agents across the Middle East and Europe. On the other hand...'

Then Lunenfeld did something extraordinary. He walked around the conference table and shook hands with all three of his visitors without saying a word. After returning to his seat, he consulted his notes, looked up and said, '*Kol hakavod and mazal tov*—congratulations to all of you. Relax. You will be pleased to learn that you are not in trouble. Now permit me to update you on some important developments relating to this case.'

The director settled back in his chair, clasped his hands in front of his chest, and made brief eye contact with each of his three stupefied guests in turn before continuing.

'The Destiny leader-elect, Azad Ahmed, now in Riyadh, has been released from our surveillance. This is because while ostensibly working for Iran he was—as he indicated to Mrs Weiss—a double agent who simultaneously served the Saudi Arabian GIP spy agency. The Saudis are delighted that we Israelis succeeded in smuggling their man out of the UK where he was—as Mrs Weiss also learned in the course of Mr Ahmed's phone call—in danger of being murdered by the IRGC. The ruling royal family have decided that their gratitude to Israel should find concrete expression. The episode has led to a revival of Saudi-Israeli cooperation and a probable establishment of enhanced relations in the near future in the context of the Abraham Accords. This is a wonderful achievement that will go down as a historic milestone in the history of the Middle East.'

His three guests burst into spontaneous applause. Lunenfeld raised his hand to cut short their celebrations. 'I could have all three of you arrested for having blatantly violated the agency's standing orders, including the submission to me of an untruthful operational report, and for taking other unacceptable risks in the process. But now that we see how your gamble has paid off, what can I say? Your status is now rather different. To put it another way, you are national heroes. Mr Ahmed—an Islamist antisemite turned pro-Israeli diplomat—was right to predict a warm Saudi reaction. That means that your decision-making, while unorthodox and fraught with danger, proved completely justified. In consequence, I am informing you now that I have recommended to the president—with the prime minister's approval—that you all three of you be awarded special recognition of your outstanding service to the state. You will receive your medals at a ceremony at the president's residence in a few weeks' time.'

Keren, Sofia, and Tamir greeted this news with jubilation tinged with near-disbelief. By now, all the initial tension had evaporated from the room. Anxious expressions had been supplanted by warm smiles. The three turned and embraced each other. Lunenfeld beamed with approval at his star team. 'One moment please, I think this calls for a special *Lechayim*.' He retreated to his rear office and returned thirty seconds later carrying a tray bearing a bottle of sparkling wine and four plastic cups.

The party at Mossad headquarters was brief. After just one sip, Lunenfeld received a text message that caused him visible consternation. He ended the meeting, excused himself without explanation and retreated to his office.

Sofia and Tamir bid farewell to Keren and descended to the ground floor to collect their children—who had bonded with the female soldiers and made known their reluctance to leave—and headed to the car pickup area. No sooner had they located their driver when multiple loud sirens wailed.

'What the hell is going on, Tamir? Are we under attack? Or is this a drill?'

'No, it's not a drill. This is for real. It means rockets are headed our way. Come on, we only have a few seconds to get under cover.'

Sofia's breathless interrogation of her husband continued unabated in the midst of the mayhem. 'What rockets? You mean from Gaza?'

'That's very unlikely, *ahuvati*. Hamas usually pick nearer targets in the south. I expect the source is Hezbollah from Lebanon. But never mind any of that just now. Just hold on to the kids and let's get the hell out of here.'

They suspended their conversation out of necessity. They ran back inside the lobby and followed the crowds descending, with practised purpose, into the bowels of the building. Before they reached the shelter, Tamir's phone rang. Sofia watched her husband's face as he answered and grew alarmed when she observed his expression—total impassivity.

As the all-clear sounded and they headed back to street level, Sofia asked Tamir what the phone call was about. He declined to answer.

That could mean only one thing. Tamir had just been sent a set of new instructions from his Mossad superiors.

Meanwhile, in another part of Israel, a second drama was unfolding.

Saturday might be the traditional Jewish day of rest, but that is more of a myth than a reality in the life of an Israeli prime minister—as Arkady Volkov had discovered. Just as he was settling down to drink his customary post-prandial lemon tea on a balmy Shabbat afternoon in Jerusalem, his phone rang. It was his director of public communications.

'I'm sorry to disturb you, Prime Minister, but there is important breaking news. We'll have to respond to the international media today. They're going berserk.'

'It would be helpful if you could tell me what this is all about, Ilana.'

'The Saudis and Iranians, sir. Both of them. According to *Al Jazeera*, they've made a comprehensive peace. A full and permanent one this time, they say. Our Ministry of Foreign Affairs have confirmed it—they're preparing a briefing paper for you now. Here is the gist: Riyadh and Tehran have agreed to restore all diplomatic, cultural and commercial relations immediately, exchange ambassadors and consuls, end all hostilities, resolve all outstanding issues of disagreement, and join forces to oppose their number one enemy.'

Volkov sighed. 'I don't suppose I need to guess who that enemy is?'

'No sir, you don't, though they don't mention us by name.'

'Let me guess—the Little Satan? The Zionist Entity?'

'Both of those and more. They call us the Usurping Cancer of the Middle East.'

'How original. Thank you, Ilana. Draft a statement and send it to me immediately.'

Volkov ended the call, closed his eyes for a moment and made another call via his speed dial. This one was to the Mossad director.

'Moshe, we have an old saying in Russia: the difference between a friend and an enemy depends only on the tip of a ballerina's shoe. Meaning that things can change in an instant. It looks like our new best friend in the Middle East may not turn out to be so friendly after all. You'd better get over here fast.'

[48]

FOR THE FIRST TIME IN WEEKS, SOFIA COULD BREATHE FREELY. The sensation of liberation was glorious and uplifting. The children had settled well into their desert home and Tamir was around most days to help with the daily grind of running the household. The unexpected meeting with Lunenfeld and his announcement of the impending award ceremony had raised her spirits. At last, she was being treated as a real Israeli and was beginning to feel like one. She knew she could never permit herself the luxury of complacency. Israel was a country where surprises—many of them unpleasant—abounded. Rocket attacks from Gaza and Lebanon were a regular reminder of that unpalatable reality, one that felt more oppressive by the day. A superficial impression of calm was misleading; it often concealed numerous sources of underlying tensions and turmoil, many of which were beyond anyone's control.

Weeks had passed since Tamir's phone had rung in the basement of the Mossad building as he and his family sheltered from an incoming rocket attack. Sofia called it 'our rude awakening' that had spoiled the short-lived euphoria of the extraordinary meeting with Lunenfeld. Tamir had remained reticent about the nature of the call, as he had about all subsequent conversations that Sofia assumed had flowed from that initial alert. Even when Tamir was relaxing at home with his family, he was never out of contact with his immediate superior, Keren Benayoun. Sofia had grown accustomed to this third adult in their family life, though she was far from reconciled to that uncomfortable reality. While she no longer regarded Keren as a potential rival for Tamir's affections, she did resent the fact that Tamir's Other Woman could snatch him away from home at a moment's notice. She had learned to interpret most of the choreography of the complex interactions between Tamir and his commander, communications from which she was excluded. When Tamir received a call from his boss and took pains to relocate himself out of Sofia's earshot, trouble was brewing, and the longer the call, the bigger the trouble.

One Shabbat afternoon, as the children slept and Tamir was winding up a particularly epic consultation with Keren, Sofia scanned the beige horizon from their lounge window and prepared herself for the worst.

'What was that about?' she asked, without facing Tamir.

'The usual stuff that Israel has to deal with every day. International relations. War and peace. Come and sit down, *ahuvati*.'

Sofia obliged and sat close to her husband on the sofa. She took his hand in hers.

'That's not an answer, darling. Tell me the worst. I assume it's not good news.'

'I wouldn't say that. Another job is about to start.'

'Let me guess—does it concern Mr Ahmed and *Destiny*?'

'You're half right. You know I can't say too much about your Islamist friend.'

'He's hardly my friend. What's he done now? Doesn't he like living in Riyadh?'

'I've no idea whether he likes it or not.'

'I thought he was working for the Saudis now?'

'He was and probably still is. But it's no secret that he's likely to be facing a new problem. Iran and the Kingdom have announced that they've embarked on a rapprochement. That's good news in one sense, as they'll have no excuse to keep fighting their proxy wars.'

'Now you're about to tell me the bad news, aren't you?'

'The two countries have vowed to destroy the common enemy, the Little Satan.'

'That's us, isn't it? Why won't they leave Israel alone?'

'They'll never leave us alone while we're in existence, *ahuvati*.'

'What a cheerful thought. But how is any of that relevant to your work? Don't tell me, I think I know—they're sending you to Riyadh to smuggle Ahmed out?'

Tamir released his hand from hers. 'Not bad. You're getting warmer. We do have to get him out, though that's not a likely role for me. Mainly because I'm not a fluent Arabic speaker, sadly. I may be involved as a backup for a colleague. Whatever his history, Ahmed has proved himself a friend to this country, so we have no choice. We owe him one. I'm meeting the team tomorrow morning for a status briefing. What happens then is anyone's guess. I'm sorry, *ahuvati,* but I may have to prepare for another spell away from home.'

'As if you haven't risked your life enough for Israel.'

'Look, that's what I do. I shouldn't have to keep reminding you of that.'

'And I shouldn't have to keep reminding you that I'm on board now too. I'm an honorary Mossadnik, remember? Maybe I don't have your lofty status, but I'm supposed to be on the inside now. So why do you keep freezing me out?'

'Please, don't. We've been over this a hundred times, *ahuvati*.'

The couple sat in sullen silence until Sofia could bear the tension no longer.

'I hate the fact that you're off on your travels again. When will you get back?'

'I don't know. As soon as I can. I'm not hiding anything, believe me, those days are over. Look, I understand your anger, especially as you're more or less one of us now. You deserve to know more than I'm telling you. But I swear to you I'm not concealing anything from you. I just haven't received the full details yet. As soon as I have them, you'll have them too, *motek*. That's a promise.'

The medal award ceremony was rather an anticlimax. Sofia hadn't known what to expect, but she assumed there would be a large gathering of the great and the good, a bit of pomp and flummery, a military band at least. None of that materialised, as it wasn't the Israeli way. What actually took place was an informal event that Sofia found, to her surprise, quite moving despite—or perhaps because of—its understated nature.

The proceedings were held in the garden of the president's residence in Jerusalem. It was a warm early summer's day and the scent wafting from the immaculate flower beds and herb garden was exquisite. About forty guests were milling around when Sofia arrived—there was no sign of Tamir. He'd warned her he might be late, but that didn't assuage her irritation—everyone was chattering in rapid Hebrew and she was growing anxious. She felt a light touch on her arm and turned round. It was Keren. She was smiling broadly.

'Relax, my dear, you're supposed to enjoy this. It's a celebration in your honour.'

'I can't, Keren, I've left the children at home with a total stranger.'

'You mean Aviva? Oh, don't worry, I'm sure they'll be fine with her. She's one of our most experienced childminders. Forget about the kids and focus on this special moment.'

'I'd find it a lot easier if that delinquent husband of mine turned up.'

'He's on his way. Don't worry, he wouldn't dare miss this. Look, the ceremony is about to start.'

The two women turned to face a makeshift podium that had been erected in the middle of the lawn. A small, slim man with a friendly face was tapping the side of a wine glass with a teaspoon. He held a microphone and began to speak.

'That's the president,' whispered Keren in Sofia's ear. 'He's a lovely man.'

As he was delivering what Sofia presumed to be words of welcome, Keren tugged at Sofia's sleeve. 'This is just a short history of the Medal for Outstanding Service to the State. Get ready to go up there when your name is called.'

Sofia grabbed a glass of white wine from a passing waitress. Her mouth was as dry as the Negev desert. 'Where the hell is Tamir? I'm not doing this alone.' As she spoke, something brushed lightly against her back.

'No need to do it alone. I'm right here, *ahuvati*. Sorry I'm late. Did you really think I wouldn't make it?' He pecked her on the cheek.

'Christ, you're cutting it fine. Where have you been?'

Before he could answer, Sofia thought she heard familiar words.

'That's us,' said Tamir. 'We've been called. Come on. Enjoy this moment.'

It was like standing on an Olympic podium, thought Sofia, except that there were six prize-winners rather than three. She had no idea who the other four were, but they all shook hands with her and each other as if they were longstanding friends. No sooner had the president presented the final medal than the small crowd applauded enthusiastically and then instantly fell silent. The distant strains of a familiar melody cut through the hubbub.

'It's the national anthem—*Hatikvah*,' whispered Tamir in her ear.

'Actually, I knew that—I'm Israeli now, remember?'

Then it was all over with an almost brutal abruptness. The medallists' families rushed forward to offer their congratulations. Only Keren could fulfil that role for the Weisses, and she had made herself scarce.

'It's a shame your parents aren't here, Tamir,' said Sofia.

She was sure Tamir winced. Whenever she mentioned his parents, he reacted strangely. 'They don't know about it, *ahuvati*. And I can't be identified in public.'

'But they called you up to the stage to receive your medal, didn't they?'

'Yes—but they didn't give my name. They called out *Efes Efes* or Zero Zero. Look at my medal. Where the name is supposed to appear, it's blank.'

'Hold on, they called me by my name so anyone could put two and two together.'

'Actually, they didn't. They called you *Eshet Chayil*.'

'What does that mean?'

'A woman of valour. It comes from a biblical text thought to have been written by King Solomon.'

Sofia blushed lightly. 'How flattering.'

'That's the whole point, *ahuvati*. You're in the history books now as one of Israel's greatest women—as Keren will confirm.' He was looking over Sofia's shoulder.

'*Mazal tov*, Sofia,' said Keren, kissing her on both cheeks. 'You deserve this honour.'

'Thank you, Keren. But why didn't you get a medal too?'

'Ah, there's a reason for that,' said Keren.

'Are you going to keep me guessing?'

'She already has one,' said Tamir with a grin. 'And that's not a joke.'

'Wow—you should have told me! *Mazal tov* to you too, Keren.'

But the doctor had turned her back and was walking briskly away. And when Sofia turned to ask her husband why, he had disappeared too.

'Permit me to congratulate you, Mrs Weiss.' It was Moshe Lunenfeld. 'A tremendous achievement. You should be extremely proud. Both of you.'

'Thank you so much for coming. Tamir is here somewhere...'

'I'm not here to speak to Tamir, I'm here to speak to you. I'm so sorry I missed the ceremony, I was distracted by official business. Anyway, I'm glad I got here in time to tell you myself.'

'Tell me what?' Sofia's pulse rate was on the rise.

'You're wondering why your husband has disappeared, are you not? That's what I was about to explain. He and the doctor have had to leave immediately on my orders. They offer their apologies for their unexpected and all too sudden departure. And so do I.'

'Leave? Where to?'

'Ah, I am not at liberty to reveal their destination. Sorry. Don't worry, they won't be gone for long. Goodbye, Mrs Weiss, and well done again. A car is waiting outside to take you home to the Negev. By the way, a couple of my strong young men will be there to keep an eye on you and your family over the next few days. A routine precaution. Have a pleasant drive. *Nesiyah tovah*.'

Tamir was away for three weeks. Of those, Sofia had lasted two.

The drive home from the ceremony had been uneventful in every regard but one—the burgeoning resentment that grew more insistent with every kilometre. It gnawed at Sofia from the depths of her gut and threatened to devour her from the inside. Her fury was so all-consuming that it would not be assuaged. But it wasn't directed exclusively or even mainly at Tamir. He was just doing his duty and she could hardly blame him for that. No, Tamir was as much a victim of circumstances as she and the children were. They were all emotional casualties in Israel's perpetual state of war against dictators, religious fundamentalists and terrorists that had all, separately or in shifting alliances, vowed to obliterate the country and a large majority of its inhabitants.

And yet she couldn't absolve the Mossadniks entirely. They had no right to keep her in the dark for weeks and months on end. Tamir, at least, should have sufficient trust in his wife to take her into his confidence. He would no doubt protest that his lack of communication was involuntary. That excuse would no longer wash with Sofia. After all, she had participated in a Mossad operation, had become an Israeli, and had been ceremonially honoured by the president. She needed no lessons from anyone about the existential importance to Israel's security of the work of the Mossad. But Tamir's hurtful habit of silence spoke volumes, with every non-articulated syllable an insult to his partner and family. If he struggled to grasp how corrosive to their relationship his secrecy had become, she would have to find a more assertive way to get her message across.

She opened the box containing the medal that she had just received, withdrew the shiny object and stroked its engraved surface. A woman of valour? A woman of worthlessness was how she felt at that moment. She was about to chuck the lump of metal out of the car window when the driver announced their arrival at their Sde Boker home. She overcame her impulse, but she had already reached an equally dramatic decision. All that remained was to turn that resolve into a plan of action.

As Keren has predicted, the children were in safe hands: Aviva, an official Mossad childminder—who could have imagined there was such a profession?—had become their new best friend. Sofia thanked the young woman as she slipped with relief back into fulltime maternal mode—minus a partner. She had no wish to be a single parent, but if Tamir didn't change his ways, so be it.

[49]

IN ONE OF THOSE STRANGE SISTERLY COINCIDENCES, LUISA LOPEZ was on the verge of calling her sister when her phone rang. Sofia had pipped her to it by a millisecond.

'Hi Luisa, it's me.'

'I know it's you, *querida*, my phone tells me. How are you?'

'Terrible. I can't stand this anymore, Luisa. I have to get out. It's like being in prison.'

'Hey, slow down, sis. What's going on? Where are you?'

'In the middle of the desert. With the kids. And a large gin and tonic.'

'And Tamir? How is he?'

'I haven't the foggiest. He's been gone for ten days.'

'Oh, sorry to hear that. He's working I suppose?'

'Yup, it's the usual cloak-and-dagger rubbish. I'm sick of it, Luisa.'

'Can't Tamir's family help?'

'Apparently not. I've only ever met them once. They live up in the Galilee next to the Syrian border. Tamir had a falling out with them years ago. I've no idea why. He never talks about them.'

'That's ridiculous, Sofia. You need to challenge him on that.'

Sofia laughed. 'You mean find another subject to argue about? You're kidding.'

Just at that moment, the doorbell rang. That was followed, as per protocol, by four short bleeps on her phone signifying that it would be safe to answer.

'What was that noise, sis?'

'It's nothing to worry about. Look, I have to go. I'll call you back later. Speak soon. Love you.'

One minute later, Sofia's visitor was sitting, bolt upright, on one of the high-backed chairs in her living room. The visitor was Keren Benayoun, Tamir's boss. She eyed the Englishwoman with a mixture of concern and wariness.

'You must be fed up with all this, Sofia. How are you coping?'

'Oh, it's a breeze. I have two young children to look after with no family support, my so-called husband has been gone for over a week and might be lying dead in a ditch for all I know, and I'm stuck here in the desert growing old and depressed. There's your answer to take back to Lunenfeld. Tell him Sofia's doing great, couldn't be better.'

Like all Israelis, Keren understood irony. She nodded in sympathy and gazed out of the window as though searching the austere landscape for a suitably encouraging response. None was forthcoming.

Sofia kept the conversation going. 'I know it's a waste of my breath asking you this, but what's news of Tamir?'

'We haven't any. None at all. He's kept *shtum* for over a week. That's not unusual in operations of this kind. I'm sure he's safe and well.'

'That's good to know. Dr Benayoun is sure my husband is safe and well. Do you think his wife is safe and well?'

'Judging from your tone—and your slurred speech—I suspect

not. You really should go easy on the alcohol. It's not good for you, especially in this heat. Try to be patient.'

That remark lit a fuse. Sofia's eyes widened. 'Patient? Are you serious? I've been patient for years and look at me. I'm a wreck. And you have some *chutzpah*, Keren, to criticise my drinking habits. No, my patience has long gone—with Tamir, with the Mossad, and with you. In fact, I think you should leave.'

'Okay, no problem, I'm on my way,' said Keren, raising her hands as though to fend off Sofia's gust of anger. 'I have one last question: what do you plan to do now?'

'I'll do what I should have done a long time ago. I'm taking the kids back to England. It's not fair on them. We fly the day after tomorrow.'

'I'm really sorry to hear that. You're making a big mistake, in my opinion.'

'I have no interest in your opinion, Keren. Absolutely none. Sorry, but that's the way it is. Now please leave. I have a lot to do.'

Twenty-four hours later, Sofia received another visitor. Two in fact. The first was the more prestigious. He was accompanied by a coterie of security men in plain clothes who deployed themselves around the house. Sofia was taken aback. But she felt obliged to treat her distinguished guest with civility.

'Mr Lunenfeld. This is so unexpected. Please come in and sit down. May I offer you a drink? A coffee perhaps?'

Lunenfeld declined. 'No thank you, Mrs Weiss. I'm sorry to spring this surprise on you, but I promise I won't stay long. Five minutes at most. I hear from Dr Benayoun that you're leaving us?'

'Yes, tomorrow. I can't stay here any longer. It's not good for the children.'

'I understand. And rest assured that I'm not here to dissuade you from returning to London. You've had a most difficult time. It can't be much fun languishing here out in the desert with two young children, effectively on your own. You have my sympathy, believe me. I don't blame you in the slightest.'

'Thank you, sir.' Sofia's eyes moistened.

'Permit me to make a suggestion. Regardless of the outcome of your husband's latest mission—and I have reason to believe it will be a success—we in the Mossad don't want to lose you. Your contribution has been outstanding.'

'Thank you, sir. I appreciate that. And the medal.'

'You fully deserved it. And I know you have your criticisms of some of our methods. In particular, the way in which we whisk your husband away at short notice without explaining why. But I'm not here to dwell on the past. What I am trying to say is this. We believe you have much more to offer the agency and Israel.'

'That is kind of you, but I've made up my mind.'

'I think you misunderstand me, Mrs Weiss. I'm not trying to change your mind to leave Israel. Not at all. All I'm asking is that you don't cut your links with us altogether. There is much you could help us with in London, even on a part-time basis. And we can arrange for a degree of remuneration. We can't pay you a fortune but it's a decent salary. What's that phrase you English like to use? Ah yes, I remember—it's not to be sneezed at. After a short few weeks of training here in Israel, you will be a fully-fledged Mossadnik. Once you are on board, we will have little reason to keep anything about your husband's work missions from you. Will you think about it at least?'

Before Sofia could gather her thoughts to compose an answer, Lunenfeld was on his way to the door. 'It's been a pleasure talking with you, as usual, Mrs Weiss. Please consider my proposal. Take a few days before giving us an answer. Dr Benayoun will be in touch with the details. As a matter of fact, here she comes now. Goodbye and *nesiyah tovah*.'

Keren entered the Weiss home as the director left. They briefly acknowledged each other without exchanging a word. Sofia felt the room spinning as she ushered her latest guest into the living room. The Mossad officer sat in the same chair she had occupied a day earlier and spoke without interruption for fifteen minutes. She set out, in outline, Lunenfeld's offer in terms of the work involved, the training course in Israel, and the likely remuneration. Sofia wished she'd had the presence of mind to take notes and made an effort to memorise the salient details. But she had been distracted by Lunenfeld's parting remark that she was desperate to memorise: *Once you are on board, we will have little reason to keep anything about your husband's work missions from you.* She was sure that's what he'd said. That promise could be a game changer. Except she detected a problem. It boiled down to one word. That little word "little."

On her way out, Keren said, 'All we are asking, Sofia, is that you think about our proposal. We have just one condition. Don't take too long. The offer will expire in one week.'

[50]

TAMIR WEISS WAS PERSPIRING FREELY. THE FORTY-DEGREE temperature that cooked the whole of downtown Riyadh in the early afternoon wasn't the sole cause of his thermal discomfort—he was, after all, luxuriating in half that temperature in the cool lobby of a five-star hotel. His ridiculous outfit didn't help matters. In accordance with his director's instructions, Tamir had dressed for this special occasion in a lightweight dark suit, white shirt and tasteful pale-blue tie. He may have looked smart enough, but he felt like a trussed chicken about to be hung out to roast in the Middle East's most unforgiving desert sun.

But the Israeli's unfamiliar clothing wasn't the sole reason for his discomfort. Nor was his chronic anxiety about the primitive state of his Arabic language skills. He was concerned with a more immediate cause of his profound unease—the potential threat to his own life and limb.

Although relations between Israel and Saudi Arabia were warming fast—Tamir had been flown direct from Tel Aviv to Riyadh on an unmarked private jet, after all—Israeli visitors to the Kingdom remained an extreme rarity and there were plenty of Israel-haters in the country who would welcome the opportunity to claim a Mossadnik's scalp. A second, though no less serious, source of danger emanated from the Islamic Republic of Iran. Since the sudden unexpected rapprochement between the two countries, Riyadh was known to be hoatching with IRGC agents and they would be delighted to gain Brownie points with their mullahs back home by claiming the scalp of an Israeli spy.

Tamir reminded himself for the umpteenth time that he held a trump card. The Saudi royal family. Or at least elements within it who were keen to progress the relationship with Israel. Lunenfeld had personally set up a meeting between Tamir and a pro-Israel prince who was known to be close to the country's ruling elite.

He checked his watch—one minute to go before the appointed time, the moment of truth. He made a conscious effort to breathe slowly and deeply. He'd been in worse situations than this one and he trusted his director to know his business. Still, the beads of perspiration formed and coalesced into rivulets that trickled down his forehead, face and neck, defying his efforts to mop up the inundation with a white linen handkerchief. *Where was the prince?*

The answer materialised moments later. An incident was unfolding at the hotel entrance. The two uniformed doormen were fussing and flapping to no obvious purpose. Tamir stood up to gain a better view. The lobby was almost empty apart from the hotel staff who had formed a line just inside the revolving glass doors. He could see a large black saloon car parked on the street outside the hotel. Three or four black-suited, miked-up young men were clustered around the rear of the vehicle. One of them placed his hand on the door handle and looked around before opening the door. Out stepped a tall, dapper figure draped in long white flowing robes and wearing a red-and-white-checked keffiyeh. He strode into the hotel as if he owned it (and probably did, thought Tamir). After a few obligatory exchanges with the staff, he spotted the Israeli, smiled warmly, and strode towards his visitor, a small entourage of officials in tow.

'Mr Weiss, I presume?' he announced in immaculate English, his hand extended. Tamir reciprocated.

'*Salam Aleykum*, Your Royal Highness. Yes, I am Tamir Weiss.'

'*Shalom* to you too. I suggest we dispense with formality. Call me Ibrahim and, if I may be so bold, permit me to call you Tamir. Let's sit down and have a cold drink. I can see you are suffering from our extreme desert temperature.' The prince turned and issued a directive to one of his sidekicks.

'Before we begin, Tamir, I bring you greetings from His Majesty, our head of state. He wishes you to know that he looks forward to establishing a close and productive relationship with your country as soon as is practicable.'

'Thank you, sir—Ibrahim. I will convey that friendly gesture to my government.'

'Excellent. I can see that we are on the same page. How is my good friend, Moshe Lunenfeld these days? '

'He is very well, thank you.'

'Please convey to him my warmest greetings, if you would be so kind.'

'Certainly, sir, I will do that the moment I return to Israel.' As soon as he's uttered it, Tamir realised he'd made a *faux pas*. The name of his country was still a near-taboo in the KSA. His host, however, seemed unperturbed.

'Ah, good, here are our drinks. I strongly recommend this iced tea—it's perfect for our weather at this time of year.' He raised a glass and held it out towards Tamir, who was clearly expected to do the same. 'I wish to make a toast,' said the prince, 'to our two countries and their respective citizens. *Lechayim*.'

'*Lechayim*,' responded Tamir, somewhat astonished at the friendly banter, as the glasses clinked.

'Now we must get down to business, Tamir. We have a mutual interest in a visitor to these parts, a British MP, is that not so?'

'Indeed, yes, we do, sir. Ibrahim.'

'This man, Mr Ahmed, has been problematic for your country, I gather.'

'Indeed, he has. He was, until recently, a senior official of a European political organisation called *Destiny*, an extremist group that showed themselves to be hostile to the Jewish people. And to our country.'

The prince shook his head in disapproval. 'That is truly shocking in this day and age. After everything your people have suffered, the promotion of antisemitism is intolerable. And as a student of history, I know that those who come after the Jews will sooner or later come after the Arabs too. It's in the interests of both our peoples to stop these fanatics. I believe that with all my heart.'

'Thank you, Your Royal Highness. Ibrahim. Sadly, not everyone shares your view.'

'Including many people in this country, to my great sorrow. I must tell you that we also had our issues with Mr Ahmed, though he was helpful to us at times. And I know that you and your colleagues were instrumental in smuggling him out of London and bringing him to our Kingdom. But his close links with the Islamic Republic of Iran were a source of great consternation here. However, recent diplomatic developments have somewhat changed the equation in this country, as you must be aware.'

'Yes, so I have heard. The Kingdom and Iran appear to be on good terms nowadays.'

The prince smiled. 'That is an appropriate choice of words, Tamir. Two words in particular—*appear* and *nowadays*. How long this new love affair will last is anyone's guess. But let's focus on Mr Ahmed. You want to get him out of here, is that correct?'

'Yes, we fear he is at great risk in this country due to the presence of IRGC agents. He believes they will try to exact revenge and he is probably right. We feel we have an obligation to help him.'

The prince's expression was quizzical. 'An obligation? Why?'

'Because of his connections with your government. We know that your leaders appreciated our intervention in London, an intervention that saved his life. And my government is keen to build on the opportunity presented by this affair to improve relations between our two countries. After all, our meeting today would not have happened without Mr Ahmed. Is that not so?'

'Perhaps so, Tamir. Yes, I think you are quite right. Unfortunately, Mr Ahmed's status in the eyes of our government has changed in the light of our alliance with Iran. He is no longer subject to the protection of the Saudi state, I'm afraid. You have presumably been informed about that new reality?'

'Indeed, I have. That is why I'm asking you—your government, I mean—to help us secure his safety by extraditing him to a third country.'

'Which third country?'

'I have no specific views about that. One of the Gulf states perhaps.'

'I see. What an interesting idea.' The prince's expression clouded. 'Unfortunately, I fear that may not be possible. We may be too late. However, let me make an inquiry.' He pulled out his phone and spoke in rapid Arabic that Tamir couldn't follow. After a few seconds, he ended the call and said, 'Come, my friend. Let's go and see Mr Ahmed. And it will be an opportunity for me to show you a few of the sights of our beautiful city.'

Settling into the upholstered rear seating of the royal vehicle, Tamir was troubled. The prince's phrase *we may be too late* was inauspicious. He had the feeling that this mission would not have a happy ending. They toured around the city for an hour, the driver slowing as each of the famous sights came into view: the Kingdom Centre Tower, the Al Masmak fortress, the Al Rajhi Mosque. The prince was proud of his capital, but couldn't conceal his mild boredom at being a tour guide, a role he must have performed a hundred times.

'You need to come back and spend some time in these places, my friend,' said the prince. Tamir assured his host that he would at the earliest opportunity, but inwardly he was growing impatient, though he tried not to show it. Small talk did not come naturally to him even in social settings. He hadn't flown to the Saudi capital for a holiday and was sorely tempted to remind his host that his top priority was to determine the fate of the man he'd been sent to rescue. As if reading his mind, Ibrahim issued a stern instruction to the driver who took a sharp left turn that caused the tyres to screech.

'Now we'll pay a visit to your troublesome MP. I must tell you, my friend, I am not optimistic. As you will see, we are about to visit the emergency department of the King Saud Medical City. This is perhaps the foremost medical centre in the entire Arab world.'

Five minutes later, a guard waved them through a checkpoint and they drew up outside the entrance of a large hospital. The prince dialled a number and spoke briefly before turning to his driver to issue new instructions.

'There's been a change of plan, Tamir. We're going round the back.'

The car drove slowly along a narrow lane at the side of the ED and pulled up outside a long low building. Tamir couldn't translate the small Arabic sign above its entrance. A uniformed soldier saluted as the driver applied the handbrake.

'What is this place, Ibrahim?' asked Tamir.

'Be patient, my friend. You'll see soon enough.'

They exited the car and were led into the facility by a small man wearing a mask and a grubby white coat. The first thing that struck Tamir as they entered was the whiff of an unpleasant chemical aroma, perhaps a disinfectant or formaldehyde. The second was the near-freezing air temperature. This was no ordinary air conditioning. When they turned a corner, they were surrounded by row upon row of storage units that looked like enormous fridges. Tamir grasped their function at once—the storage of the dead. They were in the hospital morgue.

'Please, go ahead, my friend, and take as much time as you need. I'll wait here. I hope you have a stronger stomach than me. There are two things I cannot tolerate—one is the sight of blood, the other is to find myself in the presence of a dead body. These are weaknesses that I'm confident you don't share. Not in your line of business.'

The orderly opened one of the massive doors and pulled out a middle drawer. Tamir recognized the pallid face of the MP instantly. A wide laceration across the dead man's neck—like a second grinning mouth—revealed the cause of death. Tamir pulled out his phone and photographed the corpse twice. Then he stepped back and said, '*Shukran*.' The orderly nodded and slid the late politician back into his temporary resting place.

As they walked to the car, Tamir said, 'How disappointing. Do you have any idea who did it?'

Prince Ibrahim spread his hands in a gesture of despair. 'We don't know. It could have been almost anyone—the IRGC, Saudi intelligence, or even a casual criminal. But I've been assured by my contacts that this man's murder was not sanctioned by our government or any of its agencies and my sources are, for the most part, highly reliable. Some of our people think it might have been—and I know this may come as a shock to you—one of your colleagues in the Mossad.'

'What? That's an extraordinary allegation.' Tamir stopped. His face had turned pink.

'Wait, let me finish, Tamir. It's not an allegation, merely a hypothesis. Sadly, we may never discover the truth. The fact is that Mr Ahmed made many enemies in the course of the last few years of his life. One of the most powerful was your government.'

'Can you provide me with any evidence of this—hypothesis?'

Ibrahim shook his head. 'I doubt it, but I'll see what I can do. I'm so sorry, my dear chap. I know this is not the outcome you wanted. Come, let me take you back to your hotel. If we were in your country, I'd suggest we both partake of a stiff whisky to calm our nerves. Alas, as I know you will understand, that will not be possible on this occasion. Now let's get you home as quickly as possible. I can see this has been a difficult trip for you.'

After boarding the same unmarked private jet on which he'd arrived, Tamir looked around the small cabin. He was one of only a handful of passengers. He wondered who these people were. All were middle-aged men in dark suits, all looked bored and none was keen to acknowledge his presence, let alone engage in conversation. That suggested they were in the security services, whether Saudi or Israeli (or both).

Tamir's buzzing phone interrupted his reverie. It was a message from the prince. Attached were two photos. The first was a fuzzy picture of a woman in a niqab facing away from the camera. The second image was clearer but only the woman's eyes were visible.

As the cabin crew requested all passengers to switch off their phones for takeoff, Tamir read the message from Ibrahim. *I managed to extract these two photos from a friend of mine in the intelligence services. The images were captured on CCTV. This woman was the only person in the vicinity of Ahmed at the estimated time of his death. Not much to go on, but maybe your clever chums at the agency can identify her? Have a pleasant flight.*

Tamir returned to the second image and zoomed in as close as his device would permit. A stewardess hovered over him.

'Sir, I must ask you to switch off your device.' The tone of her voice suggested that noncompliance was not an option.

'Sorry, I'll do that now.' He did, but not before he had zoomed in on the image. Two dark, beautiful almond eyes gazed back at him. He stopped breathing for several seconds. A voice inside his head was shouting, in Hebrew, over and over: *It can't be true.*

Tamir switched off his phone. By now he was agitated beyond endurance. The flight to Tel Aviv felt as if it would never end. His mission had been a fiasco, a farce. His report to Lunenfeld would be the shortest he had ever written.

He didn't need to wait to get back to Israel to identify the prime suspect in the murder of Azad Ahmed MP in Saudi Arabia. Niqab or no niqab, he'd have recognised those exquisite eyes anywhere.

[51]

As soon as Tamir was out of Ben Gurion airport's VIP terminal, he jumped in a taxi and gave the driver an address in central Tel Aviv. Forty minutes later he was in the anteroom to Lunenfeld's office. His heart was thumping and his mouth was dry.

After ten interminable minutes, the door opened and the director greeted him with his customary practised smile. 'Agent Weiss, how nice to see you back safely on home turf. Please come in and take a seat. May I offer you a drink? I recommend something with plenty of ice. You look as if you need to cool down after your trip to the Arabian desert.'

Tamir remained standing and glowered at Lunenfeld.

'Well now, Agent Weiss, I can see that something is troubling you. Spit it out.'

'Did you order the murder of Ahmed?' Tamir's tone was as hard as flint.

'Ah, I see your problem. That's quite a question. Now I know why you're here. And you've come straight to the point. You always were a young man in a hurry.'

'Please just answer the question. I must insist. Sir.'

Lunenfeld removed his spectacles and studied them as he spoke. 'Listen to me, Weiss. I understand your frustration. You promised Ahmed safe passage to Riyadh in return for his help in cementing our relations with the Kingdom. He kept his word. Now you feel we've betrayed him. And you feel complicit, naturally. But life can be complicated, much as we wish it were otherwise.'

'I must ask you again, sir. Did you order Ahmed's murder. Just answer yes or no.'

'And if I refuse?'

'Then I'll take that as a yes. And I'll have to consider my position.'

Lunenfeld took his seat behind his desk and restored his spectacles to the bridge of his nose. 'Oh, for heaven's sake, man, don't be so pompous. And impetuous. You are upset and rightly so. But you don't have all the facts. Sit down and let's talk.'

Tamir shook his head but took his place in the visitor's chair.

'Sometimes in our line of work,' said Lunenfeld, 'we are faced with questions to which there are no clear answers. There's rarely a straight yes or no, black or white. Just shades of grey. You should know that by now. I deeply regret the death of Mr Ahmed, but I am not in the least surprised by it. He played a dangerous game, playing for two opposing teams simultaneously and then claiming he had become Israel's best friend after plotting to expel —or worse—every last Jew in Europe. He was addicted to extremism and danger and he paid the price. That is about the sum total of the matter.'

'And you admit that you did order his assassination?'

'I did not say that!' snapped back the director, unable to hide his irritation. 'I must ask you to refrain from putting words in my mouth.'

'But you don't deny it, do you? The fact is that there's incriminating evidence pointing to the involvement of a specific individual who is yet to be identified.'

'Ah, you mean that CCTV image? I wouldn't get overexcited about a grainy photograph of a Muslim woman who happened to be in the vicinity of the victim.'

'I know who she is. She's not a Muslim and she's not a Saudi citizen.'

Lunenfeld's eyes widened. 'Really? Tell me more, please.'

'I recognised her eyes. She's a Mossad officer who is well known to me.'

'Ah, I see where you are going with this. Let's call a spade a spade. You are referring to Dr Benayoun, I presume?'

Tamir sat rock-still and waited.

'Agent Weiss, you know very well that certain matters in this organisation are not subject to discussion or speculation. This is one of them.'

'With all due respect, sir, that's utter bullshit.'

For the first time in the interview, Lunenfeld looked angry. 'You are sailing extremely close to the wind, young man. Perhaps you would care to withdraw that remark?'

'I apologise, sir. Yes, I withdraw that remark. It was wrong of me. But I need to know. Did Dr Benayoun kill Azad Ahmed?' Tamir spoke so quietly that Lunenfeld had to strain to hear him.

'If you are so desperate to find out, why don't you ask her yourself? She's waiting for you outside.'

The first thing Tamir noticed about Keren was that she was stressed. That mirrored his own frame of mind, though he tried to conceal it. After a perfunctory greeting, they walked in silence out of the building and headed for the café on Rothschild Boulevard.

Ten minutes later, they were downing double-strength espresso, straight. The velvety liquid seemed to soothe their frayed nerves.

Keren spoke first. 'I know what you're thinking. And I understand that you're upset.'

'You killed him didn't you, Keren? On Lunenfeld's orders I suppose.'

'Keep your voice down, please. You're adding two and two to make five.'

'So you don't deny it? That's all the arithmetic I need.'

'In that case you're far less intelligent than I thought. Ahmed was a dangerous antisemite who was capable of reviving *Destiny* or a successor movement. Israel and the Jewish people are safer as a result of his passing. But assassination is always a last resort, as you know. Look, Tamir, I'm not at liberty to confirm or deny your accusation. Lunenfeld has his reasons for ensuring that I stick to that instruction. And you should be smart enough to work out what they are.'

'What's the phrase Lunenfeld uses—"constructive ambiguity"? He stole that from his diplomatic pals. I don't get it. We used to treat each other as friends, Keren. You know I won't sell this story to the press.'

'Everyone has their weak moments. Your wife included.'

'Ah, so that's it. You're afraid I'll spill the beans to Sofia, and you don't fully trust her, do you?'

'Wrong again. In some ways I trust her more than I trust you.'

'We're not getting anywhere, Keren. You're not going to tell me whether you killed the MP this side of the end of the decade, are you?'

Keren smiled. 'That's the first sensible thing you've said all day, Agent Weiss. Now I think it's time for you to go to the Negev and pack your bag.'

Tamir's face creased. 'What? Are you sending me on another futile mission?'

'Quite the opposite, Agent Weiss. You're on indefinite leave now. You'll get a full month's salary in recognition of your outstanding service. Then you're on your own, I'm afraid. Unless the director decides otherwise.'

Tamir's face drained of its colour. 'My God, you're kicking me out, I can't believe it.'

'You brought this on yourself, as you know very well.' Keren stood.

'Wait. This is a nightmare. Don't I have a right to appeal?'

'Yes, you do. But I can tell you now that you don't have the remotest chance of success unless you change your attitude.'

'One last question before you toss me on the garbage heap. Why did you tell me to pack a bag? Where am I going?'

'You're going to fly home. To your lovely family. Go immediately. If you want to save your marriage, that is.'

'Are you telling me they're not in Israel?'

'They went back to London. Sofia was sick of sitting alone in the desert waiting for her uncommunicative husband to call. I can't say I blame her.'

'Hey, that's not fair. You know I couldn't contact her from the field.'

'I'm not blaming you. Or Sofia for that matter. But you two need to talk. And soon. She has something interesting to tell you. Call her on your way south. She's expecting to hear from you. Good luck, Mr Weiss.'

[52]

Now that Sofia and the children were back in Hampstead, the medal ceremony where she had last glimpsed Tamir felt like a distant memory from a parallel universe. Had it been real? She decided it had, but her London reality was more tangible, more forgiving and she needed that forgiveness now more than anything. Whether any of it would remain for her to share with her husband was, at that moment, an unanswerable question.

As she surveyed her garden that had grown fashionably wild from a combination of neglect and the English weather, she drank in its anarchic technicolour beauty. This was the landscape from which she had sprung and where she belonged. Where her family belonged. It was such a contrast from the monotonous pale brown of the Negev. The troubles of the Middle East—and her elusive husband—would have to wait their turn. She caught her reflection in the polished glass of the window and was amused to notice that she had nodded involuntarily. It was a decisive gesture that had banished insecurity and welcomed certainty. Life was heading back to normality again.

Her phone rang. It was Tamir. He sounded subdued.

'I'm home, *ahuvati*. All went well. The mission is over. I'm heading for Sde Boker now. How are you and the kids?'

'We're fine. Settling down again into London life. You knew that I suppose?'

'Yes, Keren told me you were fed up with the Negev. I wish I could have called you, but it was impossible. I'm really so sorry, *ahuvati*.' He waited for Sofia's response. She offered none. 'Are you planning to return to Israel?'

'Maybe. I honestly don't know, Tamir. The children deserve some stability. So do I, for that matter.'

'Help me understand, Sofia. This makes no sense to me after everything we've been through together.'

'I know, darling. This must be so hard for you. I still love you. But I've come to realise something important these past few weeks. That's why we're here.'

'Sorry, *ahuvati*, I'm still confused. You'll have to explain that to me.'

'If I have to explain it, you probably wouldn't understand.'

The conversation had ground to a halt, obstructed by mutual incomprehension. Sofia spoke first.

'Listen. Just come to London and we'll talk, Tamir. When can you get away?'

'In about five minutes. I've been given indefinite leave, without pay. They've effectively fired me, *ahuvati*.'

'Oh, no. I'm sorry. Why, what did you do to provoke them?'

'I told Lunenfeld and Keren to go to hell. Or words to that effect.'

'That's actually rather funny.'

'Is it? I can't see the joke. What am I missing?'

'You may not believe this, but they've offered me a permanent job with the agency. I'll be based here in London but I'll have to return to Israel for a few weeks. For training. What do you think?'

'Seriously? Wow, I didn't expect that.'

'Neither did I. I'm extremely flattered. And I've been giving it a lot of thought. I'm inclined to accept.'

'It's your decision. If that's what you want, go for it, *motek*. You'll get a good salary and we'll need the money if I'm unemployed. I can look after the children while you're away. The more I think of it, the more it seems a perfect arrangement. Nothing needs to change—we'll just swap roles.'

'I don't agree that nothing needs to change but we'll discuss that later. But are you sure about this, Tamir? I mean about your wife joining the Mossad?'

'I've never been surer about anything. This could be a breakthrough for both of us. Listen, I have to go now. I'll see you soon, *ahuvati*. Tomorrow or the next day. Tell the kids Daddy's on his way home. I love you.'

Sofia wiped a tear from her cheek and hung up.

'The taxi's here, *ahuvati*.'

Sofia stole a brief grateful glance at her beautiful Hampstead garden before slinging her handbag over her shoulder and heading for the front door. Tamir was waiting there with her small wheelie suitcase. They embraced and kissed lightly on the lips.

'Don't smudge my lipstick. I don't want to spoil my Mata Hari image before I've even got started. Oh, I feel sick with nerves about this, Tamir. Do you think we're doing the right thing? Will you cope with being mum and dad while I'm away?'

'Yes, I'm a hundred percent certain we're doing the right thing. As for being mum and dad, I admit I'm terrified out of my mind. But I've had a fantastic teacher. I'll be fine. We'll all be fine. The kids are so excited that their dad's going to be looking after them for a change. Now go and enjoy. Oh, just one more thing, *motek*. Be careful.'

On the drive to the airport, Sofia called Tamir to remind him —for the third time that day—of the week's timetable for school runs, shopping essentials and a weekend birthday party. As she entered the terminal, her sister called to wish her luck. Once through security, she bought a newspaper, a bottle of water and small packet of her favourite mints. Standing behind her at the cashier were a young, casually dressed couple whom she thought she'd seen before somewhere. They looked vaguely Middle Eastern, probably Arab. Was that a danger sign? She tried to put them out of her mind. Her overheated imagination must have been preparing her for her new career as a secret agent.

When she reached the departure gate, the passengers were already lining up to board the plane. The young couple were there too, right behind her. Now she was growing anxious. Were they friend or foe? Either way, Sofia's concern was offset by a paradoxical emotion. She felt pleased to have spotted them—her Mossad instructors would be proud of her.

She settled into her seat next to the window and took out her paperback thriller. She'd grabbed it from the bookshelf at home on the way out—John le Carré's *The Little Drummer Girl*. She'd heard good reports about the book, but when she scanned the blurb, she discovered that the plot was about the Israel-Palestine conflict. Maybe that wouldn't be the most soothing reading given her circumstances. She rummaged in her handbag and found a crumpled copy of a Sunday colour supplement instead. That would do nicely.

The young couple were moving along the isle towards her. They sat down in the two empty seats next to her. That couldn't be a coincidence, could it? Who were they? Should she engage them in conversation to find out? That might be a big mistake. Maybe even a fatal one. *Stop it, girl, you're becoming paranoid,* an inner voice chided her. *You're not a Mossad agent yet, remem-*

ber? You're just an English journalist. Nobody gives a fig about you.

As they taxied along the runway, the young woman in the adjoining seat leaned over, tapped her arm lightly and whispered in her ear in the accented Israeli English Sofia instantly recognised. 'Don't worry, Sofia. We are on your side. It's just a precaution. Enjoy the flight. And have a safe one.'

Make sure to join our Discord
(https://discord.gg/5RccXhNgGb)
so you never miss a release!

THANK YOU FOR READING OPERATION ALEPH BET

We hope you enjoyed it as much as we enjoyed bringing it to you. We just wanted to take a moment to encourage you to review the book. Follow this link: Operation Aleph Bet to be directed to the book's Amazon product page to leave your review.

Every review helps further the author's reach and, ultimately, helps them continue writing fantastic books for us all to enjoy.

Want to discuss our books with other readers and even the authors?

JOIN THE AETHON DISCORD!

You can also join our non-spam mailing list by visiting www.subscribepage.com/AethonReadersGroup and never miss out on future releases. You'll also receive three full books completely Free as our thanks to you.

Don't forget to follow us on socials to never miss a new release!

THANK YOU FOR READING OPERATION ALEPH BET

Facebook | Instagram | Twitter | Website

———

Looking for more great thrillers?

TERMINAL THREAT

GARRETT KNOX THRILLER

RJ PATTERSON

In a daring act of piracy, Yemeni terrorists have not only seized a special oil tanker but they've also captured a high-value asset. With President Lewis desperate to save his biggest donor's assets and protect his deepest secret, he orders Director of National Intelligence Camille Banks to deploy her secret team to recover the asset. Garrett Knox, along with his hand-picked team members of elite operatives, must attempt the impossible: infiltrate the treacherous Yemeni mountains and bring the asset home alive. Battling hostile terrain and relentless attacks, Knox and company close in on their target only to have the tables flipped on them as a far deadlier plot emerges. The terrorists offer a chilling ultimatum—the asset in exchange for a notorious bombmaker in U.S. custody. With time running out and the world watching, Knox and his team embark on a pulse-pounding mission to retrieve the bombmaker. But when a shocking betrayal threatens everything, Knox must make an unthinkable choice to save Rico and save the president. **From the Oval Office to the explosive climax, Terminal Threat is a non-stop thrill ride packed with jaw-dropping twists. As a sinister conspiracy tightens its grip, will Knox's team prevail, or will the President's dark secrets destroy them all? The clock is ticking in this electrifying novel by R.J. Patterson.**

Get Terminal Threat Now!

THANK YOU FOR READING OPERATION ALEPH BET

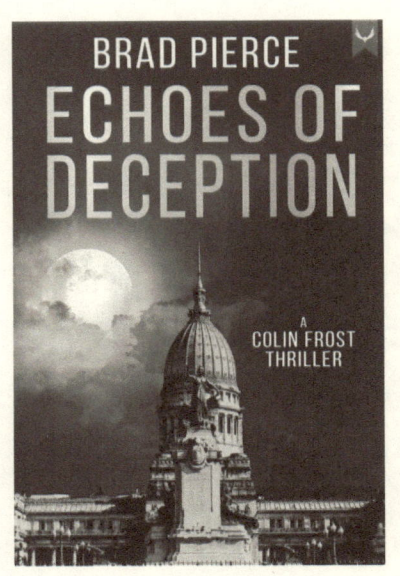

Book 2 of a debut political conspiracy thriller series by author Brad Pierce. Pre-Order Now!

Get Echoes of Deception Now!

———

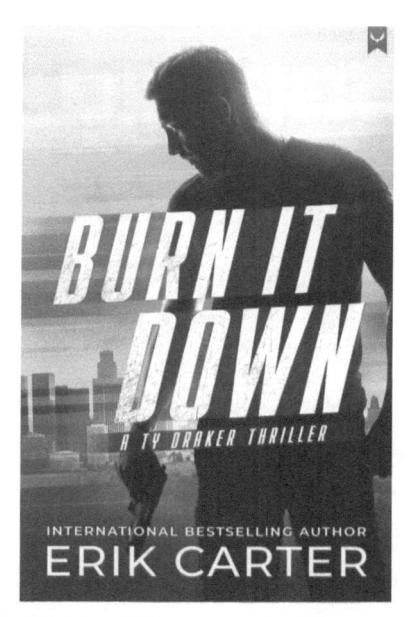

DISAVOWED. HUNTED. RUNNING OUT OF TIME. Ty Draker is a marked man with no idea why. Chased by ruthless operatives, Draker's sole ally is Beau—just a mysterious voice on the phone. In exchange for Beau's help clearing his name, Draker agrees to work as a fixer, crisscrossing the country to right wrongs. Draker plunges into a race against time after unearthing a terrorist plot with global implications. As he digs deeper, an unsettling realization dawns—shadowy threads seem to connect the terrorists, his pursuers, and the obscure events of his earlier life as a CIA operator. With the hunters closing in and catastrophe looming, Draker must solve the puzzle fast. Millions of lives depend on a man who can't trust his own history. **If you like action heroes with the steely resolve of Lee Child's Jack Reacher, the calculating will of Gregg Hurwitz's Orphan X, and the raw power of Mark Greaney's Gray Man, then you'll love Ty Draker, a new thriller series by Erik Carter, bestselling author of the Silence Jones Series.**

Get Burn It Down Now!

For all our Thriller books, visit our website.

THANK YOU FOR READING OPERATION ALEPH BET

Made in United States
Troutdale, OR
03/20/2025